CH00469797

Natasha Charles has contributed to a wide range of publications including *The Times*, *Sky News*, the *Erotic Review*, and LBC radio. She worked in London in TV development, writing, producing and presenting shows. She has had photographic exhibitions, and created a fashion collection for London Fashion Week. She also enjoyed a successful London modelling career. She studied Women's Studies at the University of East London, and journalism at Birkbeck, and now lives with her youngest son and husband in Devon, where she indulges her life long passion for horses. *The Extreme Dating Diaries...* is her first book.

The Extreme Dating Diaries of Isabelle Monroe

THE EXTREME
DATING DIARIES

of

Isabelle Monroe

Natasha Charles

Springterm Publications 2020

The Extreme Dating Diaries of Isabelle Monroe

First published in Great Britain by
Springterm Publications 2020
London, UK
www.springtermproductions.com

A Paperback Original 2020
ISBN: 979 8654450562

www.facebook.com/theextremedatingdiariesofisabellemonroe

Cover image © Susie Gunning

Edited, typeset and proofed by Andy Brown

This book is a work of auto-fiction – a fictionalised memoir based upon real life events and experiences. The names, characters and incidents portrayed in it are the work of the author's imagination, based upon those events. All names, details and identifying characteristics have been changed to protect identities. Any resemblances to actual persons, living or dead, are coincidental, or are portrayed with their permission.

THE EXTREME

DATING DIARIES

of

Isabelle Monroe

The Extreme Dating Diaries of Isabelle Monroe

CONTENTS

Just Before We Start...

I have been on more dates than anyone I know. Looking back, I see I have been going on dates for 10 years. 10 long years! 10 years of trying as many different angles as I can think of to find that man; the one who is my perfect match. Except, in fact, I ditched the 'perfect' bit many years ago.

Early on I had the following qualities on my shopping list: *Funny, Clever, Honest,* and *Integrity.* With *Handsome and Successful* as a bonus.

Now my list comprises a man who isn't too overweight. A man who isn't an addict. A man with a job.

OK, that's not entirely true. I've actually got fussier as time has gone by. Time, by its very nature, brings experience. And my experiences in dating have allowed me to quickly spot a wrong'un, much more quickly than when I was young. And with the accessibility and ease that technology allows – where we can find (and equally dismiss) a potential partner with a simple swipe of a thumb – I find myself asking: in a world of quick kicks, are dates, like plastic, becoming single use and throw away?

My online dating profile reads as follows: *A creative woman with integrity and an open mind. Bohemian leaning. Unconventional. Challenging the status quo. I enjoy art galleries, films and theatre. Girly, yes, but I'm no princess. A horse lover and a foodie who is equally comfortable in heels as wellies. I can relax on a beach, but am as happy to be challenged on an adventure holiday. I am an avid reader and am looking for an honest, clever, funny man with a sharp mind. Handsome and rich? Oh go on then, I won't say no!*

This, along with a good mix of clear, up-to-date pictures – at least one smiling, and no cleavage or body shots – has got me plenty of dates.

And I've had some fantastic dates.

Equally I've had some outstandingly atrocious ones too. I was once even a slightly bad date myself.

They are all here.

I've tried a great many dating sites. These range from *Guardian Soulmates* and *Elite*, all the way through to *Sugardaddy.com*, with good old *Tinder* in-between. I've even tried *Seeking Arrangements* for goodness sake. I have been bold, brave and taken the initiative. I have tried to be more demure and let the men come to me. I've tried rich men and poor men, businessmen and hippies. I have tried young men and old men alike.

No one, but no one, can say I haven't tried.

I've gone from my mid 30s to my mid 40s looking for the right man. And I've discovered that there are some drawbacks to dating over 40 that I hadn't anticipated. For example, women seem to continue to grow and change, whereas men seem to stop evolving, seemingly happy to just 'get by'. Do they stop right there at 40 and just agree to 'make do'? By the time they reach 40, women have surpassed men in their personal growth. Financially and career-wise, men surpass women for obvious reasons. But in personal growth, women have left men behind in the dust.

The men worth staying married to, stay married. I read that somewhere. *80% of divorces are instigated by women.* I read that somewhere else too.

"Honestly, some men are great," says my married-for-18-years sister as she skips down the road, still hand in hand with her husband. True, but I've dated the rest of them.

Men let themselves go. And women do too. We are not as attractive as we once were. When we were in our 20s, half of us were passable. We just had to find a partner with character and good prospects. If you're still with the man you married in your 20s or 30s and he's a 'good man' – a man you still like, had children with, built a life with, got a bit minging and old together with – at least he's *your* minging old man. Maybe you already did that 'lots of sex' bit that people do at the beginning of a relationship, and moved into the groove? The time invested bit. The history bit. You might as well keep him because, I can tell you, it's a goddamn desert out there later!

A man over 40 who has never committed to anything, be it steady work, marriage, or children, usually has something a bit askew. A commitment-phobe perhaps? And the man who *has* committed, but is now single again, will be shelling out half his income to his ex-wife and kids. A problem if your own child's father isn't giving you much, if anything.

Or there's the other kind of guy who's longing to be with his kids, or not bothering with them at all. Or the one who's dying to become a father and just wants to crack on with it. Yup, this is something that 40 year old women do too, but I've already had my children. Could I start again on that front? When I started out on this 10 year odyssey, I'd recently become a single parent for the second time round. With one teenage son and, now, a younger son too, I was open to putting myself out there again: I never was one to turn down an opportunity to delve into the unknown; to satisfy my curiosity.

But, there *are* the plusses to dating the over 40s too. The older man has (sometimes) good manners; knows good eateries, and has more disposable income. He has confidence and life experience under his belt and, maybe, even wisdom. He can manage to put his phone away while he's with you. *And* he doesn't send you dick pics!

I would like to date Yuval Harari if he wasn't – well – gay. Gay and married. I dream of a clever man like him. We would talk philosophy every evening until the early hours.

I'd also like to date Ben Fogle, if *he* wasn't married. He likes exploring and is a bit posh, but not-a-nob posh. My friend, who met him and knew I liked him, should have introduced us. Then he got married. He would have married me, I'm sure of it – he smiled at me a bit too long on more than one occasion on the Kings Road.

I assume this dating game is a numbers game. A game to be entered into with an open mind. Fearlessly. This is what I've done, anyway, over the years.

On bad dates, I sit and look across the table and think to myself, *Wow, I'm on a real, live, very bad date,* and I don't mind it at all. It must be very hard if you have preconceived ideas and expectations of the date you're about to go on, only to find out that it's a great disappointment. I've chatted to men online on more than one occasion who are cautious even of meeting up. I think they're afraid of wasting my time.

I never have this fear.

In my mind, every experience is valid. Go anyway and see what happens. No experience is a waste of time. Each date is an adventure. I date broadly and openly, just in case – yes, just in case – I unexpectedly stumble into the right man.

So, in these pages, I will let you into some of my most interesting and extraordinary dates, some of which even turned into relationships of sorts. Some have taken me to Paris, some across Europe in super cars, some to the best restaurants in London, and some to picnics under the stars on Dartmoor. I've enjoyed all my experiences for the stories they have given me.

Even the bad dates.

Let the tour begin.

1

Mr Bentley-Rolls-Royce

    &

Mr I'm-Your-Mr-Bond

Sugardaddy.com

Age: 40 & 38

Annual income: £250k +

Estimated Worth: £1 million +

Mr Bentley-Rolls-Royce: 6'

Mr I'm-Your-Mr-Bond: 5'10"

Watching daytime TV with my teenage son one afternoon, a piece about *Sugardaddy.com* comes on. We laugh so hard that we decide to go to the website and have a look around. Greeted with the likes of *Mr I'll-Give-You-All-You-Want* and profile captions like *I may be fat but at least I'm rich*, we spend the afternoon laughing. It's brazen, bold and without pretence.

However, it was *Mr Bentley-Rolls-Royce*'s profile that made me sign up to *Sugardaddy.com*, rather than just browse. I was curious. What kind of man calls himself *Mr Bentley-Rolls-Royce*? A preposterous name that could only be ironic, especially considering the profile pictures: rather slight and smartly dressed. He must be having a laugh, right? Although tall, this slim slip of a man doesn't quite have the Alpha Male feel he likes to make out.

Although signing up to *Sugardaddy.com* was an impulsive act of pure nosiness, I promptly message him and, before I know it, I'm getting into a hilarious rapport with this guy. "Darling, I'm totally happy with you being taller than me… you'll make me look even more successful than I already am," he says. "Mustn't worry about that at all."

"I wasn't worried," I say. "You can carry my bag for me."

He's in property and investments and I want to meet him. He seems to be, oh so very busy and, of course, 'important'. His schedule is rather tight. So tight, in fact, he says he'll have to "squeeze me in somewhere."

At the same time as I'm chatting to *Mr Bentley-Rolls-Royce* I start receiving messages from *Mr I'm-Your-Mr-Bond*. Yup, for real. He says that he's in business and lives just outside London. He seems very polite and quite shy. He's very nice looking in his pictures and, at 38 years old, a good age for me. We agree we should meet and I suggest Friday evening.

"Well," he says, "I'm actually meeting up with my brother on Friday," and mentions the name of *Mr Bentley-Rolls-Royce*.

"*Mr Bentley-Rolls-Royce* is your brother? I'm talking to him on the same site! How hilarious."

At which point *Mr Bentley-Rolls-Royce* shoots me a message.

"Hey. I hear you've been seducing my brother. Why don't we all go out for drinks together? It'll be a hoot."

"I may be completely mad, but go on then," I say. "And I bloody hope you admire my bravery. Or is it foolery?"

"Darling," he says, "what better way to spend a Friday evening than on Tom foolery! And jolly well make sure you get your best high heels on."

"Darling," I say. "If I put my heels on, I'll tower over you by a mile. I'm already taller than you without them. Can you handle that?"

"Princess," he counters, "I can handle anything, especially tall feisty ladies. Go ahead, tower over me. I'm ready!"

Now, it's possible that I'm either stupid, daring, or mad to agree to meet two brothers on *Sugardaddy.com* alone, with no female backup. Or just up for a laugh. Both of those things I guess. Safety? I'm not concerned. I tell my ex, who always has our little boy on Fridays, where I will be. The online trail is solid too. *Mr Bentley-Rolls-Royce* totally checks out in an online search. Rather than scared, I'm amused to be meeting two guys at once.

Friday night arrives. Bouncy hair, skinnies, heels, leather jacket, but no cleavage on show. Not with two guys around.

We meet in a West End cocktail bar. The boys have both arrived before me and stand up as I arrive. *Mr Bentley-Rolls-Royce* hands me a weird cocktail with chilli in it. "Here," he says, "we're trying these out. Try one," he says in his American accent.

The cocktail is truly horrible, but I pretend. "It's very nice," I say, holding back my wince.

"Don't be ridiculous darling!" he exclaims. "No need to be polite. It's totally vile."

We all laugh and order some margaritas and bar nibbles instead. Witticisms fly around the table, with *Mr Bentley-Rolls-Royce* taking the lead. He's suited and booted head to toe in Armani, while his brother's dressed more casually in chinos and leather jacket. *Mr I'm-Your-Mr-Bond* is swamped by his older brother's conversation. It's hard for the younger brother to compete; he just doesn't have the same *savoir-faire* and confidence.

I'm enjoying being with these two and the cocktails are flowing but, before long, I'm whizzed off to another bar where we down a round of drinks and then it's off to yet another bar with mini taxi drives in between. Just as well, considering I'm wearing heels of the highest variety. I have found myself on a proper bar crawl of London's finest, with intensifying heady cocktails all the way. One drink per bar, then on to another. Our feet hardly touch the ground.

We have serious repartee going – well, *Mr Bentley-Rolls-Royce* and me anyway – and both brothers are gentlemen. My gaze ricochets back and forth between them. They're both nice. Quite a predicament and I'm not sensing either one being more keen than the other. *Mr I'm-Your-Mr-Bond* is more serious, quieter and better looking than his elder brother, but *Mr Bentley-Rolls-Royce* has this sharp wit and confidence that drives the evening along.

Finally, after hours of bar hopping, we end up in the nightclub *Amika*, and dance until the small hours. I decide to leave the boys to it at a certain point and grab a taxi back home. I receive messages from both of them later and wonder what they were saying between themselves. Were they goading each other to send messages to see which one I would reply to? Was the older brother training the younger in slick dating? I reply to them both and wait to see what will happen next.

2

Mr Bentley-Rolls-Royce

Sugardaddy.com

Age: 40

Height: 6'

Annual income: £250k +

Estimated Worth: £1 million +

Since my night out with the brothers, a few messages have gone back and forth between us. The chat with *Mr Bentley-Rolls-Royce* is undeniably good. He is pure comedy with a sharp wit. An American thing maybe? When I ask him where he went to school he answers, "I'm not terribly well educated darling. The only thing I got a distinction in was divorce." Which I later find out isn't true at all, not only was he educated at Harvard, but he has also never been married. But, despite our repartee, it takes about two months to nail him down for a date. *Mr Bentley-Rolls-Royce* is, after all, "a very important and busy man."

"I don't doubt it, darling," I tell him.

He decides to prove his Alpha-ness by demanding what I'll be wearing on our date. "High heels and your best dress," he commands. He proceeds to tell me where to meet him and at what time, all to prove he's deserving of his self-appointed status.

"Darling, I'll be wearing jeans and trainers," I tell him. "I'll turn you into a midget in heels!"

I can make over 6' in some heels but I have no intention of wearing trainers and jeans. Teasing him is fun.

He is waiting for me downstairs in the bar of the restaurant in Piccadilly. I choose a party-style dress I designed and made myself, and wear high heels. I put on my best strut and shimmy up to meet him.

"Ahh, you've got your heels on!" he says. He's wearing a big smile.

"You're teeny now," I say and shoot him a wink.

"Glass of champagne?" he asks.

He has booked a table for dinner, which we go to after a couple of glasses of champagne in the bar. We are taken to a table for two upstairs, but it's not the one he specifically asked for when he booked. He's pretty curt with the waitress.

"I asked for a particular table and I'm not happy it's the wrong one," he says.

I tell him it doesn't matter and, to be fair, he gets over it quickly. He then proceeds to hand me a flower across the table. "Here," he says, "a little something for you." He passes me the rose and smiles.

We order steak and wine and talk about what we've done in the past and what we do now. Everything he says is funny and grand. He talks himself up all the time.

"I'm an amazing public speaker. I'm a fantastic lover. I'm an incredibly successful man." He's so brazen it's funny. I assume it's a comedy act and, after a couple of hours of entertainment, I address it.

"I'm assuming you know that I know this is all an act, right? All the grand statements. I mean, you know that I know it's not real?"

"Ahh," he says. "Well it started out as that many years ago, but now it's actually real. I really am like this."

I see, I think. Fake it to make it. I wonder how many people believe it? I don't. He seems quite vulnerable to me, sitting there being grand. He's funny and sweet, but I know he's not real. I bet he knows it too.

"More champagne?" he asks.

"Goodness," I say. "Aren't I a lucky lady tonight?"

I can see that our conversation isn't going to go much deeper. He's made it clear he's not looking for anything heavy and I like that he's honest, at least on that front. He's not making any pretence and doesn't *have to* want a relationship. But does he really want this fun trivia thing long term? I wonder what he's scared of. He's clearly very bright, but I can't imagine he could keep this up year in year out.

He then hands me something across the table. "Another little something for you," he says. He gives me a bottle of Chanel perfume.

"Let me take you shopping soon," he says. "That may not be your preferred scent?"

It could have been sleazy, being so smooth, but I'm not finding him so. It's clearly meant as a bit of fun.

I assume there's nothing actually special about me – giving me a rose and offering shopping, perfume and champagne.

We finish our meal and he makes a quick call. "10 minutes," he says. I look at him inquiringly. "My driver," he adds. "He'll pick us up in 10."

How nice to have a driver waiting for us outside. No walking in heels issues. No carrying presents issues. No waiting in the rain for taxis issues. We share a very nice little kiss in the car.

"Do you want to come to my place?" he says.

"I think I'll just go back," I reply.

"Damn," he laughs. "No problem. We'll just get you back home then."

"I had a really good time," I say and it's true, I did. Pure, cool, chic London dating.

"Yes, me too. Haven't got very much time though, back and forth to New York you know," he says. "Always a problem." It's pretty clear this guy doesn't want to be 'reached'. He enjoys his funny little facade and the persona that he's created for himself and has made it clear he doesn't want an actual relationship. Just some fun.

Now, it is true that if fun was to be had on a one-night stand, then I wouldn't mind doing it but, in my experience, men are frankly just not that good at it on the first try, so the chances are I'd be wasting my time.

I would have gone out again had he asked, but he didn't. "Too busy," although in reality I assume he's gone on to woo the next lady and is keeping his dating nice and light.

A few messages go back and forth to his brother *Mr I'm-Your-Mr-Bond*, but we never fix an actual date before he returns to the US permanently. The brother dating thing is all a bit odd really. Anyway, how much do they talk? Would they conspire? And who can tell if one of them actually liked me more than the other? Did they talk together about me? I guess we'll never know.

3

Mr Franchise

Sugardaddy.com

Age: 43

Annual Income: £250k +

Estimated worth: £1 million +

Mr Franchise is a *Sugardaddy.com* date and I have high hopes for him. His sane profile – just facts about himself, his more than acceptable picture – a smile, trees in the background, clean shirt, and normal messaging approach. "Hello, lovely profile, we could have a lot in common, maybe you'd like to find out, do let me know," all bodes very well.

We arrange to meet for lunch in *Sophie's* on the Fulham Road. I often suggest *Sophie's*. It's always busy, has good lighting and is within walking distance of my place, so I don't need a taxi. And it isn't too expensive if they happen not to pick up the bill. I never take the piss price wise, in case they're not as rich as they make out on their profile. Yes, this happens a lot. On *Sugardaddy.com*, a man's annual income and net worth is clearly stated and, although they can choose *not* to state it, they nearly always do.

He arrives after me and finds me waiting at the bar with a glass of champagne. It sets the appropriate standard. This is *Sugardaddy.com* after all.

It's early lunchtime and I'm wearing skinny jeans and a fitted jacket and heels. It fits all scenarios I find. I see him arriving and he looks really sheepish. Lost. *Come on dude, stand up straight! Relax!*

He is nicer looking than his pictures. And they were already good. Grey hair. I'd say 5'10" rather than the 6'2" he claimed. I try to catch his eye, help him out a bit, but he takes ages to notice. I'm just short of waving my hand to catch his attention when he finally notices me. And, no, that's not because I don't look like my pictures, thank you. I make sure of that.

As usual with indecisive men, I have the urge to take the lead. I feel the need to host him, ask him what he's drinking. Offer him a chair. I want to put him at ease. I know I mustn't. I must let him come forward.

"What are you drinking?" he asks.

"Champagne," I tell him. He joins me in a glass.

He dithers about where he's booked a table and, again, I have the urge to take charge. I can't stop myself.

"We've booked a table," I tell the *maître D* while *Mr Franchise* waits behind me. "There we go," I smile, "we can relax and enjoy our drinks now."

We pass 10 minutes at the bar talking about his journey and the weather – boring! – then head to our table. He relaxes slightly. Maybe the drink. He's divorced with one child. A businessman who runs franchises. He's had ones with McDonalds and currently Specsavers and he does indeed wear great glasses.

"I'm about to move into Cafe Costa franchises too," he says, "and I've bought a place in France that I'm going to do up." He shows me pictures of the place with its stone walls and beautiful terrace. "I'd actually rather meet a woman who has flexible working hours. I want to spend a lot of time there holidaying, doing the place up. I find ladies' work gets in the way when I want to head off at short notice."

In the UK he lives in the country – Surrey – and has land.

Hmm, a nice looking man ✔

Land = lots of horses for me and a veggie patch ✔

Surrey = easy access to London ✔

France = holidays where I can decorate ✔

No doubt his intention is to drop all this in, but yes, it all flashes through my mind.

He is awkward, but perfectly pleasant, so I wonder what he did to make his wife leave him? Led by me, we chat easily enough, but as the first hour passes he's coming across as a bit repressed. He's only a few years older than me, but already he feels like an old man. Set in his ways. Do some men get into their slot early and then stay there forever? It's like they reach their capacity for growth somewhere in their 20s and never move on. I see a lot of women who continue to evolve, but an awful lot of men just stop. They might flourish in business, but in their personal development, is minimum input really all that's required?

We stay for about two hours over a long lunch. There's not much wrong with him except he's uninspiring. Low energy. Boring basically. He shouldn't be because, on paper, he's actually very good. Still, I try to persuade myself. Maybe I'll become attracted to him. He's a good bet really. Apart from the fact he's a Virgo and you know what they can be like? Pernickety, uptight, critical and potentially cruel. My least favourite sign. Particularity in a man. I'd prefer a Sagittarius myself!

He relaxes as he gets another drink in him. "My son said that I was more fun than his Mum, right in front of her." He smirks as if competing with the mother of his child.

Is he pleased with himself about this? What he doesn't realise is that backing up the mother, even an ex-wife, is much more attractive than competing with her, or slating her. I don't join in with him as I start to detect waves of bitterness coming off him. If he had the child full time and had to contend with the daily grind of parenting; if he had to help with the homework, get those teeth cleaned, put the washing on and deal with all the objections and boring shit that goes with kids, then maybe he would be un-fun Dad too? But instead, he can pop in and do the cool, fun Dad stuff.

A trickle of ex-wife slating and resentment drips in:

"She stopped wanting to have sex."

"She wasn't very ambitious."

He orders another glass of wine.

"She let herself go a bit after the child came along."

As he tells me, the handsomeness drains out of him and that veggie patch that I had in my mind starts to turn into waste ground.

There's mention of going to the cinema next time we meet, as if we will in fact see each other again. And he must have picked up the bill when I went to the loo as it never came to the table. How lovely! He goes up again in my estimation. It takes away any awkwardness around who's paying. He's a gentleman right?

We leave *Sophie*'s and walk down the Fulham Road, politely agreeing that we had a lovely time. "Let's do it again soon?" he says although, in reality, *Mr Franchise* lacks the spark required for a follow up date. Despite the good-manners, I know we won't become cinema buddies.

And, just as I'm about to tell him, the waitress from *Sophie*'s runs down the street calling and waving something. "Excuse me, excuse me," she shouts. "You haven't paid your bill!" It suddenly occurs to me that *Mr Franchise* is one of those con men types who gets a kick from dining-and-dashing, despite being able to afford it.

All at once he seems to have found his confidence. "I'm so sorry," he says. "A simple mistake."

But was it? He pays the bill and after much laughter and apologising walks me on to his Aston Martin parked around the corner. "Don't forget," he says, "if you need a cinema companion, I'm your man."

He never did phone me; nor did I phone him. But my little boy accidently phoned his number one day and, as he was whingeing to me at the time, left a whiney message on *Mr Franchise*'s answer phone.

I wondered what he must have thought about that, but I didn't ponder for too long.

4

Mr Talky-Talkerson

Dating Direct

Age: 43

Mr Talky-Talkerson has a very agreeable face in his online profile picture, which is good because he's also super bald. But he's one of those bald men that suits it, shaving it right back. We exchange some online chats, which are sincere with no underlying agenda.

"Ahh, you like riding? I go to Windsor to ride sometimes," he messages. "I'm divorced, but my ex is great. A great mum."

I'm picking up healthy tones from little chats like these and not seeing any chinks in his profile yet.

"So you do some TV development?" he asks in his next message. "I was put in front of the camera at work for a few shows in a DIY series, but I prefer behind the scenes," he says. "Don't like too much attention on me."

I'm getting a good picture of his character. It's often what someone *hasn't* said, as much as what they choose to include, that can be a giveaway. For example, the man who says he lives in London, but forgets to mention it's with his mum. The man who says he's looking for a woman 'without any drama', letting us know he's recently had a drama queen in his life. Or the one who's looking for a 'slender woman', leaving us wondering what he would do if we accidentally became a little tubby? I'm fast becoming an expert in online profile analysis.

Mr Talky-Talkerson has an easy-going profile and straightforward messages, so we arrange to meet. He suggests going on a riding date in Windsor Park.

"Great idea," I tell him and he goes ahead and arranges it.

I've told a girlfriend where I'm going and I don't see it as especially risky, with a trail of everything from the stables' address, to details of where he works and what car he'll be in. It just doesn't feel dodgy.

The following Saturday morning he picks me up in his car at the corner of my road and we drive to Windsor. At 5'10" and slim, he's not unattractive. He launches straight into chatter. He is a TV producer and has presented a couple of shows. He has a friendly, relaxed and authentic air. Now, I'm a talker, but this guy, my goodness, he doesn't stop. I don't know if it's nerves, or if he's always like this but, within an hour, I know all about his rotund ex-wife, how much maintenance she gets from him, all about their children, all about his work, and all about his love of fishing (though how he catches any fish with all his chatter, god only knows). I know that he can fix anything, build anything, cook anything. And all about his love of life.

We collect our horses at the stables and are escorted out by one of the guides. Another punter joins us – a chatty woman called Julie, who apparently rides there most weekends. We are out for a two-hour ride. I'm a lifelong rider and he can sit on and steer a horse, but he's definitely a newbie. These horses seem to be unchallenging and forgiving though, so the ride is lovely. I had no idea Windsor Park was such a good place for a canter.

Julie has perfect nails and clean gear. I have always been covered in horse hair and mud, what with all the horses I've had. With my well-worn kit, I'm always amazed when I see riders with clean gear and tidy nails. I guess if you turn up to a clean and tacked-up horse you will stay tidy. I just never have.

In the car *en route* to Windsor I don't get a word in edgeways, and I don't seem to be getting a word in on the ride either. He just doesn't stop chatting. Julia also seems to suffer from verbal diarrhoea. The guide stays quiet like me, but Julie is a jolly soul and pushes her way in with witticisms that he responds to very well. They strike up quite a rapport with amusing anecdotes flying back and forth. It's like a comedy show.

"Well, Julie," he says. "I want to die peacefully in my sleep like my grandfather, not screaming and yelling like the passengers in his car." He laughs and she hoots back loudly.

I sit back and enjoy the ride, instead of vying for his attention. The *Mr Talky-Talkerson and Julie Show* amuses me, but he's not for me. I'm clearly on somebody else's first date.

After a couple of hours of riding we get back to the stables and hand the horses over. The couple are still chatting while I hang around the car wondering when they will finish their date. Did I see him slip her his card as they parted company? I wouldn't be surprised. I hope he did actually. Or maybe he should turn up there for a ride next week – she's made it clear it was a weekly thing for her.

Eventually we drive back and he chit-chats all the way. He drops me off on the corner near my home. I can't work out what he thinks about our date. Does he know he was on a date with Julie and not me? Is he aware of his incessant chatter? There's no weird vibe or undertone, but neither is there any indication whether he's interested in me or not. It's a mate vibe, not a date vibe I decide, and that's fine by me.

Later in the evening, when I'm relaxing in the bath, he phones me to chat some more. I put the phone on speaker, sit in my bubbles and let him natter away while I zone out and drink a glass of vino. It's nice to be back on a horse again; I haven't ridden in a while and I miss it. I want to do that more. The Julie lady with good nails, good chat and an amazing ability to get a word in should have him. They had a really good first date.

5

Mr Posh-Poor

Sugardaddy.com

Age: 41

Job: Marketing and advertising

Annual earning: £250-500k

Estimated worth: £1 million

Height: 6'2"

When *Mr Posh-Poor* messages me a couple of times on *Sugardaddy.com* saying he too likes horses and riding, lives in Chelsea and in the country, and works in advertising and marketing, he seems like an eligible match. His name is Ben. He owns horses and likes cross-country riding. What's not to like then? Seems like I might be able to start getting back into the saddle.

When I message him back he admits that Ben's not his real name. "My actual name's not so common," he says, "so I go by Ben."

"You going to tell me what it is then?" I ask him, but he doesn't want to say. Nevertheless, in the spirit of adventure, I agree to meet him.

We decide on a Sunday lunch in a pub on the river in Battersea. For some inexplicable reason he brings someone else with him. After *Mr Talky-Talkerson* and Julie on my last date, I'm beginning to worry about a pattern emerging.

"This is Ella," he introduces us. "We work together. She's also my flat mate." Blonde, with a no-nonsense expression that detracts from what could have actually been a rather pretty face, Ella is polished and astute.

"He stays with me in my house when he's in London," she says as he shifts in his seat.

A fun and boozy Sunday lunch follows. I'm pretty sure we get through six bottles of wine between us. But there's an odd vibe between him and Ella. They work together and know each other pretty well by the looks of it. He holds her glances a little too long, and she scowls at him in a familiar way. I suspect there has been something between them at some point. Does this bother me? No, not so far: in my book, people can have whatever types of relationships they want, so long as it's honest, above board and everyone agrees.

It turns out that he's divorced with a child. As we talk it also becomes clear that he's actually in accountancy, so why he's put that he's 'in marketing and advertising' on his profile is anyone's guess. Does he think 'advertising' is more enticing, or is that simply something he used to do and he hasn't bothered to update his dating profile, he's been on the dating site so long? Or is he wearing it as a mask of some kind?

"So you live in Chelsea then?" I ask him.

"Yes, I'm in the country right now," he says.

In the country? So that's *not* in Chelsea is it!

It seems he lives exclusively out of town and lodges with this girl Ella when he comes in to work. She's not *his* flat mate; he is *her* lodger! Little things from his profile – oh you know, like where he lives and what he does for a living – are simply not adding up.

Several bottles of wine later, the scowls coming from Ella have intensified, towards him not me. She's fine with me, but almost everything he says has her snapping at him. He shifts guiltily in his seat.

"Well, that's not exactly right is it?" she says to him. "You didn't come to that meeting did you? I did all the work on that project, as you may recall!"

These little personal-professional niggles deepen and, after a few hours Ella leaves us after nearly having a row with *Mr Posh-Poor.* They seem to know what this edgy atmosphere between them is about.

When the bill arrives, he covers mine, but makes her go halves. With the copious wine we drank, the bill isn't small. She flashes him a furious look.

"Expenses, yes?" she says with angry sarcasm. As she stands her anger boils over and she practically makes a swing for him, right there in the pub. He ducks away and she misses him. Then it's her turn to look guilty. She pays her share of the bill and leaves.

"Ah, she can get like that after too much to drink," he laughs when she's gone, but I suspect there is more to it than that. I love people watching, and this particular show is a god damn live soap opera.

I am left with *Mr Posh-Poor,* tall, tanned, good looking in a Scandinavian way. He's charming with a cultivated manner, but he has an edgy feel about him. Twitchy even. His legs jitter a lot. Ella's angry approach to him. His inability to look at me for any length of time.

"How long have you been in accountancy?" I ask him.

He shirks the simple question. "A while."

"So, on your profile you say advertising…?"

"Yeah, yeah," he replies. "Have been."

These indirect answers make me feel there's something slightly dangerous about him but, nonetheless, we seem to get on well and are gelling just fine. I like that he's the hunting, shooting, fishing type; I just wish there was something a little more…. arty… I suppose.

I have a skill, or a disadvantage maybe, of noticing tiny details in behaviour. I remember things that people say, and a few discrepancies in the things that *Mr Posh-Poor* says pop up. It comes up in conversation, for example, that most of his siblings had been really into drugs, but he 'hadn't touched them'. I purposely pop into conversation that I don't use drugs, but pick up from him that cocaine could well be his preferred choice.

"Oh god, yah!" he agrees. "My siblings have been blighted with problems on that front, but I've never been into the party scene."

However, I remember cocaine references from the start of our conversation and a story about a Rasta guy who had been painting his house. The job had taken double the time due to some mutual indulgences.

Still, conversation is flowing now we're alone. There's certainly something easy with him. "Why don't you come to the cottage at the weekend?" he asks. "We could go hunting?"

It doesn't take much for me to agree.

"Get the train and I'll buy the ticket for you," he suggests.

*

The week goes by and I get a train on the Friday evening. It's nice to see him waiting to pick me up from the station near his cottage. We drive up the twisty country roads in a little bashed up car. He complains that his new pick up vehicle has been towed away.

"Bastards had no right to take the car. I'll get it back in the week," he says.

Uh huh, repossessed, I think. I get the picture.

We trundle up a lane where his cottage sits nestled at the end. When we arrive he already has a roast chicken in the oven and the cottage smells delicious. The fire is blazing. Perfect. The cottage is really cosy, but the furniture is grand and oversized. He has hunting scenes on the walls and the furniture is more reminiscent of a large Georgian house.

"All my furniture's in storage from the house I had to sell during my divorce," he says quickly. "I rent this cottage for now."

I'm starting to build a little profile, one where his online image is made up of a life gone by. He's posted up a profile of his old, pre-divorce life. Like so many men, he obviously values himself on his financial credentials and doesn't want to let go of that. The man version of mutton dressed up as lamb. Doesn't he know who he is, without money to back him up?

We eat roast chicken and sit by the roaring fire and chat half the night away. He doesn't make a move at all, but we are flirty. Not making a move relaxes me and, with the presumption that anything will happen put aside, it actually makes me *want* something to happen. Even though I know he's embellished his life, I do still like him. The trouble with dissonance early on is, what if you actually find you like someone and then it's too late to go back and tell the truth? Is that what's happening here?

As we chat we connect over experiences. It seems we have a lot in common: places we've been, experiences we've had. The roaring fire and flowing wine adds to our mood and our flirting becomes charged. We are sitting on the sofa and each time one of us goes to the loo, we sit closer together upon our return. We are facing each other and our eyes meet, holding our gaze each time a little bit longer. Long enough to know we want each other. I give him a little smile and he keeps looking at me, then we stop talking and lock eyes. Slowly I lean in towards him keeping my eyes held on his and we let the tension grow. It's me making the move in towards him. I feel in control. He leans forward to meet me and, only inches apart, we stop and stare at each other, smiling. Eventually we kiss. We stay there on the sofa all night as the fire burns down.

The next morning is a bright, crisp October morning and is looking great for hunting. I get up early despite going to bed at 3am. I jump on *Mr Posh-Poor* excitedly.

"Come on, horses," I squeak, but he says he can't quite be bothered.

"It was such a late night," he says. "We can go for a ride later."

Was it actually never his intention to go riding? Has he forgotten what he invited me here for? Was I meant to just know that he never intended to go hunting at all? How did he plan to get out of it anyway? I'm disappointed, but I don't pull him up on it. I'm not sure why though. Why should I let him save face?

"Well, if we're not going to go hunting, we'd better think of something else to do," I say provocatively. "Can you think of anything?"

He raises his eyebrows and sits up. "I can think of a few things," he says. He stands up, still naked from last night, grabs my hand and pulls me off the sofa. He brings me towards him, puts his hand on the back of my neck and kisses me. As we kiss he takes my hand and leads me upstairs to the bathroom. He flicks on the shower and steam starts to fill the room.

"Hang on," I say and run to the loo down the corridor. Let's get that out of the way!

I run back and he's already in the shower. I wonder if he peed in there, because there's no other loo in the room? Oh well, I think, opening the door and jumping in with him. We lather up with shampoo and shower gel and the shampoo gets everywhere, as does the water. He moves close to me in an attempt to re-enact a scene from a movie, but I just slip around. The angles are all wrong, there's nothing to lean on and the floor is slippery. I burst out laughing – it's uncomfortable and, apart from being clean, it's just silly.

"Fuck this," I laugh and take his hand, pulling him to the bedroom. I push him onto the bed. This guy is nice. I can at least pretend he's truthful right? I don't actually mind that he's having a financial lull, but I do mind that he's not being straight up.

Later in the morning we go to the stables, where we find his horse. One horse. How exactly he intended going for a ride with just the one is anyone's guess so, instead, we take it in turns to ride round the ménage. Not quite what I had in mind, but needs must.

Afterwards, we have a slap up lunch of cold chicken and salad and go for a nice walk. We chit chat easily about places we both know in London. He has that easy, polished manner that people like him have been trained for. In the evening a dinner is planned with an old army friend of his and his new girlfriend. *Mr Posh-Poor* is conspiratorial with me. He leans in and tells me in hush-hush tones how his friend met his new girlfriend.

"My friend was in a bar talking with a man he'd met. This chap clocks that my friend is a very wealthy man and promptly makes a call to his sister. *Get yourself down here right now,* he says to her. Well, she takes his cue and, within the hour, turns up at the bar to bag my friend."

He tells me all this with a rather disapproving look on his face.

"She's a bit demanding though, this girl," he adds.

There's something very cosy about *Mr Posh-Poor,* the way he draws you into a secret conversation, as if you're special in some way. It's like being part of a team. A couple team. You know, the 'him and me against the world' bubble. That one.

When we go out that evening, the friend's house is huge, with a coach house at the entrance of a long driveway. After navigating the drive, our hosts greet us in the garden, standing smoking with flutes of champagne in their hands. The girlfriend has on long boots and tight jeans, looking pretty happy standing there with her new man. We say our hellos and go inside where the drinks start flowing. This new girlfriend then proceeds to shows us round her new man's house, describing her plans for a refurb, detailing it room by room. Bearing in mind they met just three months ago, she's certainly taken ownership of it all.

We all sit down at the long kitchen table for dinner. It's informal and lovely. I pop off to the loo before dessert and, when I come out, *Mr*

Posh-Poor is waiting. He grabs my hand, smiling and pulls me into a study down a hallway. He closes the door behind us and pulls me towards him, kissing me. We both start laughing, knowing we don't have too much time.

Just then we hear noises in the hallway outside the study. Then we hear the girlfriend's child.

"Mummy," she calls. "Mummy?"

We both start giggling, but snap ourselves out of it, quickly unruffle ourselves and get back to dinner.

"Did your daughter find you?" I say to the girlfriend casually. "I heard her when I was in the loo."

"Yes. Thanks. She just wanted some water."

I look at my date and smile knowingly. In fact, *Mr Posh-Poor* and I offer each other little flirty glances all evening. Not that the other couple would have noticed – they're pretty well in hot honeymoon phase themselves.

After dinner with lots of wine and chatting, we all get to bed. We sleep in a spare room and happily finish what we started earlier.

On the Sunday, we leave our hosts to their own fun and, before I go home, we go for a seriously fab Sunday lunch in an amazing country pub. The best roast lamb I've ever had. Afterwards I go to catch the train, but he doesn't get the ticket he offered, and I'm not about to embarrass myself asking for it. I understand the situation. The guy's in financial trouble. Probably temporary, but trouble nevertheless. He is *nouveau pauvre*.

I sympathise. It's a new breed and one I belong to myself.

Champagne taste and lemonade money.

6

Mr Posh-Poor – Part 2

After my weekend with *Mr Posh-Poor,* I don't sit around thinking too much about him. I don't have that urgent desire to know where it's going, if we will get together or not, or even if he'll call me. There's none of that checking the phone anxiously to see if he's called. Somehow I know that he'll just be some fun. But I wonder why he was on *Sugardaddy.com* if he couldn't back it up? Why didn't he just go on *Guardian Soulmates,* or *Match.com*? Why would he want to put himself in the position of not being able to afford the sugar daddy lifestyle? It's a struggle to trust him.

A couple of weeks after our last weekend, however, he invites me to a dinner party that he's holding at the cottage and, in some kind of fun-seeking desire, I agree. I've put him in my 'porky pies' category and know how to deal with him so long as I don't try to take him seriously. It's a shame he's not forthcoming with the truth. We get on so well, but there's something a little bit wayward about him. I can't quite put my finger on it.

"Get the train again," he suggests. "Saves driving. I'll get you the ticket. Do bring your little boy, there'll be kids there."

Do I really want to bring my child with me, involve him, at this stage? Then again, it's a party with other kids too, so why not? A weekend jaunt out of London with my son? Sure, I think, no harm in it.

He picks us up from the train station and, when we arrive at the cottage, the dining room table is laid out ready for the dinner party. But the table is far too big for the cottage and takes up almost the whole space. He's laid the table formally with layered cutlery and napkins in rings, even though he only prepared taramasalata and pitta bread for the starter.

I already feel at home, but not quite as at home as the assertive girlfriend of his friend. I'm not about to take over like she did last time, but instead take the opportunity to have someone cook for me for a change.

His friend and pushy girlfriend arrive and, pushy as she is, it's nice to see her again. We'd spent a lot of the evening together at their house last time, giggling, and had started to bond. I have brought my little boy with me and she brings her kid, who is around the same age as mine.

"You two aren't allowed to sit next to each other, you'll get too cliquey," *Mr Posh-Poor* instructs, so we do that girl-boy-girl-boy thing round the table. *Mr Posh-Poor* has cooked roast chicken again, with chips.

"As a man, I can get away with this," he laughs.

He actually does a great job with the roast. It's obviously his signature dish. Eight of us sit down to dinner round the dining room table. It's such a squeeze sitting round the long table, which would be more fitting in a Georgian dining room. I assume it's a keepsake from his previous, larger house. Joining us for dinner there's a Tory MP and his wife. While we're all merrily chatting, another guest starts asking the MP some awkward questions.

"So, who exactly signs off MP's expenses then? In my business I have to sign off all expenses before they're passed." He looks sideways at the MP, rather accusingly.

The room falls silent and all eyes turn to the MP. After a pause in which the tension builds, he suddenly explodes.

"What a fucking inappropriate line of questioning," he yells. "I go to a simple dinner party... and get questioned about bloody expenses! How dare you! How very dare you!"

His reaction speaks volumes. *Methinks he protesteth too much*! I start to giggle and can't stop. The more I try to repress it, the worse it gets. Then, another guest cracks a joke to try and diffuse things, but it seems to have the opposite effect. The MP, pushing 60, suddenly stands up.

"You and me, outside now!" he barks to the joker.

I can barely contain myself. I'm almost hysterical. This is superb entertainment! I wonder what will happen? Surely not a fight; a grown businessman and MP fight? God, I hope so, what fun! I sit back and watch the show.

The MP's wife butts in and tells her husband off. The joker declines the MP's offer to step outside, while the instigator of the question sits back smiling. *Mr Posh-Poor*, steps in and changes the subject rapidly. Personally I could have taken a bit more.

After dinner, I spend the rest of the night talking to various guests.

"So, where do you know *Mr Posh-Poor* from then?" they all seem to want to know.

I wonder what he has said, or if he has said anything at all?

"We met online," I say and leave it there. I'm not sure if *Sugardaddy.com* is the thing to say or not. *Mr Posh-Poor* and I simply haven't discussed it, but my answer seems satisfactory.

As more wine is drunk and the evening gets late, seating places are swapped and light stories get told. The guests start to leave around midnight, but *Mr Posh-Poor's* friend and girlfriend stay over. The kids have been playing well together and end up having their own giggles, sneaking a midnight feast. We leave the kitchen and dining room a total mess when we go to bed in the early hours.

In the morning I get up and see to the children, despite the late night. *Mr Posh-Poor* and his friend get up after me and hit the kitchen. I'm unbelievably impressed with their methodical, no nonsense cleaning.

"Army training," says *Mr Posh-Poor*. If the army trains men to clean up, well, I'm wondering if all men shouldn't have a spell in the ranks. These chaps are quicker and even more efficient than me! No mean feat.

The girlfriend stays in bed until midday. I don't really care, but *Mr Posh-Poor* isn't at all impressed.

"Party hard at night, fine," he says, "but bloody well get up in the morning for goodness sake and help tidy up, or look after the kids."

He has a point. I enjoy the little conspiratorial confides he does with me yet, in truth, I suspect he does it with everyone.

We hang out for the day in the garden and go for a walk, then we catch our train back. *Mr Posh-Poor* has offered to pay for the train ride home, but it seems, when it comes to it, he's – um – forgotten again.

When I get back home I have the same feeling about him as before. I just don't think about him. I don't wait for a call. I don't check my messages.

A couple of weeks later he invites me to a London screening of a friend's new film. I agree to go. Film and media's what I do, so I like to keep abreast of what's going on.

When I turn up, a whole bunch of his family are there, including his mother and brother. I decide not to be intimidated, or read too much into it, like, it's not a family introduction is it? The film turns out to be superb and we all go for dinner afterwards. The food bill is split. *Mr*

Posh-Poor accepts my donation, damn it. I guess neither of us can afford to be out and about in London in our current posh-poor state.

We keep in touch, but a month later his 'mad' (his word) ex-wife becomes temporarily homeless and moves into his cottage with their child, while they find somewhere to live. He is going to 'give her a couple of months to sort herself out.' She's apparently spent all her divorce settlement on saddles for her horses, amongst other things. It's probably best to stay away from ex-wives.

It would be hard to have a real relationship with someone who stretches the truth so much, however well we get on. And he's done it many times. In a way he and I do have a lot in common. I weigh it up: we both seem as equally happy in the country as the city; we have similar tastes in schools for our kids; our lifestyles are similar, and even his mum is fabulous. But that slightly wayward feeling I get from him? Best avoid that really. Does he know he can't get away with not saying out loud what we surely both know? That his stories don't tally? That he can't actually support a *Sugardaddy*-style relationship right now. Just say it man!

*

A couple of years later, I'm invited to dinner in London by *Mr Posh-Poor*. He's having the couple I met over for dinner again, as well as the flat mate girl who he worked with – the one who nearly hit him on our first date. I decide to go and, when I get there, it seems that *Mr Posh-Poor* is no longer poor. He has pulled out of the bag whatever it was he had been working on, and has restored himself, it seems, to his former glory. He's left his little rented cottage and is now living in a large house in London. His furniture fits the rooms again.

But the girlfriend who bagged *Mr Posh-Poor's* wealthy friend is no longer a fun, happy girl. She's turned into an obnoxious, shopaholic drunk.

"Why would anyone work when you can just shop?" she announces over dinner, producing some confused sideways glances that she's either oblivious to, or enjoying. Shamelessly, she continues. "Just take a card and go shopping. That's what I do."

Her fiancé glances at me uncomfortably, wondering how I'll react no doubt. Which I don't.

Although I enjoy an inappropriate dinner show, this one is sad. She's on the very wrong side of a nice drink with friends. The boyfriend looks around wondering if people have noticed. I know better than to get into conversations with bad drunks and so it seems do other dinner guests. No one answers her.

Mr Posh-Poor does his speciality cosy conspiratorial chat again. "She's bloody awful now. No idea why he's going to marry her. Maybe he's gone too far into it to back out now, but she's getting worse and worse."

I leave that evening wondering why people have these dinners at which lots of words are exchanged, but nothing is *said. Mr Posh-Poor* and the girl who works with him are too familiar to be just work colleagues.

Does he have deeper conversations with his friend about her, or anything, or is nothing ever said? What did he do to suddenly have so much money? Would he continue to be feast, or famine? Either way, I go home and we stay vaguely in touch on social media. I'm glad he's just posh now and not just posh-poor. It suits him far better.

7

g
Dating Direct
Height: 5'9"
Banking

I have tried most dating sites and *Dating Direct* is a mainstream person's website, like *Match.com* – no particular niche, just normal, standard dating. After a while browsing it, a cutie contacts me. I say cutie, but he has to send me a picture, as he hasn't put one on his profile page. You have to really stand out in other ways if you don't put a picture. 'For work reasons' they always say, as if their work precludes them from posting pictures. I never understand it. We all have work-type reasons as to why we'd rather not put our picture up, and none of us really wants to advertise ourselves. But as a lot of us are at it online now and it's become very standard, we may as well just be brave and post a goddamn photo.

We decide to meet straight away – like within an hour of contacting each other! We both live in Chelsea; I don't have my sons with me, and we can both get to the bar on the Kings Road within an hour… so why not? Let's just get on with it!

I know immediately that he'll have short man syndrome when he arrives at the bar. Men under 5'9" have a tendency to add at least 2" onto their profile's height, and this little Spaniard has put himself in the 5'9" category, but is more like 5'5". I know this. I am 5'8".

I actually don't have an issue with a man's height and don't rule out shorter men, but a lot of women do. Do these guys just try to get the date then hope their height will go unnoticed, because of their dazzling personality?

This shorty is cute enough, in that dark curly-haired, sparkly-eyed, flirty Spanish way. We meet in the bar on the Kings Road and drink wine. The bar is jam-packed and we squeeze onto a sofa with other people, like sardines.

He stares lustfully at me all evening, but doesn't have anything much to say. I can't hear what he *does* say anyway, the bar's so loud. He's a trader and runs a small hedge fund, I gather. He asks me nothing at all about myself, not a thing. This is not especially conducive to a two-way conversation. The one thing both men and women could learn about building relationships is to listen. Is being heard, being valued, the single most important thing? It should be easy, but it's so often ignored.

After an hour of non-connection when he literally finds out nothing about me, he lurches forwards for a snog. Taken aback, I lean out of reach. How can he like me, apart from physically? He doesn't know me at all. Five minutes later he goes for it again. I just hadn't realised we were getting on *that* well!

After just over an hour and lurch number three, I decide to call it a night. How many snogs would one notch up if one snogged all the men one met in bars within an hour? Time to go home.

As it turns out, he lives in the same neck of the woods as me, and so over the coming weeks I keep bumping into him in *Cafe Nero*. Sometimes we end up having coffee just because we happen to be in the same place. I've never heard anyone talk about themself soooo much! I watch him almost as a specimen, wondering how a person can be quite so oblivious.

We keep bumping into each other for more than a year. Note to self, if you shit on your doorstep... But he ends up becoming almost like someone I know. He spends half his year, the winter, in the US. "I can't stand the winter in London," he says. "I can trade from anywhere." And so he does.

One day, after bumping into him, he asks me if I want to get lunch and I agree, because, you know, lunch.

"I go to the gym every day," he says. "It's very important to keep in shape. English people aren't very good at it. In L.A., people are much more conscious of their diet and body." His dietary requirements – very low carbs. His travel plans – Miami. And where he likes to go to the gym – Virgin Fulham Road. He tells me all. "Why don't you come back to mine for a coffee?" he adds. "I'll show you how my trading works," he says. "I have all my computers open trading right now."

Interested in knowing a bit about this for a while now, *yes*, I think. And so after lunch we go to his apartment round the corner from the Fulham Road. His computers are indeed all open with his trading pages up. He looks at them, twiddles a bit then turns to me and lurches towards me full force. Did I miss something? How did he interpret this business lesson as me being 'up for it'?

"Ok, I'm going," I say, pulling away from his clutches and heading quickly for the door. I get out and down the stairs as fast as possible.

"What's the matter?" he calls down the stairs after me.

Every time I bump into him he always wants to meet for dinner, but I turn him down and, nine years later, I still occasionally bump into *Mr Short* when I'm in London. He's still spending the winter abroad. Still trading. Still in the gym a lot. Still drinking the latest special healthy smoothies on the Kings Road. And still self-obsessed.

He is also still single.

But then again, so am I.

8

Mr Super-Lawyer

Guardian Soulmates

Age: 46

I have only signed up to one month on *Guardian Soulmates*, but it's going to be enough to get me dates for several months by the looks of it. Going between this site and *Sugardaddy.com*, I'm starting to wonder what my actual goal is. Am I seriously looking for someone, or am I creating a hobby here? Is dating becoming my new evening course?

I very much like the look of one guy who pops up. He has a kind, handsome face, yet cool to boot. He's in his 40s and his pictures show he's in good shape. Googling him, it seems he's a pretty successful lawyer. He writes 'normal person' emails. High hopes indeed.

We arrange to go for dinner at the *Dorchester* – dinner proper not just a drink. This is a good start. I decide to dress up a little, so dig out a red silk dress and put a thin gold belt around it with a matching gold bag and cream high heels.

When he arrives he looks just like his picture and, at 46, is slim, beautifully suited in an Italian slim cut suit, a white shirt with no tie, flashy cuff links and good shoes. No pot belly. He's slim and toned with lots of hair flecked with grey. He's lightly wrinkled too, in a nice way. Basically, he's a dude. Pleasant, intelligent, and fairly engaging. I say 'fairly', because his performance is a bit too polished. I start to try to work out who he actually is.

We go downstairs to eat in the *China Room* and he's generous. "Have whatever you want," he says.

As we get into the flow of the date, conversation is not strained, but not quite there either. It's polite, but no banter or flare. I don't seem to be able to flirt with him. Have I forgotten how, or am I just not getting anything from him to feed off? It's the difference between me being an arty sort and him a lawyer. It's just not quite there.

His wife left him for a low-earning, arty-farty guy the year before but, oddly, he doesn't know why. He thinks she had a mid-life crisis.

"But what did she tell you why she left?" I ask.

"I didn't really ask her," he replies.

This *can't be possible, surely*? That thing that men call 'nagging' is mainly a woman trying, often for years, to save a relationship. She'll be telling him what's wrong and what's needed. She'll be trying, really hard. Followed by her withdrawal and then grieving, all while still in the relationship. Once she leaves him, it's done. And there, left behind, is a baffled man who didn't take note while he should have, wondering what happened and what he could have done to save things. But it's too late by that point – the woman has moved on and the man is left to start *his* grieving process. He often ends up chippy-shouldered and bitter and thinks she impulsively left him, taking his money and the kids with her.

"She's now living on my money with a struggling artist," he says.

I'm fairly sure a relationship with him would be a struggle for me. I mean, fancy not having it out with your wife of 16 years as to why she left you! Here is yet another successful man in his work, but whose personal development has been left far behind.

I find out that he's been dating another woman since his wife left, and has just broken up for the second time with this girlfriend of nearly a year. He's now on a dating frenzy. Unsurprisingly, this rings alarm bells.

"I meet up with a woman every evening for dinner," he says. "I figure I have to eat anyway and this is a great way to see who's out there."

While I understand this – I too have dating flurries – he seems lost and disconnected. But he *is* very nice to look at, straight out of a cashmere jumper male model shoot.

When we finish our plentiful meal, which he generously picks up the bill for, we go to leave and I have a feeling we probably won't see each other again. Though I wouldn't mind if he asked me – just to look at him. I haven't flirted once with him. As we walk out of the *China Room* and through the bar, I look across the room and there, sitting cosily in the corner, I see *Mr Posh-Poor* drinking a cocktail with a pretty woman. He's close to her with his arm outstretched behind her along the sofa. I can see that *confidante* look on his face; a look I know well myself. He'll be cosying up with her, getting into stories and observations. I enjoyed being in that bubble with him. For a while.

We acknowledge each other – it's impossible not to – and have no choice but to pass brief niceties. But we both know we don't really want to, what with our respective dates in tow. There's a feeling of being rumbled, just like when you see someone you know on a dating site. I know *Mr Posh-Poor* feels the same. We all move on quickly.

As we leave to get our taxis and say goodbye, I give *Mr Super-Lawyer* a spontaneous hug. He seems surprised and suddenly his energy shifts and it's like he doesn't want to let go of me. Maybe it's the lawyer thing. I don't think they do luvvie hugs; maybe he thinks this is a cue?

On my way home he texts me that he liked the hug, but of course I'm an arty-farty type and we hug everyone. He's a super lawyer. And they don't.

A few days later and a few messages on, he tells me that he's been on such a dating frenzy that he's lost track of what he really wants. I understand.

"I need a rest from the dating scene," he says.

Is this a nice way of telling me that he's not especially interested in me? I'm completely unmoved, so can't have been that interested myself. But I'm glad it's clear. So often things are never closed. Good manners to the end. Maybe we could be friends? One can never have too many legal friends after all.

9

Mr Stand-Up
Sugardaddy.com
Age: 35
Estimated Worth: £50 – 100k
Annual income: £250 – 500k
Height: 6' 2"

Some pleasant, normal human texts are exchanged with *Mr Stand-Up* who I found on *Sugardaddy.com.* A French reconstructive surgeon. Who wouldn't find one of those appealing? He looks nice in his pictures, in a handsome, tall blonde, toned way. And he's French. I can brush up on my conversation. I mean, I speak the language after all, having lived in Paris for a couple of years, many moons ago. I moved there in my late teens on an impulsive adventure-seeking expedition. Paris, it turned out, was the perfect place to satisfy my audacious streak, as well as the perfect place to acquire a baby, which I did, leading to my unplanned return to England.

Mr Stand-Up seems a good age at 35. The right age to happily settle down, but not so old that he's a weirdo for having not committed to a woman before. We arrange to meet one evening when he is down in London from Cambridge.

Our date comes on a Wednesday and I text to confirm our meeting, but get nothing back. I text him again to say I could make other plans if he can't make it. I have childcare to arrange, or un-arrange. But still I get nothing back. So that's that then!

Then, two weeks after we were meant to meet, I get a text from him apologising, saying his grandfather has died and that he had to rush back to Paris for funeral arrangements. Could we try to meet again?

Fair enough, handsome French surgeon guy! I agree to another meet up.

We meet for a drink one evening and, when he arrives, he certainly looks French. Loafers, slacks, hand-in-hair type of French. That smart-casual thing the French do so well, though his version of it is slightly on the boring side. He's apologetic about the last time. I'm not sure why he couldn't have jotted a message to me to postpone? But, ok.

We have dinner at *VQ*'s on the Fulham Road, even though that's the place I only usually go to at 3am after a night out. Then we go to *The Goat* for a drink. I have a couple more drinks, but he doesn't have any more, since he's driving back to Cambridge.

We get on really well – we cover travel, food, aspirations, and keep on chatting till closing time. He gives me a lift home and I wonder how quickly would be appropriate to get him to change the hairstyle that's not quite right and change his clothes into funky, rather than generic, French. Oh come on, horrible slacks with a v-neck jumper and a tan leather jacket that's elasticated at the waist! It would at least be better in a deep brown. The combo is super un-cool, as is his name. *Capuchin.* Like the monk! Why isn't he called Pierre, or Claude, like any other French man?

I do however, start fantasising about campervan-ing merrily across France in the summer. It's all fairly promising apart from the fact that he's another bloody Virgo. Virgo men, my least favourite. As I think I've said. That is... pernickety, pedantic, perfectionist fucks who really should be avoided at all costs. Still he seems really nice (well they are on the surface) and one can't be governed by astrology, right?

I come home thinking yes, maybe, maybe he could work. Enough to want to see him again anyway.

He sends me messages through the week. Nice chit-chat messages like, "Hey, I'm in London at the weekend, why don't I take you out? It will be splendid to see you again. How about *vendredi?*"

"Well that would be lovely," I agree.

On the Thursday he messages me. "Do you mind letting me know the plan for tomorrow so I can organize myself, what time, where, and will we stay late? I might need to book a hotel."

Ahh, am I deciding the schedule then?

"We can meet at the *Wine Galleries* for dinner," I tell him. "Getting yourself a hotel is up to you."

"Am I gonna get lucky and have you stay the whole night with me, lol?"

I ignore this message. He messages again.

"I didn't get an answer! Are we staying together so I can book a hotel, or do you need to get back to your kids?"

"No, I'm not coming to a hotel with you," I tell him. "We're not at that place yet."

"I'm a spontaneous, straightforward person," he replies. "French!"

Does he assume being French entitles him in some way to jump into a hotel bed with me?

After discussing and dissecting the subject, my friend and I, have gone off him by now and I don't want to go to meet him. Spontaneous? You can't get more planned than a bloody hotel!

"Ah maybe go anyway," my friend says, "see what happens."

It doesn't take much for me to take her advice. Nothing ventured, you know.

"I'll see you for dinner at 7.30 in the *Wine Galleries* then," I say. "I've booked a table."

7.35pm on Friday, I turn up for my second date with *Mr Stand-Up* and settle with a glass of white. At 7.50 I message him to see where he is, but get no reply. I call him. Straight to answerphone. I've given him a bit of leeway due to the Cambridge thing.

I sit at the little table on my own, surrounded by people laughing with their friends. How long does one wait? I decide to post this question on *Facebook*. "How long should one wait in a venue for a date… what's the protocol people?"

Minutes later messages start coming in: '17 minutes' someone writes. '15 mins'… '20 mins tops'… 'Certainly no more than 30 mins'… in come the responses.

By this time I've been around 35 minutes. He's not coming. I've actually, for real, been real live stood up for the first time! Wow!

Right, excellent, this is a great opportunity to sit with this feeling: the feeling of rejection, the feeling of embarrassment, the feeling of sitting on my own in a busy restaurant having told the waiting staff that I was waiting for someone. I decide not to run away at all, but instead to indulge the feeling. I sit back and get comfortable with myself. I take a breath and relax. I'm going to get into this. I call the waiter and say my friend isn't coming, and order another glass of wine. I get even more comfortable. It's working well. I'm getting into people watching and I'm enjoying myself. I feel as if I've jumped a hurdle: the hurdle of dining alone, of sitting alone in restaurants, of having a drink alone. It's ok, rather nice actually.

I then get a message from a guy who has edited a trailer for me for a TV series I'm pitching to the networks. He has seen my *Facebook* post.

"I've been stood up," I tell him.

"Let's meet up then," he suggests.

"OK great." I leave the restaurant and go to meet him on Battersea Bridge.

"What are you like!" he says laughing. "Putting that on *Facebook*?"

"Ahh, what the hell. It's actually fine being stood up. It gave me the opportunity to meet up with you instead, right?" I laugh.

We go to my girlfriend's house, the one who had persuaded me to go on this date in the first place. Her bad. We take a couple of bottles and I proceed to tell them my evening's woes.

"I bet he has a wife," I say. "Yes that's it, he's got a wife and he's sneaking shags on the side, spontaneous-not-spontaneous shags!"

Appalling and hilarious and... my first stand up!

See, Virgo fuck. And he had a stupid name. *Capuchin.*

10

Mr Littleboy

Age: 26

I had managed to wangle a meeting at the *Evening Standard* because I told my friend, a director there, that I thought the newspaper's *Londoners' Diary* was rubbish. I wanted it to be more like *Tatler* – more of what parties were on, what events or restaurants were opening, who went to what party. A huge cosmopolitan city like this and the *Londoners' Diary* didn't reflect it at all. I decided that I should be the one to shake it up. As someone who was out a lot, I was their target audience and they weren't reflecting the scene in the slightest. I was switched off in the very section that should have switched me on the most.

I persuaded my friend to get me a placement in the department. "Just go in and say I sent you," he said, "then it's up to you."

I went through security, up the escalators, said a quick hello to my friend in his office and was sent into the news room with an aloof guy called Jeff Jones, who seemed to be the one heading this section of the paper.

Although Jones knew I was coming and a couple of email exchanges had passed between him and my friend, he couldn't really see why I was there and had a purposeful unfriendliness about him. Maybe he did know why, but just didn't want me pushing in?

He showed me to a desk and a laptop. Figuring it to be a good start, I asked where the press releases came in.

"Oh we never use those." He waved his hand without looking at me.

"Well what do you use?" I asked him.

"You just find stuff," he muttered.

Right, well, find stuff I can. I'm out in London all the time, always at gallery openings, fashion parties and restaurant openings. I can find things. All I needed to know really was what the process was. Should I find what I want, or was there a theme? Should I go and write stuff up and send it in? Should there be an equal balance between openings and restaurants? What about pictures?

Jones was not about to make any of this easy. There wasn't much point in sitting staring at a screen in an office. I needed to be out doing. I decided to go to some events. My friend suggested a PR company that runs events. There was a big themed party happening that week and, in fact, I already had an invite anyway.

That evening I also had an invite to a nightclub event where Jay Z was going to be, and another event to follow – a huge Banksy exhibition of unseen work I'd been invited to. That's where I'd start. That would be a good story, right? And a press pass from the *Standard* couldn't hurt, could it. Of course Jones didn't help at all on that front.

The Banksy exhibition was in *Il Bottaccio* in Grosvenor Square, a beautiful building with sweeping staircases and huge walls perfect for an exhibition. I've been to fashion shows there, which also work very well, and I've been to New Year's Eve parties there too. The perfect venue for such things. I invited my older son to come with me – the one I acquired all those years ago in Paris. He was doing an art project for his Philosophy A-level, and this was a good opportunity for him. We went together. Champagne and canapés aplenty and a good look at the art. I genuinely love Banksy's work.

My son wandered off chatting to people and made a beeline for one of the prettiest girls in the room. He brought her over to me and introduced us. It was not un-amusing to watch him in action. Accompanying the girl was her colleague, *Mr Littleboy*, a Zac Efron look-a-like in a Tom Ford suit, sharp, fitted, with no tie and good shoes. Looking good, so he was! Both he and the girl worked in an accountancy firm.

My son was not in luck with the pretty girl in the end. Aside from her being about nine years his senior at 25, she also had a boyfriend. *Mr Littleboy,* however, was attempting to chat me up I was pretty sure. But at 26 he was some 11 years *my* junior.

"Are you actually his mother?" he asked. "Like for real, or is this a wind up?"

We assured him it wasn't a game. *Mr Littleboy* is cute, very cute, and insisted on my number. But would I actually want a date with a little boy like that?

Later that evening, when I get home, I get a message from him.

"It was nice to meet you. How about we meet up?"

Having a rule never to drink'n'dial, I decide to leave it until the next day and think about it.

The next day my phone pings again. "Hey, let's meet up at the weekend."

I've had dates with rich men, poor men and old men so, yes, maybe a young man might be what I need right now? No ex-wives to rant about. No chippy shoulders and, basically, just cute. Let's be honest, that's the main reason.

I agree to meet up with *Mr Littleboy* at the weekend, despite my underlying reservations, like "What's the actual point?"

Cuteness, I remind myself, cuteness is the point.

"Where shall I meet you?" he says.

"In Sloane Square," I tell him.

"Yes, but where in Sloane Square?"

"Well, at Sloane Square. *In* Sloane Square."

We go to and fro and I can't work out what's not to understand.

"Yes, but I need the actual address. I'll bring a couple of bottles of wine."

Oh for god's sake! He assumes he's coming to my house with a couple of bottles, presumably followed by a shag fest! Presumptuous, entitled little boy. Is that what Friday night dating in your 20s is like now? Get drunk and shag? I simply can't imagine the sex will be so fabulous to be worth it. Not for me anyway.

"You're not coming to my house if that's what you had in mind. We're going out."

"Oh, ok," he replies.

"So, Sloane Square – the bloody tube! – at 7pm," I direct him.

We meet at Sloane bloody Square tube, and I guide us to *The Phoenix* pub on Smith Street where we get a bottle of wine. He likes rugby and hockey, comes from Herefordshire and is in accounting. I can't help thinking the whole time, hot as he is, what's the point in this? I'm never gonna marry him and, if I went out with him, it would be short lived. Is that what I'm after? Not really, no. I feel too grown up for him, and I have no desire to fulfill what is fast becoming apparent – his fantasy of getting it on with an 'older woman'. Maybe I'd become a nice story for his friends. I don't resonate with the cougar role and, as a woman only in my 30s, I don't think I want to get into that just yet. I prefer a man to be a man. The little boy thing just isn't appealing.

As another bottle of wine arrives at our table I go to order some chips and olives. I can't take this drinking and not eating thing. Men do it all the time. When I get back from ordering, there's an old lady sitting next to my seat. I sit down and resume conversation with *Mr Littleboy*. The old lady keeps butting in. She picks up my bag and looks in it. I watch her, but don't grab it from her. She looks confused.

"Is that my bag?" she says.

"No," I say gently. "It's mine." I hand her another bag, which is sitting nearby. "I should think this is yours?"

She continues to repeat the same comments and is clearly very vulnerable. Dementia of some kind probably. She leaves her wallet lying on the table and doesn't know it's hers, making me quite uncomfortable. I keep answering her when she asks me things, which displeases *Mr Littleboy* immensely.

"Leave her, talk to me instead" he says. "I hate old people. They give me the creeps. Yuck! I don't even like my grandparents very much."

It's at precisely this moment that *Mr Littleboy* becomes incurably unattractive. He doesn't look like Zac Efron anymore and, just like that, if there was anything there at all, even a quick shag for fun, I've gone off him.

The elderly lady then tries to get up to go to the loo, but is struggling to get out of her seat. I'm one side of her and, to the other side, a girl at the next table. As the old lady stands, she nearly topples over and the girl and I both jump up to help her. Neither of the boys we're with – my own little boy and the random girl's little boy – move out of their seats to lend a hand. The bar lady comes over and tells the old lady that her taxi has arrived. She mouths *thank you* to me.

"Margaret's a regular," the bar woman says. "She lives in the home just down the road," she adds quietly.

I'm ready to finish my evening and get up to leave. Cute as he is, *Mr Littleboy* is looking uglier by the minute.

"Right, I'm off," I say breezily. He gets up too and comes with me. As we get to the Kings Road, I point him to Sloane Square. "Tube's that way," I say. "I'm this way," I add, pointing in the opposite direction.

"That's ok," he says, "I'll walk you home."

I sigh, but accept. A gentlemanly offer to walk me home is no bad thing after all. We get to my house and he lingers. What now?

"Would you like a cup of tea?" I say, dutifully, figuring that tea doesn't have quite the proverbial connotations of coffee or 'a nightcap'. I'm still working on the 'Go home, I'm going to bed and, no, you can't come in' option. The best option of all.

He comes in and, as he sips his tea, doesn't look like he's making any kind of plan to leave any time soon. The cat climbs on him and starts to knead his very nice Tom Ford suit. He panics slightly and, as he attempts to remove the cat from Tom Ford, a little thread comes loose in the creature's claw. I sit and watch in amusement as he dives into a spin, throwing the cat down.

"Oh dear," I say casually. "Will your lovely suit be ok?"

Poor moggy.

But still he doesn't leave. It's now 12.30am and why I don't just tell him to fuck off I don't know. Some sort of ridiculous politeness thing that I'm still struggling with?

Finally at 1am I've had enough and decide to say what I should have said after leaving the pub.

"Off you go home now then."

"But… but… I can't now, I've missed the tube," he complains.

"Get a taxi then."

"I haven't got any cash," he whines.

"Jesus Christ, we all know you can pass a cash point!" I say.

"But it's miles to East London," he says.

By this point I'm getting irritated and want to go to bed. I open the drawer where I keep some cash, get a 20 pound note, shove it in his hand and practically frog march him out.

"There you go. Problem solved. Off you go now. The Kings Road is that way." I point him in the right direction. "Bye," I add, ushering him out. I shut the door and go to bed.

The next day he messages me. "Let me take you to dinner?"

I wonder if he has asked advice from someone on proper dating. "Nope," I reply.

"Oh go on," he says. "Wherever you'd like to go."

"I don't really like you," I say. "You don't like old people."

"Oh please! Let me take you out. How about next Friday?"

I keep saying no, but he literally pursues it on and off for a month until, finally, I snap.

"I don't think you're very nice," I tell him. "Unhelpful, uncaring to the elderly, preoccupied with your own appearance and not an animal lover. You're pushy as well."

He leaves it a month then sends a final attempt. I decline again. Full marks for persistency though. I'll give him that. Oh, and cuteness. I'll give him that too. And Tom Ford... it suits him. As for the *Standard*, you guessed it – every suggestion I sent in, Jeff Jones rejected, making it clear that this was his gig and he wasn't having anyone else muscling in.

So he's the reason that section's so lackluster. What a missed opportunity.

11

Mr Cocaine

Sugardaddy.com

Age: 39

Annual Income: £1 million +

As usual, the pictures on *Sugardaddy.com* are grainy. All of them. The site is in need of updating – the minimum effort, minimum budget and low maintenance means I can't see what *Mr Cocaine* looks like. I like to give people the benefit of the doubt, but there are some tell tale signs that he's a bit of a twat. Maybe he's not a great emailer? Maybe he's good in person? I can't dismiss everyone for goodness sake, can I? For example, he bigs himself up massively: 'You won't find a more successful man on this site... You won't find a richer man on this site... I am the most handsome man on this site...' Really?

On his profile he's ticked the 'Worth Over 5 Million' box. There are also boxes for 'Average', 'Above Average' and an 'Exceptional Looks' box. I kid you not. *Mr Cocaine* has ticked the 'Exceptional Looks' box but, judging by his picture, I'm not sure he has this quite right. Is he winging it? Even the best-looking people usually tick the 'Average' or, at a push, 'Above Average' box. But I don't think I've ever seen anyone tick 'Exceptional Looks'.

I often wonder why people lie like this. Apparently it's not just men who do so. I've heard from men that women do it too. Especially about their age, knocking off a few years. While men add a few £'s to their earnings. Why would you put a picture that's very old? Why would you say you're worth much more than you are? You'll obviously get rumbled sooner or later. But people still do it. I have an inkling, nay, knowing, that this man is of that breed but, in a compulsion to see for myself, I agree to a date.

Friday night comes. I dress up good and proper, with my highest heels, silkiest frock and teeniest clutch bag, to match and meet my date's very impressive credentials. I meet *Mr Cocaine* in the *Sanderson Hotel* in Mayfair, although I hadn't realised that the *Sanderson* was such an escort joint. Lovely expensive escorts.

If I'd known beforehand, I might have been more prepared for this date's expectations. There are beautiful girls dotted around the bar in expensive clothes, not looking overtly hooker-y, but it's obvious: look at all these good-looking, single women clutching cocktails at the bar.

Mr Cocaine walks straight up to me. "Woah, you're a knock out babe," he says taking my hand. "Just like your picture." He looks me up and down. "Garden, babe?" he asks twitchily and leads me to the garden at the back of the hotel. On the way he grabs a waitress. "Bottle of white wine, gorgeous," he says.

He's a very average looking man: average height, average weight, average everything, despite the 'Exceptionally Good Looking' box. Either he hoped I wouldn't notice, or he is, in fact, deluded.

We take a table and he disappears to the bathroom. When he comes back, we drink our wine quickly and, within the half hour he excuses himself to go to the gents once again. Can't he hold his wine, or is there something else going on?

I'm wondering whether there's a reason chaps want to meet at 7.30pm without wanting to feed me properly? I really don't want to drink copious amounts of booze without some proper food at dinnertime. What on earth is wrong with people? My 'Best Date You'll Ever Have' has plied me with drinks, but not an olive or canapé in sight! Meeting at a swish venue to impress, but then not really impressing properly by pulling out an *actual* great date, smacks of 'fur coat and no knickers'. I do love to see how these men live up to their profile promises. Aren't they embarrassed? It's as if they hope by simply saying it, it'll simply come true.

He comes back from the bathroom and I ask him to order some olives, which arrive shortly. I start to hoover them up.

"Wow Babe, you're gorgeous," he tells me again.

"Gosh thanks," I reply.

"I only say what I see, and you…" he says, standing up from the table to take a good look, "are gorgeous!"

A waitress walks past and he grabs her. "Another bottle of wine for the beautiful model, please," he says. I look around to see if anyone has noticed.

Apparently he lives in Spain, in what he describes as a 'super villa'.

"I live three months of the year in London on business," he says. "The rest of the time I live with my wife and child in Spain and we are…" he pauses, "…*sort of* separated."

One wonders what 'sort of separated' *and* living with your wife actually means?

"We agree to see other people too," he says.

"I see," I say. "And does your wife know about this agreement, or is it your very own special arrangement?"

"Yeah, yeah!" he replies inconclusively, standing up. He then pops off to the loo again! How many times in an hour?

While he's gone I sit and polish off the olives, wondering what he's up to. Either his wife doesn't know, doesn't care, or maybe she's in on it and once he's picked up a woman in London, he takes her back to Spain for a threesome with his wife?

When he comes back, he seems very restless, disconnected and innately sad. Quite vulnerable and childlike even. He struggles to find interesting things to talk about at all, so I probe into his life. When did he go to Spain? When did he meet his wife? How old is his child? All the things that interest me about people's lives.

"Well, I don't know which direction to take next," he says and, all of a sudden, it starts to pour out of him. "The only reason I'm in Spain is because my wife wanted to go there, now I don't know what to do."

I listen politely.

"Work is better in London, but if I come back here then my child's still in Spain and when will I see him? What d'you think I should do, babe?"

All that male bravado he displayed at the beginning has gone and, before I know it, he's asking me for advice about his life and how to manage his relationship with his child. I can't really help but offer him some, from what I can see, rather obvious pointers.

"Perhaps try to breathe and relax a bit? You know, calm down. And possibly stay away from stimulants for now. Try to nurture your relationship a bit. D'you think that might help? I mean, would you like to stay with your wife?"

He doesn't really have any coherent answers at all and the 'Best Date Ever' descends into nervous self-pity and a couple more trips to the washroom. By 9.45 I've had enough.

"I'm off then," I say, bringing the date to an end. He tries to persuade me that going to his room would be a great idea. "I've got a room here. Let's have some fun, get some more drinks?"

"Shall I be honest with you, my lovely?" I say. "I feel like I've been your marriage and drug counsellor this evening. As such, it would be unprofessional to go to your room. There are however a few lovely ladies here whom I suspect might be interested. Try them at the bar."

He looks a little sheepish. I tell him straight.

"You know when you said this would be the best date I've ever had?"

He nods, a little confused.

"Well, think about that," I say. "Was it really?"

I decide not to go so far as to call him out on his average looks too, and leave him in the garden. The bar is really buzzing now as I walk through to leave. Looking at the escorts I think what a straightforward transaction that must be – everyone knows what they're doing, agrees on it and understands. This *Sugardaddy* malarkey is neither one way nor the other. Wine and olives followed by a two hour counselling session? No thanks. If he wanted an escort, he should have said so. This date was just a cheap ruse to get out of paying for one. Maybe I should become a *Sugardaddy* counsellor? At least I'd get paid properly.

Many dates end up like this. But it's not just *Sugardaddy.com* that has this problem, *Guardian Soulmates* has been surprisingly similar. Given all the men in London, is it that hard to find a compatible one? Is this dating game ending up a hobby instead of actually meeting a real match? I'm just grateful that I always find people's lives fascinating – for a couple of hours anyway.

Poor *Mr Cocaine*. What will he do now it's 9.45? Will he go to his room and keep snorting the coke, alone, get online to some porn, or book himself an online service? Maybe he'll go to the bar and try one of the escort girls. Or maybe he'll just go to bed, alone.

I wonder what his wife and child are doing tonight in Spain?

12

Miss Bad-Date & Mr Lawyer
Guardian Soulmates

At 59, and more than 20 years my senior, *Mr Lawyer* is a bit out of my age bracket, but he sends a very convincing message to persuade me that I'm his ideal woman and insists we meet, to which I agree. An affirmative approach goes a long way with me.

He writes lovely emails and says to 'give him a chance', which I'm prepared to do, although I'm fairly sure he's not for me – he looks nice in his photos, but a little too dad-like.

Before I meet him, I meet up for a drink with a girlfriend with whom I sometimes get a bit wayward. We just seem to egg each other on a bit too much. Anyway, the weather is lovely and we sit in a pub garden in Chelsea, with a cocktail that soon turns into a few cocktails. A jug in fact. As laughter sets in, I see myself pushing time to the very edge, and don't leave my friend until the time I'm actually meant to be meeting my date. It seems terribly funny while I'm with her.

"Don't bother going!" she says. "Just stand him up."

"I'm not going to stand him up," I tell her. "That's just bloody mean."

I text him while I'm still with her, to say that I'm *en route*. Eventually, I get to Notting Hill a naughty 45 minutes late and, when I arrive, apologize.

"I've been drinking with a mate," I confess, and he seems fine with it, although I wouldn't have been fine with it had it been the other way around.

We guzzle red wine and share a platter of cheese, cured meats, olives and the like. I talk absolute rubbish nonstop. I totally know I'm doing it, but the more confused he is by me, the more compelled I am to continue. It's like I just can't stop.

I keep changing my accent from Chelsea to Essex, which just keeps popping out of my mouth randomly. "Know what I mean innit," I keep saying. Then occasionally a bit of Scottish pops out. "Och I wouldn't be waiting too long for any wee man tae turn up lach yoo do fur me." Although I've been told my Scottish is actually more South African.

I can see he's intrigued as well as confused, but I just keep going. "Come on mate, when we gonna go party then?" And I'm back to Essex. The more it continues, oddly, the more the power dynamic shifts in my favour and the more theatrical I become. Then the French starts coming out. "And where is zee petit *maison* you 'ave in France zen? Ow often you go zere?" I ask him in my best Franglais. I have a good accent.

He asks me what my real accent is, and I think he's probably a snob. Am I picking up he doesn't like my Essex? "How does your mother talk?" he asks.

I just can't help winding him up. "Wot, you got a problem with Essex or summink mate? You a snob are-ya?"

I don't know why, It just keeps coming out. He's perfectly nice – lawyer, divorced, three kids, place in France, all that jazz. But he bores me. He's conventional. A stay-in-the-box guy. A colour-inside-the-lines sort of guy. I know he's baffled by me, poor chap. He stares at me trying to work me out.

And what about this sort of man? A couple of decades of marriage and a few kids. Divorced, with half the money going to the ex-wife. What about the three children and the three lots of school fees and all the maintenance and the like? Would I, the new girlfriend, get a raw deal? I haven't come out of my previous relationship with a good deal and a house. Should I consider the practicalities here? I'm certainly not going to go for the 'in love but poor' angle again. Poor doesn't make a better man. Are they any more virtuous for being poor? Nope. Poor men are just as wanky as rich men. But with less frills.

Not that this guy is poor and, to be fair, if I really felt drawn to him, knowing me, I'd go for it. Finances aside. But I don't feel he could handle me, and I'd be bored. We aren't on the same wavelength at all.

"Tell me," he says, as the few glasses of wine bring him his voice. "Did you have any lesbian experiences in your school days?"

It's a little surprising, the question. "Darling," I reply in my best Oxford English. "I'm straighter than the pole your mum dances on." He looks at me bemused.

I got that line from my teenage son. And, all of a sudden, I'm back to Scottish. "Och, I'm going to whack yer wee behind."

I would have liked more than some charcuterie with all the alcohol we're drinking, but that's all we have and, frankly, I realise I've been very badly spoiled in the past, what with some of the amazing dinners I've had on some other dates. A plate of charcuterie and a bottle of wine doesn't cut it.

This poor man has no idea how to manage my one woman comedy act. Although he's desperately trying to keep up. I'm really sharp this evening. Damn I'm on fire!

At least I *think* I'm on fire.

At around 11 o'clock I announce I'm off. I thank him for a lovely evening. He leaves with me and hails a taxi, handing the driver some cash.

"Thank you, you wee sweetie," I tell him in my best Scots. I do appreciate the gesture. When a man hands you cash it can feel pretty vulgar, so paying the driver directly is a gentlemanly thing to do.

It's not just women who have bad dates. Men have to suffer them too and, on this occasion, I was the bad date. I turned up late. I was tipsy. I was snotty, loud and entitled. I ran away with my power, then flicked my hair and left. And he paid for it all.

Still, I did message him to thank him the next day. He messaged me back. "I had a great time. Did you? Would you like to meet again?"

How? How could he possibly have had a good time?

Maybe I wasn't as bad as all that? Maybe I'm actually a good comedienne after all? Or maybe he's a glutton for punishment? Surely he wouldn't want to come back for more of that? But yes, it seems he did.

He messages me a couple more times, but there's just nothing there. I don't want to get into a dialogue, so I ghost him.

The final nail in the bad date coffin.

13

Mr Doctor-Handsome

Guardian Soulmates

Age: 38

Height: 6' +

Mr Doctor-Handsome's profile is promising. He's 6'2". A surgeon, no less. In his thirties. He describes himself as 'Not taking life too seriously' and 'Enjoying his work'. He'd like to 'Take off at a moment's notice to – say – Paris for the weekend'. Nice, right?

We meet at the swish West End cocktail bar, *Sketch*. When I see him sitting there at the bar, I'm very happy. He's even more handsome than the pictures on his profile, as if that was even possible – he looked delicious in those. A damn good start. I'm in a dress-up mood and have my very nice, strappy, shocking pink shoes on, and a black silk shirt-dress with a gold belt cinched at the waist.

When I arrive, *Mr Doctor-Handsome* has already decided what I'm drinking. Is this a rather gallant gesture, a decisive gentleman unafraid to take the lead? Quite rare these days! Even if I didn't actually want the ginger so snazzily shoved in my drink, it was nice of him to take the lead.

After we finish our weird drink, *he* also decides we're going to eat, and leads us through to our booked table. I didn't even know we were going to eat. This is definitely a 'Take Charge' kind of man. I may like this.

Before I know it, he's ordering my food while I'm still scanning the menu.

He feeds me oysters – the one and only thing I don't like. Then he feeds me salad and paté. I wanted the haddock actually.

"Here," he says, as a hand with a fork comes towards my face. He's decided he would like to feed me *his* food from *his* fork. It's a nice thing to share, right? I like a sharing man.

Then he undoes a couple of buttons on his shirt. "I'd show you my muscles," he laughs, "if only this place wasn't so damn full." He raises his eyebrows and, for once, stunned into silence, I say nothing. He *is* jolly handsome. Like, really handsome. He's 'tall, dark and handsome' in fact. But as he runs his hand through his hair, I get the feeling he's a bit too suave.

"The lady will have mango for pudding," he tells the waitress.

It's all a bit too slick; a creepy sort of handsome, what with the shirt buttons coming undone.

"I've been in the gym a lot recently," he adds. "It's part of my work package."

"Really," I reply, a little disinterested.

"D'you like my Armani suit?" he asks.

"I... I do," I falter.

"And the shoes?" He pokes a foot out from under the table.

"Um, sure I do," I say, trying not to laugh.

"I like a woman in Louboutins," he says. "It's the red soles. Know what I mean?" he adds winking. "I do like an adventurous woman." Those eyebrows go up and down again. "Are you an adventurous woman? You have children, right?"

"Yes, I do," and, before I can add their ages, he's all over it.

"Your children wouldn't get in the way of our spontaneous weekends, would they? Because I'm all about the spontaneous. You'd need to be ready with child care at all times."

"How does that spontaneous thing work if you're a surgeon?" I ask.

"Sweets," he says, "I work in Harley Street in cosmetic surgery. I only have scheduled surgeries. I can get you a very good price, if you know what I mean," he adds, his eyes dropping to my chest.

As a *Guardian Soulmates* date, I wasn't expecting this sort of thing, yet somehow, after only 45 minutes, I find I've somehow slotted into this 'Sweets' role for him. It's all getting a bit seedy.

What would it be like to be with a man like him? He's sleazy, yes, but what fun it could be to a totter around in Louboutins with a Chloe handbag. I could get my hair blow-dried every other day and get a manicure and pedicure whenever I wanted and a massage in a beauty parlour. I could toss my hair around while browsing in Harvey Nicks. Hell, I could even get a knock-down boob job! So long as I was available to dine and be whisked-off at short notice. Could I be *that* woman?

But all those raised eyebrows, Louboutin and boob job insinuations! *And* he forgot to ask me what I do, or the ages and names of my children. In fact, he pretty much forgot to ask me anything about my life at all.

He does remember, however, to tell me where *he* works; where *he* has lived throughout his life; what sports *he* has participated in. Apparently he was a child junior fencing champion. I even know what happened to his last girlfriend. "She left me for a musician with no money – silly girl."

As we wrap up our date and wait for a taxi, he lurches in for a kiss. I don't kiss him back. After having my face licked, I turn my head away and wipe my cheek.

"Would you like to have a quick cheeky look at my muscles now?" he asks.

"Ooh yes please," I laugh, "but next time, eh? Bit chilly for you right now." I raise my eyebrows knowingly and he raises his back. On the way home, he texts me and calls me *baby* and *sugar*. "Can't wait to see you in your bikini and Louboutins," he says.

I hover over a reply. I mean, how simple could life be if I just took one of these *Sugardaddy* type men? How hard could it be? I could surely get my intellectual stimulation elsewhere couldn't I?

In the cold light of day, I decide not to answer him. He's just too silly with his muscles and his sleaze, his boob jobs and 'spontaneous' fantasies.

He texts me over the next few days, saying "Babe, where are you? Sweets, what's wrong? We got on great didn't we, sugar? Let me take you shopping."

Realizing I must be a bit of a whore at heart, my fingers linger over the phone, contemplating a reply.

Eventually, I ghost the shit out of him.

His messages last six weeks. Determined – I'll certainly give him that.

14

Mr Conveyor-Belt-Dater

Sugardaddy.com

Age: 50

Annual Income: £250k +

Estimated wealth: £1 million +

This *Sugardaddy* user's name is a bit of a give away. *Perignon007*. He looks younger in his picture than the 50 years stated, and he's smiley. I like a picture with a smile. I decide to meet him because he writes perfectly reasonable messages and suggests *The Dorchester* in Park Lane. That's not far and, presumably, a glass of champagne will come my way. *In for a penny, in for a Dom Perignon,* as they say.

We arrange to meet at 7.30pm, but it's the time that's the problem. What is that – a drink? dinner? I'm reckoning on dinner but, as always, eat something before I go. Even a banana's good before a drink.

I'm 20 minutes late – naughty! – but I do message him *en route*. As I walk through the *Dorchester* to the piano bar, I feel like I've got 'hooker' written on my back. Could this possibly be a reflection of my own state of mind? Or maybe I'm picking up the vibe in the place – the well-trodden path in these hotels. Either way, I think I like it: the theatrics, the game. Yes, today, I'm going to play escort. I strut through the piano bar swinging my hair in what I imagine to be a confident, expensive hooker kind of way.

When I find him, *Mr Conveyor-Belt-Dater* – from Norway, actually – looks 50, and some. His picture was taken, at the very least, 10 years ago I'd say, and he's now somewhat heavier. It's a very odd thing to do – put an out-of-date picture on your dating profile. Does he not see himself as he actually is? Or does he, but doesn't care? How do people think they'll get away with it when they actually meet?

That said, I must admit to getting carried away on my own *Guardian Soulmates* profile with the 'languages spoken' category. I can now speak French, Norwegian, Urdu, Arabic, and Welsh, apparently! Only the French bit is true. But then I did also tick the '*Not very'* box, in the 'How honest have you been writing your profile?' category.

Mr Conveyor-Belt-Dater is dark, but greying, with a full head of hair and a little potbelly. He feeds me champagne in the piano bar. He's not my type at all. He's a businessman with the feel of a man who buys what he wants. Including women. We chat away very well together, nevertheless, probably because I know I'm not interested and he is. Is it precisely this that makes the power shift in my favour? He has more money than me no doubt, but I'm younger and prettier and, well, just nicer. And he knows it. These dynamics are always interesting. When a man can feel a woman isn't interested, does he feel he has to conquer her to make her like him? Of course it happens the other way round too. But here, it's him who has to work harder.

Divorced with four children, he's not my favourite type. Will he have given all his money to the ex-wife and paid a shed load of maintenance for the kids too? I didn't get a house or much maintenance at all from the fathers of my children. I don't even know why I'm thinking about it – I'm not even interested in him.

He keeps looking at my chest, even though I never reveal too much cleavage on a first date. Is he a sleazy old guy? If I did the same back to him, you know, stared at his crotch, I bet he'd just think I was flirting, rather than making a point?

I start to become very hard on him with scathing comments, ripping him to shreds. Something – maybe the chest staring – compels me to.

"So, do you always say you're younger that you actually are? How do you plan to get out of that?" I say. I just can't stop myself. But what's this? Does he like it? Does he enjoy being put in his place after all?

He's disparaging about his ex-wife. Bitter, despite having had four children with her. This is not the first time I've found a man talking about his ex ungraciously. "She never worked, always complained that I was away, and always wanted more," he says.

"Was raising four children her work do you think?" I say sarcastically.

He ignores me and hands me his business card. "I come to London every month on business," he says. We're two glasses of champagne in when he adds, "maybe next time we can have dinner?"

Precisely 45 minutes later, he gestures that it's time to go. It's only 8.30, but I'm hungry. I must have looked disappointed. "I'm kind of meeting someone," he says.

"Business?" I query.

He looks sheepish.

"What, like another date type of someone?" I thought he was joking, but it seems not. *Mr Conveyor-Belt-Dater* is conveyor belt dating right here, right now! "You have another date coming, like now?" I ask, astonished.

"Trouble is, you never know what will turn up," he says.

I laugh, bemused. Do I take it the 8.30 date got the dinner part? Do I assume he had a 6.30 before me too? Was I just the 7.30 drinks girl?

"You're going to regret that," I announce. I'm in full movie mode by now, standing up and sticking my nose in the air. I flick my hair and get ready to flounce away. His business card lies discarded on the table. I feel him panic. He picks it up and follows me as I leave.

"My card, my card!" he calls.

I take it and chuck it in my hang bag flippantly, turn on my heels and strut off with him following. "Let me at least give you a fifty for the taxi," he says.

Changing my mind on the 'playing escort' front, I reply, "I'm not a bloody hooker you know!" then pause. "Actually, give me a tenner," and, with that, I'm off without even a backwards glance.

In the taxi I get straight on the phone to see if my friend is in, and relay my evening so far. It's not even 9 o'clock by the time I reach Sloane Square. I had, after all, planned to be out all evening and have childcare covered.

From Park Lane to Kings Road is £8. I get out of the taxi and go to pay the driver. I hand over the bill from *Mr Conveyor-Belt-Dater*.

"You not got anything smaller love!" he asks, disgruntled. I look down, and there's a fifty quid note in my hand

"No sorry," I say, laughing.

"Don't worry love," the driver says, roaring with laughter himself. He'd been listening to my phone conversation. "At least you're quids up."

15

Mr Fun-Man

Sugardaddy.com

Age: 49

Annual Income: £1 million

Estimated Worth: £1 million +

Height: 5'9"

I decide that if I'm going to mess around on *Sugardaddy.com* I might as well do it right by selecting the men who earn over £250,000 a year. Isn't that what's it's for? I'm certain the men only select the women on the basis of looks, after all.

Whether this is a good way of choosing a partner is questionable. But what's not in question is that I can't possibly go for a broke artist again. You know the sort – the highly charismatic film maker; the intriguing, pontificating artist who listens to opera, while drinking red wine from a chipped tumbler; the wandering philosopher who looks deep into your soul while he listens to your thoughts on life. The father of my youngest child has taught me that love does not conquer all. You must have a little bit of money at least – you know, to eat, for example. And poverty doth not a worthy man make. Of this I can assure you. I've done poor men, and now I'll try rich.

I still can't resist striking up a conversation with *Isle-Of-White-Man* though – a cute, jam-making, campervan-ing, Indian head-massaging, wild flower meadow conservationist hippie from, you guessed it, the Isle of White. With annual earnings of £24k, I can't work out what he's doing on this site! But then the same applies to me in a way. I'm from bohemian stock and not a typical sugar babe, except that I am blonde and like snazzy restaurants and high heels and getting taxi's everywhere and going to nice theatre productions and nice cars and nice clothes... and... hang on...! I recognise this *Isle-of-White-Man* in spirit. But we just converse online. I can't really see how we would meet – I mean, The Isle of White?

In the meantime, *Mr Fun-Man* gets in contact with me. His profile name is *I-Love-Fun*. And he does actually look really good fun. He's all smiles. I like that. And he's quick to strike up a conversation. I like that too. But he's also quick to name drop left right and centre in our email conversations although, strangely, I don't seem to mind. I don't know if he's doing it on purpose, or if it's actually just his life, rather than bravado? He's very prompt in making a date. God I love a decisive man. The affirmativeness speaks to me. It's one thing I love about this site – the men just get on with it. There's no dithering about. On *Sugardaddy.com* a man will make contact and a meeting within a few short sentences.

We meet for lunch at *Scott's* in Mayfair. He is small and I am tall. The 5'9" on his profile is more like 5'6". This is an on-going theme. I actually don't mind a shorty, but a man saying he is 5'9", doesn't actually make him 5'9" in the flesh. Men take note – we can see you!

And that Age: 49, there on his profile? When he's actually more like 60?

As I walk through the restaurant to our table, my legs are one stride to his three. I can see people looking at us and know what they're thinking. We've got that mismatch look. I have that 'been hired' feeling of recent dates. I'm a lot younger than he is and we're not a physical match, so I must be there with him for some other reason, right? Oh what the hell! It's an experience, I think, lobbing any thoughts of being in the spotlight out of my mind.

He's a businessman, originally from Greece, in the world of nightclubs, restaurants and art dealing. The staff at *Scott's* seem to know him and are coming off a little bit sycophantic as they bow and scrape.

Despite the mismatch, I quite like the guy. He's funny and generous. We drink champagne. "It doesn't have so many calories, isn't that right?" he says. "And we'll eat oysters. No fat right?" he adds, as if he's checking in with me on the facts. "When I was younger I was as skinny as a bean pole and couldn't keep the weight on. Now I've got to try and keep it off."

He's wearing black skinny jeans and has big rings on his fingers, a black silk shirt with several buttons undone and a large necklace – dare I say medallion! He's sporting sparkly shoes. It's proper fun! I'm dating an actual real live medallion man.

We talk about art and I complain that Damien Hirst's 'dots' look like an *Argos* children's bed set.

"Oh no!" he says, "I bought one of those. D'you think it was a bad investment?" again checking in with me.

"Oops!" I laugh, assuming he's bullshitting me. I'm used to men talking nonsense, and assume they all are, all the time. "No babe," I reply, "it's a totally good investment."

At the end of our meal *Mr Fun-Man* takes a pill container out of his pocket. In each compartment there's a single pill. One section to be taken with breakfast, one with lunch, one with dinner. He knocks the pills back with water. "I'm keeping healthy," he announces without a trace of self-consciousness.

Mr Fun-Man takes my hand and looks at my nails. Fuck it, I haven't been to the nail bar and have no polish on! "Hmm," he mumbles. He seems like the kind of guy to mind that sort of thing. I think I might have failed. Note to self: must do better as a sugar babe. Sugar babe's attention to detail needs work.

He tells me he has restaurants and clubs and I don't think anything, although it doesn't quite feel like total bollocks. I still just assume he's talking himself up. He does feel relaxed and quietly confident. He's quite sweet in a way, sitting there with his vitamins and medallion. He's just too much like a caricature of a Greek businessman, or is it mafia I'm thinking of? And, with those tight jeans and prominent jewellery, I can't take him seriously.

He tells me that he gets on with his ex-wives – plural. "I take care of them very well," he says.

Somehow, I believe him. I get the feeling he's enjoying his life. He's going to hang on to his health and fitness and live well for as long as possible. This aging malarkey is getting in his way and he's going to do his very best to keep going in tip-top condition for as long as possible.

At the end of lunch *Mr Fun-Man's* chauffer is called and I am popped into his Range Rover and chauffeured to my youngest son's school in time for pick up. It is not a bad way to spend an afternoon.

*

A couple of weeks later, a friend of mine is curating an art exhibition near the West End and I decide to invite *Mr Fun-Man*. He's in art dealing after all. He turns up, but I'm quite busy with friends. I quickly introduce him and we have a couple of glasses of champagne. Then he moves on to another event and I stay on at the exhibition.

As the weeks pass and some light communication continues, *Mr Fun-Man* occasionally offers me VIP tickets to art events, or *soirees* he thinks might interest me. Or my son. Which is jolly nice of him actually. But each time we try to meet up, the timing is always wrong. I invite him to a gallery. "Damn, I'm in the country shooting," he says. He invites me to an art preview evening. "Damn, I'm at a birthday," I say. Then the contact gently fizzles out until I see a story in the news about The Presidents Club charity event – you know, the men-only charity raiser with all the sexual harassment? – and spot *Mr Fun-Man* in the press stories. I *Google* stalk him, which I've never done before. Luckily he's not accused of any of the bad behaviour, but *Google* throws up endless photos of him with a different pretty girl in each one. He really is a big restaurateur. Businessman. Art collector. Womaniser. The lot. In fact, all the things he said and a whole lot more.

Note to self – not all medallion men are full of shit!

Apart from his age.

And his height.

Well, we can't have it all now, can we?

16

Mr Eastern-Prince

Sugardaddy.com

Age: 48

Annual income: £100k +

Estimated Wealth: £1 million +

Non-smoker

If a guy has a picture of himself on a horse, I always message him back. As long as he can actually ride. And I can tell immediately whether a person can really ride, or not, from a photo. I can see through the holiday snaps. Such is my experience in this subject. And so it is that this 48-year-old *Sugardaddy* date invites me to go for a ride in a London Park. He lives close by and has horses. The pull is irresistible.

We arrange to meet at a tube stop where he will pick me up.

When he meets me in his car, he has a cigarette in his hand, which he then proceeds to smoke in the car.

"Ahh, you smoke," I comment.

"A bit," he says. "We can never say that in our profile though."

"Can we not?"

"No, no one ever says that they smoke," he says, lighting another. It's a short car journey. Thankfully.

We arrive and enter the park via large electric gates. I had assumed it was a livery yard we were riding at but, no, it's a large house with a stable yard and a groom handling the horses. As we wait for our horses to be readied, we're served coffee by a submissive male servant. He offers me sugar and I take the bowl, although it becomes apparent that spooning the sugar is also his job. I watch as he spoons sugar for *Mr Eastern-Prince* while he smokes.

By now the groom has finished, tacked up, and the horses are ready. We finish our coffee with few words passed between us. I'm unsure of the rules.

In the stable yard there are three beautiful horses waiting. My date mounts after me and, lastly, the groom, a tall thin woman with a rich Eastern European accent. Slovak, I think. We have a little ride round the ménage, "To warm up," says *Mr Eastern-Prince.*

My date is wearing a flowing cape that flaps behind him as he canters through the park. He wears no hard hat but, instead, a little round colourful Kufi cap. He looks like Lawrence of Arabia. No joke! And he chain smokes, even on the horse!

"No hat for you?" I say.

"Some days," he replies. "Depends if I'm feeling mortal."

He seems pleased that I can actually ride. Apparently other dates say they can when, in fact, all they've ever done with a horse is pootle on a pony as a kid a few times. That's why he took us round the ménage first, "To make a quick assessment."

It turns out to be a fantastic ride. I had no idea a London park could be so wild and vast, with such good riding. Although there's hardly a word of conversation between us. Instead, the Slovak groom chatters to me non-stop about her own love life.

As we arrive back at the stables, the groom takes over the horse care. *Mr Eastern-Prince* and I don't even get a chance to start to un-tack. The groom simply whisks the horses away while we go into the house to be served a fabulous lunch made by the male servant.

I think he must do everything in the house. He hovers around at the ready and I feel uncomfortable and restricted with him there.

Mr Eastern-Prince, on the other hand, appears to feel completely comfortable with his man-servant listening in. Once again I find myself with three of us on the date. I don't know how many dates he has the same drill with, how many lunches the servant makes, but it's all rather awkward for me. It's an intriguing experience certainly and, for that, I love it, although for him, I note, it looks increasingly like a daily routine. Going for a ride, having the servant make you lunch – it can't be bad, but there's no real effort on his part.

As we chat over lunch I find out that he's a landlord and his business pretty much runs itself. He wants to move to the continent, "Where the climate is good and the food is better," he says, although his quality of life is already pretty good here. I find myself thinking that unless you can find something inside yourself, you'll always be dissatisfied and searching for something else.

Apparently, the man-servant turned up when he got divorced. "A gift from my mother," he said. "*You'll need someone to cook and clean for you now*, she told me."

He can't move abroad until the man-servant has his passport, which will be a couple more years to wait yet. "I don't need staff," he says, "but I've got him for life now. He sends his salary home to his family."

He seems slightly begrudging of the commitment that has been placed on him by his mother. The servant lives in a mobile home on site and the hierarchy is shamelessly apparent. But the man-servant has a genuinely happy air about him.

Mr Eastern-Prince tells me that he hasn't seen his own daughter for a couple of years now. I wonder why his ex-wife won't let him see his eight year old? As I understand it, women like their children to spend a weekend with their fathers – it gives them a break and, unless they have a very good reason, why would they stop their children seeing their father after separation? And yet men repeatedly say that their exes withhold access to punish them. I'm just a bit suspicious about *Mr Eastern-Prince*'s story.

He drives me back after a long lunch. It's been interesting. His set up is cool – talk about the best of London and the country right on your doorstep! He asks me to think about what I might be looking for. A monthly allowance? If so how much? Live in with him? Marriage?

What?!

Warning bells start ringing.

I tell him I'll think about it.

He's fun and jaded in equal measures. Bizarre and intriguing, but without any interests apart from the horses. His business runs itself and he feels unfulfilled. I don't trust him. He doesn't feel like a romance match for me.

A few days later he messages me for a follow up.

"How about an afternoon ride, dinner and a DVD?" he suggests.

Without wanting to be greedy, or an ungrateful cow, I do wonder if he should have asked me out for dinner instead of a night in. Dinner (no doubt cooked by the man servant) and a DVD at home? Come on, where's the effort! Where's the investment? He just wants a shag, doesn't he? That, or to just slot straight into domesticity, skipping the dating part.

I text him back. "I don't see a romantic match, but if you fancy a riding companion, I'm up for that?" I like unusual people who don't wear riding hats.

"Thanks for being straight forward," he graciously replies, "and for not messing around."

And so we now meet up regularly, have coffee and ride. I always like it when the groom accompanies us and I get an update on her love life. Sometimes, his English friend (who rides in a hunting jacket) comes with us. I get to hear about his love life as well. But *Mr Eastern-Prince* doesn't ever talk much. He leaves it to everyone else.

One day he tells me that he's had an offer from a student who he's considering as a possible match. He's very factual about her, not excited or anything, just matter of fact. She wants £500 a week, wants to live in and "be his girlfriend". He says it's too much. They're in negotiations. He may get her for £200 a week.

"Parents used to make the arrangements," he says, "but these days, we do it ourselves. Online."

And she's the living proof.

17

Mr Needy

Sugardaddy.com

Age: 30

Estimated wealth: £1 million +

Annual Income: £1 million +

Height: 6'2"

Hair: Blonde

I'm standing outside Victoria station, by WHSmith, waiting for lunch with *Mr Needy*. He looks good on paper, but he's 35 minutes late. Just when I'm beginning to mind, he texts me and I go for a coffee and watch the world go by. It will be whatever it is.

From our online correspondence I know that he runs a successful property business, but no more than that. When he arrives, he is indeed tall. But he's a red head. Puzzling. His profile clearly says 'Blonde', though his pictures were blurry. He isn't unattractive, but truth-stretching isn't a good start, is it?

Showing his inexperience in the *Sugardaddy* dating scene, he hasn't booked a table anywhere and asks me what I think we should do. Sensing that he's probably not *Sugardaddy* material (and, at 30 years old why would he be?) I save him by suggesting my favourite. "Salad wrap from *Pret a Manger*?" I smile. Affordable and simple. He clearly hasn't organised himself, so I'll do it for him. Without taking the piss, in case he can't afford it.

But *Mr Needy* doesn't like the idea and, instead, we dive into one of those ribs and steak places with the all-you-can-eat salad bar.

We get chatting over his ribs and my salad.

It seems he runs a property business, which he started after university. "I started it on credit cards," he explains. "I used 0% interest credit cards, bought a property, turned it over fast, re-sold, and did it again and again." He has a slight Nottingham accent. "I now have a property portfolio with several properties but, my god, I've flown close to the wind several times, when the turn-over hasn't come in on time."

He shakes his head stressfully. I strongly suspect that at 30 and only four years in business he isn't bringing in the £1million+ it says on his profile. Nor do I think he has a portfolio of equal worth. But I like a driven entrepreneur and a guy who's done it for himself. We get on well enough. He's into his politics and was a political journalist before his property business. Not bad for 30. It's a good age too – old enough to be grown up and ready for a proper relationship, but young enough not to have an ex-wife and kids to be dishing out to. But I get a strong feeling that he's winging it; trying the *Sugardaddy* businessman role out for size. He's like one of those kids at school who lacks confidence but, now that school's out, has got a bit of success and is trying to change himself.

Good for him!

But he's not there yet.

As he drops me at the tube and we go to say goodbye, I'm pretty sure he's going in for the kiss. As in, proper full-on kiss!

I turn my head to make sure it's cheeks only. Jeez, we only had lunch!

He must have been comfortable and I'm guessing he wasn't put off by the wellies. Well, it *was* raining hard.

Later he texts me. "OMG!" he says, "You're by far the best date I've ever met online. I loved meeting you. You're really hot, and you're so intelligent. I can't believe how well we got on…"

I can feel the excitement building in his tone. It's way over the top. *Take it easy*, I think. *It's just one date.* After one date, all you have is someone's dating persona; their immediate image and, although you can get a good idea of someone in very little time with good intuition, you don't necessarily know their quirks, their habits, their values. He shouldn't get excited just yet. He's getting excited by the idea, not the reality. And that's a dangerous thing. And a harder fall in the end.

We arrange a second date. I'm assuming 7.30pm is, indeed, a dinner date. It has to be right? We meet for a drink in the French *brasserie* in Sloane Square. After three drinks I'm wondering if we'll order here, or if he's booked somewhere else. After the second bottle of wine I decide to order some chips.

He's feeling young and inexperienced to me. I wonder why he chose the *Sugardaddy* site? You *can* be young on *Sugardaddy*, sure, but it's somehow assumed that the man will be assertive and know how to date. This guy just doesn't. I keep having the urge to take over, but resist. If I take charge, that's it, I'll end up being mother. Roles will be set. I just wish he'd take the lead.

By 11.30 he walks me home and we kiss on my doorstep and then kiss again. This is why one absolutely must eat before drinking for goodness sake!!

The wine made me do it!

He is not a good kisser. He's a face licker.

But anyway, wine or not, it's good to get this out of the way, crack on and see if there's anything there.

I know he's a bit over-keen, but he tries really hard not to contact me for a couple of days. Then a few text conversations follow. His first text comes while I'm in the cinema. When I get out, there's a line of messages waiting. He's clearly imagined that I've seen his messages, each getting a bit more frantic than the last. In fact, he's having a conversation with himself.

6:07… "Hi, be lovely to meet up."

6:18… "Hey, did you get my message? We could meet this evening. You don't have kids tonight do you?"

6:27... "Everything OK?"

6:51… "I hope I haven't done anything wrong?"

6:59… "You would tell me if I'd done something wouldn't you?"

7:03… "I would rather you did say than ignored me. Just say so."

He seems slightly nuts. I message him. "I was in the cinema with my phone off. Fancy meeting for a steak in *Sophie*'s?"

"Thank goodness!" he replies. "Thought I'd upset you! I'd love to, though I had a big lunch."

Damn, looks like I'll be eating on my own.

He arrives some 40 minutes late. Now I do this all the time, but I'm not that keen when someone does it to me.

"It took longer from the tube than I thought," he says. Quite why a person who earns £1million+ a year can't just hop in a cab, I don't know. I mean, I take taxis. Lots of them. Then again, maybe that's why I don't have a million in my account.

During dinner (which he decides he *will* now have) I find him a bit annoying. He has a neediness about him, which he knows and tries very hard not to show. But he can't help himself.

"Oh, you like riding horses do you?" he says, with raised eyebrows. Is that him trying to flirt? The more I don't respond, the more he can't help saying crass things. "How am I doing?" he asks.

"Pardon?"

"How am I doing, on the dates?" he says. I pat his knee and tell him he's doing fine. You have to encourage them, right?

"Maybe we could go away for a weekend mini break," he suggests.

It's sweet, but he really isn't reading the signs very well. We're nowhere near that point yet. And, as it was me who suggested dinner, I offer to pay my part of the bill.

"Are you sure? You don't have to," he says.

I want him to say, *No, no, don't be silly* and, better still, insist. But he doesn't. He walks me home and I feel obliged to kiss him, not wanting to hurt his feelings. I'm still working on this little problem I seem to have. I was hoping that he'd be a better kisser this time but, yes... sloppy. He kind of gobbles my chin along with my lips. Afterwards, I need to wipe myself dry.

When his texts start coming in the next day, I'm sitting in the pub with my friend Jon. I tell him about the sloppy snogging and the not-bill-paying and how *Mr Needy* can't seem to make a decision.

"I think you know what to do," Jon says.

18

Mr Perfect

Sugardaddy.com

Age: 34

Height: 6'2"

Annual income: £100k +

Estimated Worth: £1million +

This *Sugardaddy* guy is dark and handsome in his pictures. He earns well, likes yoga and spiritually, travels and likes to cook. At 34 he is younger than me and has some time to go before he becomes one of those weird 40-year-olds who has never committed, won't move into adulthood, wants to keep partying, or has a disorder. Women are different. Although a woman can be desperate for children in her late 30s or early 40s, it will usually be because she hasn't found someone suitable to have children *with*.

Mr Perfect and I chat online and get on perfectly well. I'm in '*get on with it mode*' as usual and tiring of the tendency to chat online for too long. I'm simply not prepared to invest in online chat forever, only to then be ghosted, or to be the ghoster – which I am also capable of doing. One or other party simply zones out and, unless it's specifically online chat that someone is after, it's pointless to dedicate so much time to it.

"I'm not looking for a pen pal," I prompt him.

"Let's meet then!" he says.

Et voila! I pin him down for a date for a couple of days' time.

We meet in the *Blue Bird* on the Kings Road at 8 o'clock. When *Mr Perfect* arrives he is indeed dapper and just like his pictures. Sharply dressed in jeans, a crisp shirt and fitted jacket. Excellent shoes.

We get talking and I'm looking forward to hearing about his spiritual side – the depths he mentioned in his profile. His travels. His beliefs. But it seems that he's not that forthcoming. In fact, he doesn't have anything much to say at all.

He's of Persian and English origin, proverbially tall dark and handsome. But, try as I might, he doesn't disclose much and it occurs to me that someone else might have written his profile for him? Or perhaps he just wrote what he thinks someone *should* write? How could he possibly be so boring in comparison?

"I'm a bit of a runner myself," I say. "I love to run on a tread mill. Once I've pushed through the first 10 minutes I just zone out. It's meditative. The body just keeps running and the mind settles. D'you find similar with yoga?" I'm hoping this will prompt him to tell me what he likes about it.

"Hmm, similar," he murmurs.

And that's it. Nothing back.

I try again, remembering the 'spiritual'. "Have you read Steve Hagen's *Buddhism Plain and Simple*?" I ask.

"Um, no," he replies.

"Great book! Takes all the religion out of Buddhism and just addresses the state of 'being'," I say, hoping to pique his interest.

"Ahh," he replies. The lack of engagement is deadening. Pretty as he is to look at, I can't find *him* inside his pretty picture frame.

He does tell me a story of a date he had with a woman though. "I met up with a woman who said she was 40 and had pictures to match that, but when she turned up for a dinner date, she was more like 60! How... just how...! does a person imagine they can get away with pictures *that* out of date?"

Ok, now he's getting more interesting. A story to tell. Maybe he'll come out of himself. Maybe it's the second drink?

No. That's me on my second drink. He's on the soft drinks now.

"I didn't leave then and there," he goes on. "I still dined with her, but I made it clear that she wasn't for me. *You did say you were 40*, I told her. Then she turned it around on me," he says. "*OK fine*, she said. *If you're not interested in me, perhaps you'd like my daughter? She's 25. Maybe you'd prefer her?*"

What weird things people decide they'll try.

We both end up in hoots at his story. I should like him really. He's opened up, but that date story's the only one he has. He's *supposed* to be the right combination of alternative-thinking-but-not-a-hippie. Someone who likes the good life, but not superficial. He's supposed to be the boy version of me for goodness sake. I like a Buddhist with money. That could be my type. But I can't quite work out why I'm not that keen on him. I like a clean man, but maybe he's too clean – well, too polished-perfect? Perfect jeans, perfect designer shoes, he can even pull off a white jacket. Contrived perhaps? No it's not that... I don't like the gel in his hair, for sure, but that's not it either. I prefer London proper, or proper muddy countryside, but he's neither. He's kind of suburban. And yet that's still not it either.

I think it's called a spark.

He doesn't have a spark. Or *we* don't have a spark.

And it continues, until 10.30, when we leave. We kiss cheek to cheek and go our separate ways. He heads off to his perfect Porsche. I pretty much forgot about him by the time he followed up a long week in dating life later.

19

Mr Young-And-French

Raffles Club

Age: 28

In between the very hard and erratic work (to say the least!) of pitching programme ideas to TV networks and articles to newspapers, I spend time going to gallery openings and fashion parties creating a network for myself as a freelancer.

I also spent a lot of time sitting with my mother while she was bed ridden. During that time, I ended up creating a whole line of clothes: knitted dresses, silky evening dresses, and funky jumpers. At the time, a designer friend of mine was putting on a fashion show for Great Ormond Street Hospital. He was showing his own collection and, as well as other designers' work, he invited me to show my clothes too. I'd often considered a career in fashion and had created enough clothes for a show. I organized a photo shoot with some models, but also modeled some of the clothes myself. I'd been a model for a few years in my 20s after all. We did an outdoor shoot as well as using some funky venues for the evening dresses.

The day of the photo shoot was very long, but I had already lined myself up a fashion party that same evening. The party in Sloane Street was, of course, full of models, designers, photographers, make up artists and everyone to do with fashion. It was organized by the founder of *Superstar* magazine, who held regular networking parties for fashionistas.

They were always fun and great for networking. I took along the models I'd used for the photo shoot and we schmoozed around.

I still don't know why *Mr Young-And-French* was at this party. We got chatting over mojitos. He did something financy. Cute indeed, in a tall, toned, medium dark way, *Mr Young-And-French* was like a *Milk Tray* man. Classic handsome.

"Let's talk zee fashion darling," he said. "My suggestions ees you take your funky jumpers to zee boutiques in East London where zey will be well placed."

"I may well do that."

"And are your clothes as lovely as you?"

At around 11.30, the models and I decided we'd head off to *Raffles Club*, to party on. *Mr Young-And-French* pushed the point and I didn't object. "We will accompany you guys, non?"

In *Raffles*, we get a table, some drinks and start dancing. Am I the oldest of our group, I wonder? The models are about 20 years old and *Mr Young-And-French* is 28. I'm 38. Yes, I'm out-olding them by a decade! Am I getting too old for clubs? I suddenly wonder, but promptly throw those thoughts away on the dance floor.

Mr Young-And-French and I start dancing together.

"You are a very nice lady, very sexy," he flirts. "I bet your fashion line ees just as fabulous as you. I will come to your fashion show. I will model for you, I will help you sell your line."

The sexual tension is building right there on the dance floor – either that or the prosecco. We're dancing almost nose to nose, but just far enough apart to create stories of desire in our minds. We're not quite kissing, and the more the tension grows by not giving in to the desire, I remember why I often go for French men. They stay the right side of drunk, unlike English men, but they also know the importance of building desire and holding on to pleasure before giving in to it. Do English men have to get drunk to enable them to do anything?

I'm well aware that *Mr Young-And-French* is too young for me and don't see anything here other than a bit of fun. So, after plenty of tension, this 38 year-old mother of two does in fact kiss this 28 year-old French dude, right there on the dance floor. A good quality French kiss. Then I look to my side, and one of my models is firmly stopping one of *Mr Young-And-French*'s friends who is trying to take photos on his phone of us kissing.

The models and I call it a night, while *Mr Young-And-French* and I exchange numbers.

As I climb into bed, it occurs to me that I'm at that point where I don't know whether I'm in the young, or the middle-aged camp. I'm partying with 20 year-olds. Equally, there are all ages at fashion parties – designers and photographers aren't all young after all. But I can't help feeling that maybe I'm in the middle camp. Shit, am I middle-aged? Or maybe it's just kissing guys in their 20s, when I'm nearly 40 that's highlighting that feeling? Either way, the age gap hasn't passed me by. Do I even want to piss about with little boys?

Maybe I do?

Maybe just part-time?

Maybe just the cute ones?

Age gap aside, when *Mr Young-And-French* messages me to arrange meeting up, I agree to do so.

It's true that in London, dating reflects the wealthier, more cosmopolitan side of the city. Cocktails are standard and dinner is often on the cards. *Mr Young-And-French* suggests drinks in the East End and we arrange to meet outside the tube, near the swanky bar, outside my usual stomping ground. I console myself with the thought that he might actually still be really cute; or was that just the night lighting, last time?

My fears are laid to rest when he swaggers from the tube – brogues, black slim fit jeans, black polo neck, a flowing overcoat. He's tanned, despite the winter and his hair is cropped short. We walk to the bar together and he gets the drinks in.

"What do you do exactly?" I ask.

"Ah, zees and zat," he says.

It's something entrepreneury, but I can't work out what he does exactly. Something financy. He's got fingers in various pies.

We sit in silence sipping strange cocktails, looking at each other, me and this silent, hot, French dude.

"What do you like doing outside of work?" I ask him.

"Ah, zees and zat," he says again.

"What about sport: d'you have one you like?" That's usually a winning conversation starter.

"Hmm, football is a passion," he replies. "You are one lovely lady."

Ignoring him, I attempt to squeeze a conversation out of him. "Ok, do you play or watch?" I ask.

"I play," he says.

"Weekly, or what?" I continue while he fidgets.

"Two times a week," he says without adding to it.

So he likes playing football.

I know that much.

"You are very beautiful," he says again, out of the blue. "Let's move on," he suddenly adds.

Ey? I think. How did we get to this part so soon? But I agree, and off we go to get a taxi.

I assume we're going to another bar but, before I know it, with no discussion, we're arriving at his flat.

Given his record on the intriguing conversation front, I can only imagine what it is he thinks we'll do in his flat.

"You wanted to go to your flat?" I say, surprised.

He looks blankly at me. "Of course."

"No discussion? No need to ask?" I say and, suddenly finding myself enraged, slap him hard around his *Milk Tray* face, sending him flying backwards into the gutter where he cracks his head on the pavement. Well, in my mind anyway. What I actually say is "I don't particularly want to."

"Just come in for a drink zen," he says.

"I suppose now I'm here I might as well," I sigh unenthusiastically. Had I known he was taking a taxi direct to his flat, I wouldn't have come.

He has a large maisonette and no flatmates it seems. He puts on some music and I sit on the sofa looking around. He goes to the kitchen to get us drinks. When he comes back he's wearing nothing but a pair of tight boxer shorts outlining his package, and a bottle of champagne with two glasses in his hand!

Is this how the 20's are dating? Is this what men that age expect? Are girls dishing it out so freely that men don't even need to ask anymore? If this is the case, I pity both the young men and women. They're missing out on building connection and valuing their worth, all for the sake of quick kicks, but never experiencing substance, or depth.

Nevertheless, I can't help laughing at his comic arrival. He's certainly fit, all that football – and, by the looks of it, regular workouts in the gym – has paid off. But one kiss in *Raffles* and a couple of drinks does not a shag make.

He pours me a glass and I take a few sips. He holds his hand out and I take it, you know, to be polite. Let's see what he's going to do. He pulls me up from my chair to stand with him. He leads us to a long mirror and stands behind me. He then flicks on some music with a heavy bass beat, and starts swaying behind me looking in the mirror. He peels my silk camisole top off and sways me in front of the mirror, both of us facing it. And then he starts running his hands up and down his body, watching himself in the mirror.

Not my body you understand. *His* body.

I stand there wondering what the plan is for me. Does he think he's in an actual porn movie – with himself? Is that what's going on here? He starts to make porn faces in the mirror, followed by porn noises. He flicks the music higher and takes a swig of champagne straight from the bottle.

Boom shak a lah, the music booms as he writhes in front of the mirror, all the while not taking his eyes off himself. He's performing a lap dance on himself.

I can't see any real need for me to be here at all. It wouldn't matter if it was me, or someone else standing there with him. I'm not interested in entertaining him, or watching him entertain himself, except on an anthropological level.

"I'm off then,'" I announce.

"*Mais non!*" he suddenly says, surprised. "Stay! Let's drink. You no having fun?"

"Nah, not so much," I say. "Entertainment's a bit lacking." I grab my top, put it on fast and dash for the door. "I'm off," I say, swiping the bottle of champagne. "For my journey," I add. "Oh, and this," as I spot a packet of cigarettes. I take one out and leave it on the table for him, putting the rest in my bag. "I'll leave you to have sex with yourself."

"*Mais*, come on!" I hear him call down the stairs.

Laughing as I go downstairs, I wonder where I am. Somewhere in North London, I think. I light one of his cigarettes and sit on a bench. Right then, get a taxi! But first I drink a bit of the champagne and smoke his cigarette, chuckling to myself.

While I'm smoking, a homeless guy sits down next to me and asks for a fag. "Have these," I say, handing him the packet and the lighter. I take a few swigs of champagne while I wait for a taxi to appear.

"Here, why don't you have this too?" I say and hand him the bottle as I climb into my taxi.

20

Mr Lamborghini

Sugardaddy.com

Age: 44

Worth: £1 million +

Annual income: £500k +

I know by now that men are choosing women based on their looks alone, and being pretty ruthless about it. I also know they are looking for women 20 years their junior, so, in for a penny in for a pound!

By now, I'm actively only searching for those men online who've put an annual income of £500k upwards. They are searching for the best looking or youngest women after all. But how can you know if they're telling the truth? Are we within our rights to ask for proof? You know, *It was lovely to meet you, thank you for dinner, you can see I am who I said I was, now can you please show me your bank account before we take this any further?*

It is here, on *Sugardaddy.com*, with the £500k+ annual earnings box ticked that I find *Mr Lamborghini*.

Mr Lamborghini has a picture of a car on his profile instead of himself. This is always dubious. It's really hard to strike up a conversation with a car. Still, *Mr Lamborghini* messages me and it turns out that he's got good chat and a normal profile: *Used to be in shipping, now retired and investing in various businesses. Love travel, restaurants, and getting together with friends. Looking for a lovely woman to enjoy those things with. Age immaterial — a connection is what matters.*

He calls me and sounds pretty nice on the phone too. Neither does he hang about in making a meeting. My kind of guy. "Expect me in a very interesting car," he laughs.

When he arrives outside *Cafe Concerto* on the Kings Road, it's in an Ariel atom – a very fast two-seat track and race car.

Mr Lamborghini is cheekily giggling, trying to squeeze a reaction out of me.

"Very nice," I say to please him when, in fact, I can't see the appeal. They clip you in to those with a harness instead of a seat belt.

I don't really care about cars and this one looks like an uncomfortable toy. He continues to talk about the car rather than himself, or me.

"So this car is one of the fastest on track, but it's legal to drive on public highways too," he educates me, raising his eyebrows to encourage my reaction. "There are only a few available and mine is the only one on the market currently. It'll sell very quickly." He waits expectantly for my response, which is, at this point, not forthcoming.

"Yes dear, it's a lovely car," I have to stop myself saying.

I nod and smile.

After we've finished lavishing admiration on the car, we go for lunch. Now, I love people-watching so, while we eat, I pick out other diners and imagine their lives – who they are, and what they do.

Mr Lamborghini listens to my observations and gets into the game.

"Well," I say. "That lady over there is called Sandrine. She's French by birth, but has lived in the UK all her life. She's mother to four boys, ranging from 15 to 25. She was a teacher, but only for five years, pre children."

"Ah yes," he agrees. "And what's her husband called?"

And with that *Mr Lamborghini* and I hit it off. He's good fun, open, and quite intense. There's more to him than just the 'ex shipping man' on his profile.

After lunch he drives me home in the Atom thing. It attracts attention as it roars down the road.

It was a good meeting and I'm up for another one, although there's one major problem. He's ugly. Googly eyed ugly. Like Garfield.

But maybe what he lacks in looks he can make up for in character? A man surely can't be both ugly and nasty? I've tried handsome men who haven't turned out well, so maybe ugly is the way to go? Yes, I'll try an ugly man!

He messages me later and fixes a second date. "I'll pick you up from your home," he says, "and take you for dinner in Shoreditch where I live."

This time he picks me up in a Lamborghini. Now, is this all slightly too cliché – a blonde bird in a red Lamborghini with an ugly bloke driving? As I get into the car, I sink in my seat hoping no one I know will see me.

We go for dinner and, again, get on really well. He seems open about his life, his businesses check out online – yes, I *Google*'d him! – and conversation flows. He picks up the bill and is very gentlemanly, opening doors and driving me home after dinner. There's nothing letchy about him and never a lewd word uttered.

So, two dates in and I'm thinking, yes, this could work. I like this guy! Turns out he likes to go on 'driving experience holidays' for people with super cars. He's got a fleet of super cars himself. Can't be bad.

He invites me out to dinner for our third date, again near where he lives.

"I can take you home after dinner or, if you want, you can stay at my house. I have a spare room," he says, making it comfortable.

I agree and, as it's on the evening my little boy stays with his dad, I take a few bits in my bag should I decide to stay.

"I'll send a taxi for you at 6," he says.

I arrive at his place and he meets me downstairs at the entrance of his apartment block. I'm wearing an off-the-shoulder jumper dress – one of my own designs – long boots and a fur jacket. I bounce out of the taxi.

"Oh hello," he laughs, "you look like you're ready to be entertained."

We go to a nice restaurant. Chinese, my least favourite food. But, as Chinese goes, this is a good one. He doesn't know about wine I notice, and orders a Diet Coke. Doesn't he know that the 'diet' bit of the Coke is as bad as sugar? Would it be too greedy to order a bottle of wine to myself, I wonder?

I go for a glass at a time instead, hoping it's not as noticeable, even though I'm drinking a whole bottle's worth after all.

After dinner we walk back to his place and, *en route,* he takes my arm. He goes in confidently for a kiss and I'm with him on it. Thank goodness he's a good kisser! The ice is broken and we make that connection.

His apartment is a huge, flashy, modern warehouse conversion, open plan and minimalist, with kitchen and bathroom doors that slide in and out with a flick of a finger. He has expansive brick walls that are crying out for giant pieces of art. But there is no art. In fact, his open plan living area looks a bit like a lobby. There's nothing that says who he is, just open space, like a show room. I imagine my kids chucking crap everywhere and cringe.

He puts on some music and, of course, he has a great sound system and a great music collection. I'm relaxed.

Now, many men reach this point of the evening and then just ask directly: *So, um, are you in the mood?* to which you may think, *Well, seduce me and let's see.* Or else they clumsily fumble at you, or never even dare. *Mr Lamborghini's* approach works. He looks me directly in the eyes and asks if I'm ready to go to bed. I'm willing. He's a gentleman and giving me the option to stay in the other room makes me comfortable enough to want to stay with him in his room.

He continues gazing at me intensely as he takes my clothes off. He doesn't seem so ugly now. He's dark and has a cuddly, but strong, body. He's got that 'in charge and knows what he's doing' feel. He really studies me and definitely likes what he sees. He looks me up and down and takes his time. More than anything else, he seems genuinely interested in pleasing me. It's like that's where he derives his pleasure from.

We both sleep well and, in the morning, kiss goodbye, natural and relaxed.

It feels like we're an item already.

21

Mr Lamborghini – Part 2

Mr Lamborghini and I seem to have made a rather nice connection. It's like we just slipped comfortably into coupledom with no dithering around. In the days to follow, there isn't any of that 'will he phone me?' bollocks. No. Messages ping merrily back and forth and we start to meet up a couple of times a week, on the days that my little boy is with his dad. Always in his place, never mine. He always sends a taxi. A pretty nice perk of dating a sugar daddy. No more public transport for me.

On Tuesdays I go to his place in the late afternoon, while he's finishing some work in his home office. I hang out in his big, clean apartment with gym equipment in one corner, him working in the other. One Tuesday when I arrive he holds up a bottle gleefully.

"You like G&T?" he declares. "Here, I've bought you the Bombay Sapphire you like." With the gin in one hand, he pulls his other hand from behind his back and produces another bottle. "A good supply," he grins.

"Wow thanks!" How nice he's thinking of me.

I start to stay over at his apartment regularly. We spend the evening chatting and listening to music and, on a Friday, we visit a few of the restaurants in Shoreditch, none of which I'm familiar with.

This Friday *Mr Lamborghini* has one of his driving rally guests with him. The man is staying in London from Greece, for the whole summer. He's bought his super car over with him, to drive around London and take it on tour. We decide to take him to *Gaucho* in Sloane Avenue for some serious steak eating. As it's in my area, I invite my older 19-year-old son along too. He likes a steak. My younger boy stays with his dad, although he has met *Mr Lamborghini* briefly, on a school pick up. "My daddy's car has four seats and yours only has two," my little boy told him. That's perspective!

We order our steak at *Gaucho* and chat while we wait for our food.

"I'm thinking of getting another tattoo," my son says.

"Well, wait on that for a bit", I reply. "The one you have is really nice, but people can get addicted to tattoos you know. Hold off for a bit while you decide what to get."

"Sure, I'll think carefully," my son replies.

"Tattoos would look great on you," interjects *Mr Lamborghini*.

"Well, yes, but think on it," I prompt again.

"Nah, he's a big boy now, he knows what he's doing," *Mr Lamborghini* says, nudging my son.

"I think I'll wait," my son replies.

Our guest from Greece rattles his cutlery awkwardly. I smile at him, then glare at my date.

"Mums always say that kind of thing," *Mr Lamborghini* continues, ignoring my look. "But at some point, a kid's gonna grow up and do his own thing, hey!"

"Yeah, but she's kind of got a point though," my son says. "No hurry."

Our food arrives and my son and I are the only ones sharing wine. *Mr Lamborghini* always drives. You would, wouldn't you, if you had the cars he has? Our Greek guest has his super car parked outside and doesn't drink either.

"It's just us then," I nod to my son.

"She likes her wine, doesn't she?" *Mr Lamborghini* observes, laughing.

"Don't we all?" my son replies.

"Likes her G&T too!"

My son refuses to be drawn.

"Don't worry," *Mr Lamborghini* goes on, "I keep a good eye on her."

I sit quietly smouldering and we finish our meal.

"Right, let's get going," says *Mr Lamborghini* once he's paid the bill.

"I think I'll go back to my place tonight," I say pointedly.

My son chats with our guest and *Mr Lamborghini* pulls me aside, "Everything ok?" he asks.

"Was that your attempt at undermining me just then?" I say through gritted teeth.

"What!" he exclaims. "What have I done?"

"Unacceptable," I say, refusing to believe he didn't know what he was doing.

"Ok, cool," he says. "No problem. Won't happen again! Now, come on. Come home with me." He smiles. "Please?"

"I'll talk to you tomorrow," I say and, smiling at our guest, head off into the night with my son.

22

Mr Lamborghini – Part 3

One must give someone the benefit of the doubt, right? No one's perfect. *Mr Lamborghini's* subtle attempt to undermine me in front of others didn't go unnoticed. It's not the first time I've experienced it, and I know it starts like that and slowly escalates. But I figure nipping it in the bud may set the dynamic straight from the start.

Later that week we settle back into the routine of me going round to his apartment. He always hands me a G&T upon arrival.

"Thanks, but I don't actually want to auto drink."

"Oh go on, treat yourself!" he usually says, despite not drinking himself.

There's often chocolate, too. I think I must have mentioned that I love a bit of Green & Blacks. He's gone for it though. 12 bars on a 3 for 2 offer. I realize how much I note my intake of both alcohol and sugar. I have them, but I moderate both and have a little inbuilt monitor. I would never have 12 bars of chocolate in the house – they'd be guzzled in no time. I thank him, but wish he hadn't bought so much. He buys cartons of cigarettes in bulk too. I don't want to commit to chocolate eating like he's committed to smoking.

One Saturday, we go to the supermarket and, after he has stocked up on cartons of cigarettes, as though he was at the duty free, we do a shop for a house party he's holding the next day. I head for the olives, and the ricotta and spinach parcels, the sun blushed tomatoes and calamari. He heads for the giant bags of sausage rolls and onion rings. It makes it interesting at the check out.

"We don't need this," he says, putting aside my calamari pieces in light chilli oil. "Or this," he adds, discarding my sun blushed tomatoes.

"How come?" I say.

"We have enough with these," he says, pointing to the giant bags of sausage rolls and chicken wings.

All he leaves of my choices is the olives. He's paying, so I can't really dispute it, but sausage bloody rolls… what is this, 1985?

The day of the house party arrives and so do lots of people, from lunchtime onwards. The apartment is perfect for a house party: open plan, bags of space, great sound system. As I get chatting to people, I realise that his friends are mainly car people, all connected in some way to super cars: showing, racing, owning, or wanting them.

I speak to a guy called Darren. "Hello you," he says. "How do you know *Mr Lamborghini* then?"

"We met online," I say.

"Oh yeah," he laughs, "is that how it works now then, online?"

"It can do," I answer, dryly.

"Oh right." He dips in to the olives. "What do you do then?"

"Well, I write and I've just made a documentary."

"Oh ay," he suddenly shouts over to *Mr Lamborghini*, "you've got a clever one here have you?" He roars with laughter. "Better than the last one," he says turning back to me.

"Oh, right?" I say, wondering who the 'last one' was. And with that he has nothing more to say and wanders off with a beer.

In fact, I struggle to find much in common with *any* of *Mr Lamborghini's* friends. There's just not that much that interests me in cars and that seems all they are interested in.

*

As the weeks go by, the dining out in the little restaurants seems to have fizzled out.

"Shall we go to a restaurant this evening?" I ask one Friday night visit.

"It's a pretty expensive way of eating," he responds.

"Oh, yeah I guess so," I say, rather dejected. It's a shame. Food is a big passion of mine, but it doesn't seem to be high on his agenda. Unlike his work, which is. He was in shipping, now retired. He's in his 40s and has set up several businesses and seems to have invested in other companies too. He frequently tells me his work stresses him out.

"You just don't understand the pressure I'm under," he fumes one evening. He seems to think his stresses are really big. Bigger than I could understand. But I have to worry about my kids, how to pay my bills, my rent and where my next bit of freelance work is coming from.

"What you actually need is life management skills," I tell him. "How to strategise your new business challenges. It needs thought and planning. But they're not actual stresses if you learn how to manage yourself."

He stares at me. "Hmm," he murmurs. "Maybe, yes."

He has a Skype call with a PR company that he's invested in, and pulls me into shot for them to see me. Does he want to show them he has a girlfriend? He seems to be pouring money into this PR company, but it's his own cash, rather than a 'new business' type of investment.

"I haven't actually made any money in the two years since I retired from shipping," he says. "I'm investing heavily in my businesses."

"OK," I say. "Doesn't tax planning and clever accounting help, rather than putting in all your own savings?" And then, just like that, despite my best efforts, he invests another £30k of his savings into this failing PR business.

I sit waiting for him to finish his call. These calls seem to increasingly be creeping into our time together. He strikes deals and invests more of his savings and hands me endless G&T's. I start to rebuff them.

"I thought you liked G&T?" he sighs. "I was just trying to be nice."

"Thanks, but I don't want to drink all the time," I say.

Undeterred by my rejection, the G&T's keep coming. The same happens with the Green & Blacks chocolate. And Magnum ice creams. They come out after every meal.

"No thank you," I start to say a bit more firmly. "I don't want chocolate or G&T on tap."

"Woah, hey!" he says. "Just taking care of you!"

It seems that food and drink are starting to become a bit of a thing between us.

"Shall I make some seafood and salad?" I suggest one evening, trying to be enthusiastic.

"Ah no, we'll eat what I have here. No need to get other food in," he replies flatly. Sadly he's more of a pasty and iceberg lettuce kind of guy.

He also drinks several Vitamin C drinks a day. I look at the ingredients and tell him they contain aspartame. He doesn't know what it is.

"Maybe you could get your vitamins from your food?" I suggest. "From avocados and the like…"

He looks at me blankly and sprays a jet of freshener into the room.

"What's that?" I ask.

"*Febreze*," he says. "It eliminates the smoke."

He often sprays *Febreze* around the place in vast quantities. He smokes a lot indoors, but I imagine suffocating on the *Febreze* more than the smoke.

"Shall we take it easy on the spray?" I say.

"Anything else I'm doing wrong?" he rolls his eyes.

"Well, I guess a bit less smoke wouldn't hurt, seeing as we're on the subject," I joke. The weekend hasn't really got off to that good a start.

At weekends, we usually go to car events. I didn't know car events existed, but I do now. We drive to some venue or other, take the Lamborghini, park it with other Lamborghini's, then watch people walking around and admiring all the Lamborghinis. *Mr Lamborghini* very much enjoys letting people look at his Lamborghini. Whenever we stop at petrol stations, people talk to *Mr Lamborghini* about the bloody Lamborghini and I watch his ego inflate. One time, I come back from the service station loo and find a child sitting in the car. The child's father is taking a photo. *Mr Lamborghini* proudly allows it.

After a few weeks of letting my life be integrated into *his* – the car events, his friends, his food, his work issues – I suggest a visit to an art exhibition that I'm keen to go and see.

"Maybe next weekend," he replies.

"It's actually the last week this week," I say.

"But we're taking the car to an event in Buckinghamshire this weekend," he replies.

"Never mind then," I say.

*

I arrive one Tuesday afternoon, and *Mr Lamborghini* has a girl with him.

"This is Tina," he says "Remember Tina from the house party? I was going to hire her as my PA?"

I nod, vaguely.

"Well, here she is!"

"Fantastic," I say. "You can get some help with your work."

Suddenly he looks annoyed. "I don't need 'help'," he says angrily. "Are you suggesting I'm not managing?"

An awkward atmosphere slinks in and fills the gap between us. I'm baffled. "Well..." I say. "Nice to meet you Tina," and walk out of the room.

Tina turns out to be a bossy, loud, posh girl who says she's a natural blonde, but isn't. She and *Mr Lamborghini* talk in riddles and seem to understand each other's in-jokes. I don't. There's a clique developing here and I'm not in it.

Later that week I turn up mid-afternoon on Friday, as usual. It seems he's hired himself a personal trainer. The gym equipment he keeps in his apartment hasn't been used for months. We have an hour-long session with the personal trainer and groan about our aches and pains. It's apparently going to become a regular thing and I'm up for it.

After the session, Tina goes home and *Mr Lamborghini* shows me the brochure and marketing material they've been working on. I take my time reading it, in order to give proper feedback. We talk a lot about the business.

"So you're going the sponsorship route then?" I say, offering him a couple of suggestions.

"Hmmm,' he replies distractedly, "I'll think about it."

I stay over as usual. It's only been a few weeks, but we are already in a routine. I notice that he still concentrates just on me in bed and always takes the lead. Today, *Mr Lamborghini* decides to introduce something else into our relationship. Poppers.

"See this?" he says. "Ever used them?"

"No, I haven't. What's 'Poppers'?"

"Perfectly safe," he says. "Really intensifies sex."

"No thanks," I say. I never use any kind of drugs at all."

"It's perfectly legal," he says. "You can buy it on the high street."

"Still no thanks," I say. I don't care if something is legal. I care if it's healthy. I never do shit like that. "Can we just do it normally, without that?" I say.

He looks disappointed. "It's perfectly safe," he continues. "No side effects. You'll love it! You just sniff this." He opens the little bottle and waves it under my nose.

"No thanks. Gives me the creeps that kind of thing."

"Alright," he sighs.

We do have sex, but without the Poppers. Only today, it's not straightforward.

"Twist my nipples," he says quietly.

"What did you say?" I ask.

"Twist my nipples," he demands more loudly.

"Um… right… ok." I wonder quite what he's after. I give his nipples a little tweak.

"Harder," he pleads.

I squeeze them harder.

"Harder!"

I twist and squeeze his nipples as hard as I can, but he's still yelling, "harder!"

I'm at capacity. I can't twist or squeeze any harder. And I'm not enjoying it. For god's sake, how hard can one twist nipples anyway?

Undeterred, he tells me to scratch his skin. Again I start fairly lightly, but it's soon apparent that it's a case of 'the harder the better'.

"Excuse me," I say, not wanting to interrupt his ecstasy. "I'm twisting and scratching as hard as I can here."

"Do it harder!" he shouts.

I oblige and he moans, but I'm not sure I believe him. I'm sure that's a fake moan!

He never finishes during sex. In fact – hang on! – I can't remember him ever having come during sex at all. Not once! At the beginning, I thought he was being considerate, waiting for me kind of thing. But in the six weeks we've known each other, he's never once come.

"I don't need to come to have a good time," he says, but suddenly, I suspect that, actually, he can't. Has he taken things to such extremes in his life that he's now not getting there without Poppers and nipple clamps?

The next day I ask my teenage son if he knows about Poppers.

"Yeah, gay guys love them. They enhance sex," he says.

"How the hell do you know that and I don't?" I ask him.

"It's the twenty-first century, mum. People *know* stuff."

23

Mr Lamborghini – Part 4

"We have a road trip coming up," *Mr Lamborghini* announces one evening. "A week across Europe. Tina will be coming. Why don't you come along with us? It'll be great for you to come on a driving tour."

Yes, *Mr Lamborghini* has invited me on the 'Alps Driving Tour'. I will be his passenger.

"God yes, I'm in!" I'm pretty excited about it. Five days of driving in the Alps among the super cars. What's not to like?

"We'll be taking the best driving roads and views through France, Italy, Switzerland and Germany," he tells me. The routes have been carefully planned by the tour leader. "We drive at least six hours a day, sometimes eight, and each night we'll stay in a different hotel. Want to go shopping beforehand?" he asks.

"God yeah," I say, beaming.

"Tomorrow?" he says.

"God yeah."

The next day after breakfast and a slow morning, we go shopping. "*All Saints* first stop," I instruct as we hit the shops. I rummage around *All Saints* and find a sequined dress, a few funky T-Shirts, a little skirt and a weird shaped wrap dress. He buys them all.

"I need a few bits too," he says and so we go to *Gap* where he picks a few items.

"I think you need to go up a size?" I suggest, "those are a bit tight on you."

"No, no. I lost three stone," he assures me. "This is a good size."

"Well ok, but you know not to worry about the label size right? Just feel how they fit instead."

I find him a nice jacket, but it doesn't look good on him. I try more styles on him but, whatever combination I pick, I just can't seem to style him right. We do get a few things, all of which are too tight, but he won't budge on it. I'm going to have to get really creative to get him looking good.

Clothes shopping done, he suggests lunch. "Let's get a *Subway*," he says.

"A what?"

"You know, the sandwich place?"

"Never been," I say. "Is it good?"

"You've *never* been to *Subway*…? What the hell!"

"It's never appealed," I reply, a little put out. "I'll try it though."

"You'll see," he says. "They have great bread, all sorts of fillings."

So we go to *Subway*. I order 1 tuna sandwich, but can see that it's just not going to be very good. The bread's poor quality, or have I just got too used to the artisan bakeries of Chelsea?

"Good huh?" he mutters through a mouthful.

"Mmm, nice," I reply, not wanting to be snotty. But it just ain't worth the gluten!

We end up in Camden market. "There are some great shops here," he says. "I'll show you."

He leads me into a shop with some 'unusual' clothes hanging on the walls. Clothes with chains on them. Dresses with lace-up corset backs. Leather jeans with studs up the sides. Platform heels and boots that lace up above the knees.

"How about this one?" he says, pointing at a corseted dress – a Halloween witch's outfit.

"For me!" I sputter, conscious of my classic silk shirts and bouncy Chelsea hair. "I'm more of an *Yves Saint Laurent* girl, don't you think? *Reiss* at the very least? Or a silk dress maybe."

"OK," he says, a little disappointed. "Let's try another." He leads me further along the market. "This one has great clothes. I'm sure there'll be something in here. How about this?"

He pulls out a 1950's style burlesque dress, frothy and cute.

"It's cute," I say, "but I'm more classic chic, with a dash of funky."

"Ok, how about these? These would look great on you!"

He hands me a pair of studded, thigh-length PVC boots.

"Erm, noooo," I say, feeling irritated. "Not my style."

"You should try them, you'd look good."

And I'm thinking, I would not bloody look good. I'd look like a bloody dominatrix.

"To go with this?" I say, and point to the bottles of Poppers arranged along counter. "No more shopping for me. Can we go now, please."

24

Mr Lamborghini – Part 5

The day before the trip, I arrive at *Mr Lamborghini's* with my two little cases and we set off on the first leg. Tina is in the Porsche with the tour leader. I'm *Mr Lamborghini's* passenger. In the Lamborghini.

We spend our first night in Kent, where we meet up with all the other rally-ers. Supercar after supercar pulls up. Aston Martins, Maseratis, Porsches, all sorts. As people arrive I look around waiting for someone to connect to. But so far I'm uninspired. Once they've all arrived, we go to a buffet dinner. It all looks as middle-of-the-road as the people eating it. I ask if there's any balsamic for my salad leaves, but there isn't. There's coleslaw. And salad cream. Yes, welcome back to the 1980s.

A lot of car talk goes around the table. Is this collectively the most boring bunch of people that could have gathered in one place? Are all car people like this? Middle-aged, middle-of-the-road, some in couples, and some men on their own. There's normally at least one person in a group that I'd befriend, a woman usually, but anyone would be fine tonight. I'm wearing some glitzy eveningwear and heels, but everyone else is in jeans. And bad jeans at that. *Stop it!* I tell myself. *It's the first night, it's going to be fun.*

After dinner, there's an introductory session. It's as much as I can do to keep my eyes open. Afterwards, we all go to bed early. I'm trying to remain upbeat. I just love road trips and surely this will be the ultimate one. In a Lamborghini!

In bed I make a little attempt at intimacy.

"I'm really tired," he says, so I don't push it.

Next morning, we get up early to leave. "You have so much stuff!" he says, picking up my bags and making much of carrying them. My two small carry on cases.

"Yes, I have stuff," I say. "I like to have all eventualities covered and I like my products."

We trundle in to France and, of course, our troupe causes quite a stir – 10 super cars together causes a stir wherever we go. But the attention is all slightly vulgar. I have a bag in front with me, and take out my knitting. *Mr Lamborghini* is decidedly unimpressed.

"Why aren't you paying attention to the views?"

I've knitted so much that I can knit without looking. I take in the views as I knit away and let the hours of driving roll by.

Finally we stop for lunch, although it's basically a pit stop. Time to fill up cars and people, empty our bladders, and off again. It's all a bit manic. Whatever happened to taking it all in? Eventually we arrive at our evening hotel. There's just enough time for a shower and then everyone joins together for dinner. Again, no one dresses up. I still haven't found anyone to bond with. We drink a glass of wine and go to bed.

The next day, we drive for hours and hours again, without stopping. I want to get my kids something to take home, but we don't stop long enough even for that. We re-fuel for lunch and petrol in supermarkets on the edges of towns, then drive again to the next hotel.

Mr Lamborghini decides to give me an unprompted lesson in how to handle a super car.

"The way to handle her," he says, "is to look to the furthest point and drive towards that. That way you can assess the right speed."

I don't reply. I have no desire to be mansplained. But he simply doesn't get what's wrong with his unsolicited lessons.

"Yes," I say. "We do the same with horses. Don't look down, look to the next jump. It's pretty obvious."

He stops the car. "What's the matter? What's wrong with you?"

"Don't tell me how to drive," I tell him. "Please. I haven't asked for a lesson."

"Well excuse me," he says and we drive on in silence.

That night we stay at a hotel – a youth hostel on the top of a snowy mountain. *Mr Lamborghini* and I don't have sex. Again. I can't work out why not. We're on holiday, right! Maybe he's still brooding over my rebuff at his driving lesson. I think it's put him into a very bad mood.

The next day, we stop at a supermarket to get lunch and petrol. It's encouraged on this trip to occasionally swap passengers to get a feel for other cars, so I decide that this is the perfect moment to ride along with someone else. I pick a guy with a Bristol accent who has been piping up humorously over the walkie-talkies that all the cars communicate through. He's doing the trip alone, so doesn't have a passenger to swap.

"Of course," he agrees. "Why not? Hop in!"

I go to *Mr Lamborghini* and tell him that I'm going to be driving with someone else for a while. "Maybe you'll be in a better mood at the other end," I say. I get into the other car and have a fun few hours driving and bantering with *Mr Bristol.*

We lunch at a picnic site in the mountains. But I've left my lunch in *Mr Lamborghini's* car. Along with my bag. So I have no cash or card to buy anything.

What's more, *Mr Lamborghini* doesn't even turn up.

The PA, Tina, is getting her lunch. The tour leader is getting his. Everyone. I simply can't bear to ask anyone for money for lunch, and no one notices I haven't got anything to eat. I sit with Tina and the tour leader and they ask where *Mr Lamborghini* is. It's awkward. Some of these are his work colleagues. I have to be careful.

"*Mr Lamborghini* is in a very bad mood," I tell her. "I think he's unhappy about me driving with *Mr Bristol…*"

She seems completely unsurprised. "Ah yeah. He does that," she says, like she's seen it all before.

"Oh really!" I answer.

"Yeah," she says. "He did the same to the last girlfriend. Once, you know, a girlfriend phoned me in the night asking me to come and get her. They'd had an altercation and she said she was scared of him."

I listen intently and start to get the picture, but I'm feeling pretty alone. *Mr Lamborghini* still hasn't arrived, and he has all my stuff – bag, money, passport.

And then, finally, just as we are getting ready to leave, he arrives. He ignores me, but recounts some adventurous story about waiting for an ambulance after some guy got knocked off his motorbike. It looks to everyone else like he's a wonderful, caring man. I get in to the Porsche with the tour leader.

How I can get off this trip, I wonder? We're nowhere near an airport, a train station, anything. The tour is pre-set and we drive more or less in convoy. All the way we meet up at check points. I can't see how I could possibly leave.

In the evening, we all dine together as usual. *Mr Lamborghini* doesn't utter a word to me and, when we go to bed, he continues to ignore me. I wish I wasn't here and go into the bathroom and cry. When I think he's asleep, I climb into bed, thinking how ugly he's getting by the day. I know I don't want this man. A man who will brood over something for days. It's not a good night's sleep. At all.

The following morning is the last breakfast of the tour. I rise early, eat on my own and meet *Mr Lamborghini* by the car. The drive is silent. It has been four days since he last properly spoke to me. And then the vibe suddenly turns.

"So," *Mr Lamborghini* jokes, "I'm guessing you won't want to see me anymore. Is this end of the road?"

I look him in the eye and wonder what he's doing.

"He is a bit of a wanker that silly old fart isn't he!" he says of himself, laughing.

He begins to make self-aware, self-effacing jokes that are genuinely funny and, just like that, a switch has been flicked and he's happy and fun to be with again. I'm not a grudge holder. I'm easy to get back on side. I can't find it in me to punish him, and so I find myself laughing along.

"Don't do it again," I tell him in my best joke schoolteacher's voice.

*

The rest of the tour passes enjoyably and soon enough we find ourselves back home. He drops me off and I call up my friends to tell them all about it. They're envious that I've just toured several countries in a Lamborghini.

"Well, that *Mr Lamborghini*'s a bit of a twat, to be honest," I tell them.

"But, still," they say, "the super cars!"

Once we're back, *Mr Lamborghini* messages me with nice words. "Thanks for coming on the tour and putting up with me. Coming over Friday? Let's go for dinner."

Somehow, I agree. Maybe his twattery was just a weird blip?

Now, I've made no secret of my love of the country and horses, so when *Mr Lamborghini* comes to pick me up on the next Friday lunchtime, I'm delighted to find that we're driving to Oxfordshire where we stop at a converted barn with stables and paddocks.

"It's coming up for sale," he says, "in a few months time. Do you like it?"

My heart skips a little beat. "I love it."

"Maybe we should get it?" he enthuses.

The possibilities start racing through my mind.

"If we still know each other in a few months time," I joke.

Suddenly he pulls me towards him, looks intensely into my eyes and holds a long silence.

The Extreme Dating Diaries of Isabelle Monroe

"You won't be my girlfriend in a few months time," he says. I wait for the next bit. He bites his lip, building tension, continuing a long pause. "You'll be my wife."

The words fall between us. It doesn't quite ring true. It's all drama without substance. I nevertheless have a moment's panic at the thought of it. He's looking at me knowingly. "Well, the stable and paddocks are certainly very nice," I say. "C'mon, let's look around."

I stay over at his place that night. He is very attentive when he leads me to the bedroom. Very intense. Taking my clothes off slowly and seductively. Lowering me onto the bed. Balancing his touches, between strong and passionate, to light and seductive. He runs his hands up my legs, all the time looking in my eyes. I look back at him and remember why I was here in the first place.

I bring my hands across his back and pull him closer to me, but all of a sudden he's only half there. The finger that is gently stroking the side of my face moves to my jaw, then down my neck, then suddenly his hand is on my throat and he starts to put pressure on. I can feel him on my leg. He's quickly getting hard. Really hard. The more pressure he puts on my neck, the harder he gets. I'm starting to lose my breath as he cuts off my air. All the while he's staring at me, staring intensely into my eyes as if to see what I'll do.

I shake my head and take his hand to get him off my throat. I can hardly breathe now, but he is rock hard. I start writhing and chocking and pull his hands off my throat.

"What the fuck are you doing!" I pant.

"Seeing your limits," he replies.

We sit in silence for a bit, then he picks up his phone and fiddles with it.

"Fuck's sake!" I seethe at him, turning my back to him in sleep position.

I wonder if we'll ever have normal sex? I don't think we ever have, so I don't imagine we ever will. Sometimes he can't get it up, and I'm casual about that. I don't want him feeling bad and I don't especially mind. Other times he has the biggest hard on ever, and there's no other explanation but Viagra. He even pretends to come once, making groaning porn noises, but I know he faked it. And then there's the poppers, the nipple twists… and now this!

He tosses and turns in bed. "I tell you what," I say. "If you're having trouble sleeping, I'm going to sleep in the other room," and I go to the other bedroom and switch off. I don't care about him. *You're a twat and a perv.* I fall asleep without much effort, when suddenly *Mr Lamborghini* bounds into the room.

"Did you want me to follow you in here, is that what you're doing?" he rants. "You want me to persuade you, don't you?"

"I really do want to sleep here," I say. "Please. Leave. Me. Alone."

He starts to pace up and down, ranting and, as I watch him, I see him go to lock the door. I'm overcome with repulsion.

"Ok, so I'm going to go home now," I say very quietly. I get up and start to get dressed. It's 1am. *Mr Lamborghini* stomps into the other room and, as I go to put my shoes on, a book on mindfulness that I've given him as a present comes flying past my head and knocks a vase over.

I stay calm, but head quickly for the door. Mindfulness? You've got to be effing joking!

This is the last time you'll ever see me, I think, mindfully closing the door behind me.

25

Mr Italian

Elite Dating

Age: 46

A combination of my mother dying; a back operation; a housing situation, and my son's father's drinking issues, instigated a move out of London. A need to decompress for a bit. Re-charge, do some riding, let my son run wild. A change of scene, to rural Devon, where I know no one at all.

I rent a small cottage, get a horse and spend the summer breaking it in, teaching my son to ride. I then take the first job that comes up – a cleaner in my son's new school. When they see me cleaning the school in my flowery rubber gloves and fur coat, they know I've arrived. Later, I find that looking after holiday properties is a more lucrative business, so I start doing that too. After a while I also join a supply teaching agency, but zero hours contracts is, well, shit. Although rent and life is cheaper in the country, the earning opportunities and type of work is very different to London.

Dating takes a back seat for a while, but not for very long. Once I've settled in to country living, I decide to get back online. The first thing I notice is that there are hardly any men on *Guardian Soulmates* in Devon so, after one month's subscription, I don't bother again. *Tinder* has sailors in Plymouth, or hippies in Totnes it seems. I try *Elite* and find *Mr Italian,* who catches my eye. Every woman should experience an Italian man, right? But here's the thing. He's in London. A corporate man. Top of his career.

He's got a great profile and doesn't mind putting his pictures online. He messages me first and, after only two exchanges, he gets straight to the dinner date.

"What kind of food do you like?"

"Almost everything," I say, "but fish is my preference."

"Excellent!" he writes. "I'll let you know the venue and time when I've booked it."

Bloody marvellous! A man who can make a god damn decision, take charge, book a restaurant!

Seems simple, but god knows the to and fro-ing that can go on in this area. Endless messages back and forth. Get on with it already!

He has a slick picture of himself, looking rather serious. Slick in that Italian way – dark, thick hair flopping around, Italian loafers – and he seems to take his slickness rather seriously. He's not smiling, more sultry. And he's taken care of the background in his pictures too: there are no unmade beds, or drawers hanging open, or socks on the floor. He looks good at 46. In his pictures anyway.

We continue to make contact before we meet, which makes me confident that he's serious. Then he lets me know the venue. "One of my favourite Mayfair restaurants," he enthuses. "We can have a drink at the bar and then dinner."

I love being told where to meet. I have so many other things to take care of in life that the relief of someone else doing it is quite immense. *Imagine a life of not having to be in charge of absolutely everything,* I think.

I arrive there at the bar, in *Novikov* in Mayfair. He texts to say he's *en route*. I'm in my favourite skinny jeans, fitted leather suit-style jacket and very high heels. I'll be 5'11" in heels. Taller than him. And I'm good with that.

"Get a drink at the bar," he texts me, and I get a glass of champagne to set the standard. I wait for about 10 minutes, comfortable in my people-watching and being alone, something I learnt a long time back, thanks to *Mr Stand-Up*. Eventually he arrives, and I enjoy watching him walk in. We instantly recognise each other – we're both as described.

He's warm and we hug, but in a polite, contained way, rather than a Devon 'tree hug' way. I am indeed taller than him by a long way. He's wearing a fitted Italian suit jacket, with a handkerchief in the breast pocket, jeans and polished shoes with a buckle. He has a well-made half-length wool coat over the top. His hair is thick and floppy. His hands swipe it off his face often, as if he's proud. In slow motion.

He orders champagne to join me, and we eat olives at the bar. Then the *maitre d*, who seems to know *Mr Italian*, comes to tell us our table is ready. We sit down and study the menu. *Ahh*, Italian food. Probably my favourite. Seafood interestingly prepared, salads. Perfect. He tells me some of the things he's tried before and what he recommends, and asks me what wine I'd like.

"This," he says slowly and passionately, "is a superb white wine from the southern part of Italy, un-oaked and light, perfect for the fish dishes we've chosen. I've had it before and it's very good. You tell me what you think."

"Lovely," I gush, rather enamoured by him.

I learn that he's divorced, has been in London for two years and will probably be here a few years more, unless he sets up an office for his company in South Africa. Which is an option. He has lived in Russia, the US, Japan and now the UK. His ex-wife didn't want to travel around like that, following him around once she had children, and their relationship broke down.

"She knew what my work was like when she married me," he says.

Mr Italian is hot. Proper hot. Once into our 40s we have to really tune into the personality zone more than hotness. There are only a few remaining hotsters left anyway. But *Mr Italian* has still got it. He's slim, fit, got loads of hair and a few lines around the eyes. I like that. His teeth are white and his manners impeccable.

When our food arrives it looks so damn good that I pretty much want to dive right in and gobble the lot. But *Mr Italian* is still talking about life, and has more finesse than me. He refrains from diving straight in and talks slowly, in a quiet, measured and controlled way. He's formal and correct. A little nervous, but super polite. We are getting on really well, and I'm very happy to look at him, to stop my eyes dropping to my plate and drooling over the fish.

The wine he's chosen is superb and he loosens up a little with a glass or two, becoming quite flirty. He twinkles his big dark eyes at me.

We take a good amount of time over dinner and have full courses, dessert, coffee, the lot. When we finish, he asks if I want to go downstairs where there is music and a bar.

I do want to yes. Hot Italian, drinks, dinner, now dancing – this date couldn't be going better!

We get G&T's downstairs and chat. The music is good and the lights low. We start to slowly sway in time with each other. It's like the good old days, when guys were still hot and flirting was still in. I realise I've been deprived of hot guys of late. We dance looking into each other's eyes for ages, but not actually kissing. This, of course, like waiting for good food, is even better than diving straight in.

Finally, he slowly goes in for a kiss, but I keep him just far away enough to tease him. He knows exactly how to play the waiting game, and build that desire, and I'm taken right back to my days travelling around the Mediterranean, where men and women know the art of seduction; where men can be men and women can be coy, and everyone can flirt.

Slowly we move in to kiss, right there on the dance floor like god damn teenagers. We look into each other's eyes and smile and he pulls me in close to him. We carry on kissing for a while and dancing slowly. Then we sit and people-watch for a bit and have another G&T. He makes good assessments of where the people are from.

"Mainly Greece," he says of the men. "The women are mainly Russian," he adds.

People-watching, one of my top pastimes.

It's past midnight and we decide to leave. We're going in the same direction and share a cab.

"Would you like to come in to have a drink?" he asks.

"Sure," I say casually.

We're in Chelsea and we take the lift to the top floor of his apartment block. He's a hold-the-doors kind of guy, manners still perfectly intact.

His apartment is like him. Super slick, modern, and minimalist, with a large dining table and a chandelier of bunched light bulbs.

"A drink?" he asks.

"Yes, water please," I say.

"Ah, excellent," he says. "You know when to stop drinking. Unlike a lot of English women."

We laugh. We both drink lots of water.

Mr Italian is demonstrative and unafraid. He's put some music on and takes my hand, pulling me towards him. He goes in for a kiss, all the while looking straight into my eyes. I follow him as he leads me into the bedroom. It occurs to me, shouldn't I be waiting and all that jazz? But as I now live in Devon, and won't see him every week, I decide to just crack on.

I stand at the end of the bed looking out across London through a wall of windows. We're in the penthouse. He's very warm and affectionate in bed and, afterwards, pulls me towards him. When we eventually fall asleep, we turn over in the night, and I'm aware that he's a night-time snuggler.

I sneak off before he gets up. I woke early. I don't have my earplugs and I want my stuff. I send him a message.

"I didn't run away. I just couldn't sleep. Let's talk later."

"Sure no problem," he replies. "I'm off to Italy later today, but see you soon hopefully. I'll call you later."

And, with that, I walk away, relieved somewhat that there are still some appealing men out there.

26

Mr Italian – Part 2

I go back to Devon after the weekend, feeling revived and happy that there are still options. He calls me in the week and fills me in on his thoughts.

"While I'm looking for a soul mate, I understand that's hard while I travel so much. A woman's time is important and I don't want to waste it. I'm open to falling in love, I wouldn't prevent it, but I want to make sure I'm offering something. I can only offer my company about two times a month, so I propose I make your time worthwhile. We will have dinners, discover the best restaurants in London together and maybe you could travel with me sometimes if you have time? How does it sound?"

It sounds like that could definitely work, yup! I think.

"Message your account details?" he suggests. "I want to make sure your travel is covered."

"Lovely, thanks!" I say and, within an hour, there's cash in my account. I don't know whether this is what it's like to be an escort, a mistress, or a kept wife. Am I on a retainer?

I do that 'thinking about him a lot' thing over the next few days and am looking forward to seeing him again. A few pictures go back and forth on *WhatsApp* – pictures of him skiing, and of me riding; pictures of him shopping. It's good text talk. Nothing needy, but no stupid long waits between replies either, making you wonder if there's a game going on.

Ten days later and I'm still keen to see him. I'm nervous, good nervous, butterfly nervous. Is he as hot as he was first time? Will I still like him?

We meet upstairs in the *Blue Bird*. He's there before me this time, sitting in the corner looking slightly shy, in a perfectly fitting Italian suit, straight from work, drinking a glass of champagne. He stands up and hugs me. He's still hot. I wasn't wrong. He gets me a glass and we catch up.

"I've booked *The Ivy*," he says, "near to home."

After drinks we have a lovely meal in *The Ivy*, and then go to his apartment. He's genuinely interested in what I've been up to. He's a quiet, concise man with a good sense of humour. I take the piss out of him running his hands though his hair.

"Who's' this?" I joke, imitating his motions. He's good-humoured and joins in. We open a bottle of champagne, listen to music and chat.

He sees his kids who are abroad every month, and works at least one week a month away. I imagine how easy it would be for him to lead a double life. It suddenly occurs to me that, if he's actually still married and wants a London girlfriend too, how easy it would be to do that. But nothing he says indicates to me that he's lying about his life. Everything's consistent.

He asks me if I want to stay, and I appreciate his lack of assumption that I'll automatically stay, just because I did last time. Ever the gentleman, he makes it my choice and, in turn, my choice is yes.

I sleep better this time, coming prepared. I've got earplugs and a toothbrush with me.

In the morning he's relaxed. He makes good coffee and looks good in the daytime too – he has casual joggers on and he's even got those right. His t-shirt says "I prefer to do, rather than talk".

I look across the London skyline views. *Not bad at all.* He's off to work soon and I don't hang about. He walks me to the door.

"Oh here," he says causally, pointing to the side table where there's an envelope. He doesn't hand it to me. "You know, travel and things."

This guy is super subtle, smooth and ever the gentleman.

"Oh thanks," I reply, putting it in my bag. It's a good job he's generous – I haven't sold one article this month, and no teaching work has come in.

Three weeks go by in which I don't see him. We message though and send photo's of where we are. If I don't message for a couple of days, on the third day he'll message me and we make a good exchange. After three weeks, we arrange to meet up.

I go to his apartment. Ever polite, he comes all the way down the stairs to meet me and to escort me back up.

"We can go and eat now if you like?" he suggests.

I ate a late lunch with a friend earlier that day and, as we over-ordered, I've got a huge doggy bag with me. "Well would you like to eat this with me?"

He gets out two plates, a candle and some wine. We listen to each other's stories and he tells me he still believes in finding 'the one'. He's an incredibly balanced, optimistic guy who seems to be successful at everything and, as far as I can see, living a blessed life.

I stay the night again and, once again, I'm asked if I want to.

We sleep well and, in the morning, drink coffee together again. Then the same side table money ritual. It doesn't feel at all sleazy. He's so casual about the money that it seems normal, just like handing me a key or a letter to post. But I can't work out what it means. Am I a girlfriend, or am I something else? His escort? Does it even need defining?

We message to-and-fro for the next two months. I send him a picture of a pair of fabulous stilettos that I've bought.

"We'll certainly have to go somewhere nice with those," he answers.

But he's away a great deal. The USA, Italy, Portugal, South Africa. To see his kids. Our timing just doesn't match up. He's only been in London for one weekend in the last two months. And when I find that he went to Italy on a clothes-shopping trip over a weekend without me, I realise there isn't really much time for me in his life. I now understand why he said what he did about 'offering something'. Is this what an 'arrangement' is, after all? I've never been suited to the role of side kick. I'm far too much of a leading lady. *Mr Italian* is certainly fabulous, with a generous spirit. He has been straight about his situation from the very start. And he has the most impeccable manners I've seen. So I'm left with nothing but good feelings about him.

Every woman should experience an Italian man at least once, right?

27

Mr Polo

Facebook

Age: 47

Mr Polo keeps popping up on my *Facebook* feed as a friend suggestion. I don't think that much about it, but *Facebook* keeps pushing him on me. That face keeps showing up.

It's a nice face – a professional black and white headshot with penetrating eyes. Some algorithm somewhere will have linked us together I take it. We become *Facebook* friends and have several friends in common. We start chatting. "How outrageous, that you're single!" he messages me. "How on earth have you not been snapped up. We absolutely must meet up!" he enthuses.

I'm in Devon. He's in Oxfordshire. A couple of months go by. When I message him to let him know I'll finally be in London the following week, he seems keen.

"Darling that would be wonderful. I'm going to be in London too for some meetings. Let's have dinner."

The afternoon of our date, I sit in a cafe with my laptop writing for a few hours. But come 6pm I haven't heard from him. I don't want to do text nagging, but I do want to make sure he's on track. I need time to spruce myself up after all. So I decide I'd better message. "Still good for the *Blue Bird* at 6.30?"

"I'm running late," he replies. "Still in my meeting."

I can't stand sitting around waiting for messages, but that's what I end up doing. By 7 he messages to say he's on his way. We were going to have a drink first then go on to dinner for the table I've booked at 8.

"Go straight to the restaurant, no time for that drink," I tell him.

I change into skinnies, silk top, leather jacket, and high heels. Enough make up, but not too much effort put in. How nice to get the heels out and shimmy a bit. By 8 o'clock, there he is in the corner, looking out for me. He's lean and tall, in a silk shirt and jeans. He has the biggest smile on his face. Charismatic more than conventional handsome. I stride towards him and we lock eyes. He stands up and initiates a hug – bear like and warm – like old friends. He doesn't let go quickly.

When we sit down the conversation flows along like old friends. It just clicks. We're on the same page, with the same interests. Our work crosses over and he has horses and plays polo. We share an understanding of culture, of the country and the city. It all falls into place easily, like you just know and understand who you are. Me, slightly posh but poor; him, just posh, but not Hooray Henry posh. No, he's media, like me.

"What on earth were you doing moving to Devon?" he asks with a smile on his face. "I mean, what on earth is wrong with Oxfordshire? Couldn't you have moved there for goodness sake? Good riding and even better people!"

He's charming, self-effacing, confident and nice to look at. We just know we like each other. He doesn't drink at all with dinner – he's having a liver detox.

"Had a health check that showed I drank too much. Doctor and I think it may have been my extreme indulgence during Ascot week. I did my health check straight after that," he jollies along.

Good, I think. Someone who can stay off drink for a month. Can exercise self-control. Check.

After dinner we walk to the train and it seems totally natural to kiss. Relaxed, no fumbling, no clashing teeth kissing. Just sensual, hot, spot on kissing. Kissing that makes you want more kissing.

We separate and he goes towards his train. I go the other way. Do I sneak a quick look back at him as he leaves?

No, don't do it, don't look back.

But I do. And there it is – he too has snuck a cheeky glace back at me. We flirty-smile at each other knowing we've caught each other out.

I bounce away on cloud nine.

He messages me about an hour later.

"Home and heading to bed. Such a wonderful evening... how impossibly beautiful and incredibly lovely you are. I love kissing you. One of those evenings I really didn't want to end. Let's do it again soon please??!!! Xx"

"Agreed!" I reply.

When he messages me the next day to tell me he's distracted at work, I tell him I'm art gallery hopping. "Be nice to do that sort of thing together," he replies.

We start talking follow-up dates. Will he come to stay the weekend at my place in Devon? I'm miles away, so a sleep over is the only way. Or will we meet again in London? A steady stream of messages go to-and-fro, all utterly charming.

"I think I'd better just get on and visit you, don't you!" he says, "Can't possibly wait until you're next in London, for goodness sake!"

I tell my friend that he's going to come down and see me.

"Don't you let him stay with you in your house!" she says to me.

"But what am I going to say? *You can't stay with me, get an Air B&B...?*"

"Yes, that's exactly what you say!" she says.

Needless to say, I don't say that to him.

Instead, I think about what we can do for the weekend. I assume he'll come the Friday night and go later on Sunday. A proper weekend.

"Darling," he messages. "I'll arrive on Saturday. I'm passing friends *en route*, so I'll get lunch with them and come on straight afterwards. Can't wait to see you."

So, not Friday then. Better book a table for dinner in a pub for the Saturday evening. I also book a table for Sunday lunch in my favourite country pub, knowing they'll be busy.

"Is it bad that I'm literally counting down the hours to see you?" he messages. "I actually dreamt about you last night."

"Can't say you haven't crossed my mind," I reply. We're warming up nicely for the weekend.

He arrives on the Saturday at 5, in his little convertible Audi with its roof down. It's a lovely warm evening and, when we see each other, I get another super warm, 'old friends' style bear hug. I bring him into my tiny cottage and give him a G&T and some olives. "You can have the rocking chair," I say. "Sorry it's so tiny."

"Darling, I've come to see you, not your lovely little cottage," he replies.

Conversation flows and we continue where we left off last time. "Right then," he says. "Where are the shops around here? I think it's time we got some champagne, no?"

I take him to the local shop for some champagne. It's possible we're the only people in town who buy champagne – there's only one choice. We go back to my cottage, drink the champagne and eat olives. "Dinner's booked for 7," I tell him.

A rare warm summer evening, we sit in the pub garden having dinner. "I've got plans for my house. It's very exciting, let me show you," he says.

He pulls up *Google Maps* and shows me his land.

"This is where my fields are. This is where my stables are. This is where the house is, and where the neighbours' house is. I plan to knock this through here." He proceeds to tell me his plans for knocking down walls, building a pool, extending this and that. Where he'll landscape garden an area. Where the party room and wine cellar will go. "I'll put my organic vegetable patch here," he says.

"I prefer organic too," I say. "If you're going to eat meat, I'd rather go shooting for it. Can't stand factory farming. Free range all the way, me."

We look at each other knowing we're on the same page.

And here we are again, my mind runs wild: a veggie patch, horses, frolicking in the country, and this guy can even ride, has horses and plays polo! Yes, he's like my man mirror, my man match. He's theatrical like me, likes to wear a flashy shirt to a red carpet event, but is happy to get his wellies on and get muddy. He grows vegetables for goodness sake. He has horses! It's perfect. I would straight up marry this guy tomorrow, I just know it.

And that's it! My mind has gone… I'm now married, I'm cantering through fields with my husband in slow motion. I'm writing screenplays and he's producing them. We're an actual real life power couple who attend film premiers on a Tuesday, script meetings on a Wednesday, and we dig up the vegetables we've organically grown together on a Saturday. I'll cook the dinner we've grown and shot together, for the dinner party we'll be having for friends in the evening. He'll pour my wine and tell me funny stories while I cook in our open-plan kitchen. On Sunday we'll ride our horses together and, in the evening, we'll sit by the fire drinking red wine, with dogs at our feet, chatting about our friends, our holidays, and plans for the next film.

That's it! This is the guy I've been waiting for. We have everything in common. Even the humour.

Apart from one thing.

He's a Tory. A proper, full on Tory.

He was even going to become a Tory MP. He's *that* Tory.

Inevitably, we touch on politics. But not massively.

"I can't bloody stand the school and their stupid attendance rules," I vent. "I don't bloody need permission for my child not to be at school

170

for the day. D'you know, they can even fine you for non-attendance? Telling me how to live! Fuck off nanny state!"

I'm on a roll.

"Ah, you see, you're Tory at heart," he says. "That's fundamentally a Tory philosophy, being in charge of your own life, and not being run by the state."

I might just have to ignore my hatred and despair of the Tory cuts and the real poverty I'm seeing around me. I'm one step away from the bloody food bank myself, working as a supply teacher while planning my next work move. I've seen the consequences of the cuts first hand, all around me in the last couple of years. People in work who can't afford to make ends meet. In fact, I'm one of them. Just a bit posher. The new downwardly mobile middle class – educated, middle class values and expectations, middle class hobbies, middle class food. The *nouveau pauvre*.

How quickly could I forget all that and move straight in with him and live happily ever after? Could I pretend I don't actually know what I know about being poor?

After dinner, we come back to my cottage, drink copious amounts of prosecco and talk and talk. My cottage is so small there's no sofa. I remember my friend's advice. "Whatever you do, don't sleep with him. It doesn't do them any harm at all to wait," she says. "You can't snog without a sofa, but you certainly don't want him straight in your bed."

Mr Polo and I sit opposite each other, one on an armchair and the other on a rocker. We both put our feet on the footstool and touch toes.

"Hello lovely dog," he says to my pooch as he jumps up.

Ahh, nice to my dog. Check.

He tells me about his childhood and fills in some of his life stories. He has flashes of vulnerability. He tells me about his ex-wife. How she'd had multiple affairs and they divorced, then even got back together again after the divorce!

Ahh, I think, he attempts to conquer the unavailable woman. I do hope he's grown out of that by now.

He doesn't, however, ask me about what I'm currently writing about, or what projects I'm working on. But never mind, he does tell me about the events that *he's* working on.

We munch on some nibbles and drink until the early hours, my friend's words ringing in my ears. I momentarily wonder if I should put him in another bed, but it seems totally contrived and unnatural to do so. He's practically my husband for goodness sake! Why would he not sleep in my bed?

We're not wasted drunk, just gently merry and relaxed. We simply go into my bedroom and start kissing. The clothes come off. He looks into my eyes with those incredibly intense ones of his. Please don't fuck me over. Please just save me instead and let my search end here.

And then there's the wake-up. The something's-not-quite-right moment. Nice and relaxed as all this touching is, I realise from the touch of my hand that he's hairless.

Has he shaved or waxed his balls?

Yes, he definitely has. Those balls are definitely smooth!

Why oh why has he done this? Where did he get the idea from and why would he think that in any way it would be nice? Does a guy just say to himself one day, 'I know, I think I'll shave off all my pubes?' In fact, how do you even wax or shave balls? I have trouble enough clipping my horse! You have to pull the legs forward to tighten the skin and clip around the legs. How do you even go about smoothing off your balls? Did he go to a salon?

Then I get it. Porn! It's a porn thing, isn't it? I know women go hairless. Oh god, are men doing it too? And how much porn has he been watching to have been influenced by it? Poor men, if they're getting their idea of what women want, their idea of masculinity from porn, then they'll never find what they, or we, really want.

What we all need, what we all want, is connection. Being able to connect, being present, being real – those are the things that we want. Not some bizarre, big dick, shaved-ball-sack fakery.

But he's so warm and cuddly that I decide to try and put it out of my mind. He's going to save me, right? I'm going to have to forget he's done it, because I want to forget it, like the rampant Tory thing. He will be perfect, he will, he will…

I snuggle up to him.

"Oh no, you're not a snuggler are you?" he says laughing.

I pull away.

*

In the morning, it all feels natural again and I assume that he'll be staying for the lunch I've booked in my favourite pub. Maybe we can have a country walk, or take my horses out for a ride?

"I'm on mother watch," he suddenly says. "My mum's very old. I need to check in on her."

Breakfast suddenly doesn't taste so good.

"I do want to see the horses, though," he says. "Please?" he adds.

We go and visit my horses in the very un-flashy farm I keep them at. And, by 11, he's gone.

I need to find an alternative afternoon plan, sharpish, in order not to sit around with my own wandering thoughts. I go for a ride myself and meet up with a friend instead. Then, as we're out on the horses, I get a call from my youngest son's father to say that his mother just died. My little boy's grandmother. I have to now work out how to get my son back home from London, where he's staying with his father, who will now inevitably get so wasted that it will be unsafe for my boy to stay with him. But I also have to work in the morning. It's a four-hour drive to London. I have some dilemmas to face.

Mr Polo messages. "Had a lovely time! SO good to see you." He asks me what I've been up to. A few hours have gone by and so, by now, my son's dad is, as predicted, wasted and I tell *Mr Polo* that I don't know how to get my son back. I briefly fill him in. Then apologise for the offload.

"I'm about to watch *Game of Thrones*," he says.

"Oh right!" I reply.

"I wish I could help," he adds. "Offload anytime, just not in the next hour and a half…"

I let the hour and a half pass. In fact, I let a couple of weeks pass, with just a few messages between me and *Mr Polo*, enough to keep connected. But he never does follow up on how I juggled picking up my drunk grieving ex, getting my son from London, and getting myself to work.

I can feel my fantasy lifestyle picture gradually slipping away…

28

Mr Polo – Part 2

After a month, I decide to try and keep my fantasy picture alive a little longer, and invite *Mr Polo* as my plus one to an art exhibition that my friend is having in the *Saatchi Gallery*. The timing ties in with London Fashion Week and I'm modelling for a friend in that as well. *Mr Polo* agrees to come to the exhibition after a work meeting as my plus one.

I spend the day having fun modelling for my friend, and then make my way to the *Saatchi Gallery*. I was hoping to meet up with *Mr Polo* before the opening, so we could go in to the exhibition together but, since his meeting is running on, he meets me there. Several old friends are there already, so I just get on with it without him. When he does arrive, he has that lovely smile on his face and bounds over to me. "Aren't you just a vision, darling!" he says as we hug.

I watch him holding his own, talking to people, asking my artist friend questions about her exhibition, and mingling with my friends. He's talking to one of them when he suddenly turns to me.

"Are we a *thing?*" he asks. One of my friends has obviously asked him.

I decide to take the bull by the horns. "Yes, we are," I reply theatrically. He laughs. We drink some champagne and chat to people some more.

"Hey," he catches me. "Shall we get out of here and get some dinner?" And in that moment I feel connected with him again.

"Yeah, come on," I reply.

We link arms and leave for a nearby restaurant. He tells me excitedly about his success of the day – he's being paid a tidy sum for a re-write on some project he's done. It's one of the many projects he's had success with. He seems to have forgotten, though, to ask me what the modelling job I did today was, or how it went. He seems quite feisty today in fact, on a high, and he talks a lot.

"Darling, why did you have to bloody move so far away?" he complains.

"Well look," I say. "If I fall madly in love with you, then I'll move ok?"

"IF?!?" he jokes, and looks at me with those intense eyes. He takes my hand across the table.

We finish dinner and walk through night time London to the tube.

"You don't *always* have to stay with your ex while you're in London," he says. "I mean, there are a million hotels you know…"

Well you bloody book the hotel then, I think. Or better still, *Invite me back to your place!*

I don't want to tell him I have no money for hotels. I want to be on an equal footing. Still, we do that passionate embrace thing that we do so well together, and we leave each other at the tube.

He texts when he's home. "Why aren't you here with me? You should choose to live here…"

*

The next two weeks are spent with a few messages going back and forth, a bit sporadic really. I want to move this thing on. I message him.

"Shall we try and meet up next weekend?"

"That sounds like a lovely idea! What do you have in mind?"

"I haven't got a plan? I say, "but maybe I should come to see you?"

He doesn't reply. And he doesn't reply the next day either.

I need to sort my childcare plan and need to know, so I prompt him, which I don't want to do. I don't want to be pushy, or needy and it's certainly against the rules!

"I'm on mother duty on the Sunday," he finally replies. "Shall we do another weekend where I'm free the whole weekend?"

"Sure, another weekend then," I say. "I like seeing you, and want to do it some more," I add.

But despite the messaging, a meet up doesn't materialise and I totally can't make another offer. It needs to come from him.

Days go by with nothing from him. I'm not keen at all to do the chasing, but my friend has created a message to send him and so, despite my reservations, I decide to go ahead:

"I really like you *Mr Polo* and, while long distance isn't ideal, I'm ready to make the journeys and see where it leads. I get the sense you don't feel the same way. I'd love a reply that directly addresses whether we want to move forward, or let it go?'

Three days go by. My friend and I decide it's a lost cause and are both hugely disappointed for me. Then, after another three days, he sends a message.

"Hey you. Insane week! I really like you too, and I'd love to see where it leads. I adore your company and you know I also think you're one of the most beautiful people I've ever met. I'm ready to make the journeys too. But I wish you lived closer and that you had somewhere else to stay in London! Work's frantic right now. And mum! But I'm not going anywhere and would hate to just 'let it go'! XX"

And, again, just like that, I'm back on him!

But, hang on a minute! Although that's not an ambiguous message, he's not actually doing anything about it, is he? Actions speak louder than words don't they? Yes, I'm pretty sure he's messing with me.

I get that you can't have it all – a man available to meet all the time; a busy, working, successful man. How would he fit it all in? But *The Rules* say that if a man wants to see you, then he *will* make time. And I just have to accept that he's not making time. For me.

29

Mr Polo – Part 3

Several weeks later, he has a big work event one evening in London when I'm back up there for work again too. I wish him good luck.

"I'm very nervous," he replies. "Fancy a bite early evening before I go to the opening?" he suggests.

If I want to see him, which I do, I have to accept. Even though he's only given me two hours notice. Am I at his beck and call?

Nevertheless, I agree and we meet for dinner. He's casually dressed and hasn't shaved, or showered.

Am I in fact just keeping him company while he eats, I wonder?

Despite these niggling doubts, we get on like a house on fire, as usual. He's worried that an elderly speaker at the event he's hosting will fall off the stage during a presentation. I make a suggestion.

"Have two nice ladies accompany him either side, as part of the presentation," I suggest.

"Excellent idea," he says. "I think I'll do just that!"

We finish dinner and walk to the tube. He goes his way and I go mine. His event is on his mind and we hug, but don't kiss. Later, he rapidly sends that oh-so-charming 'Sooooo good to see you' message, which keeps me dangling there as usual.

A few days go by and I don't hear from him, apart from the news that his event went well. I make a last ditch attempt to invite him for the weekend.

"I can't keep inviting you for the weekend now can I?" I say.

"No, no of course you can't," he replies. "As soon as I have cover for the horses, I'm there."

A week goes by and, instead of just going on other dates that I'm being asked on, I have a stupid sense of loyalty, like I shouldn't be seeing other people? Why, just because he sent that message? Just because I told him 'we're a thing'? So, instead of accepting other dates, I message him.

"So, when I'm asked on other dates, am I accepting them, or not? Are we 'a thing' or not?"

Is clarity too much to ask from him, I wonder?

"Sorry darling, I'm in hospital with my mum who's had a nasty fall. I'll call you tomorrow when I'm home."

Well what can I say to that?

"Oh dear, I hope she's ok?" I reply.

That will be the last message I send him if he doesn't call tomorrow.

He doesn't call tomorrow. Or the next day, or the next.

In fact, six weeks go by…

*

My friend sends me the *New Rules* book. I read it years ago, but it now includes social media and smart phone updates. "You need a re-cap," she says. "Also, watch Matthew Hussey's videos on *YouTube*." I watch him, and then re-read it, and find I have, indeed, violated every goddamn rule.

"That doesn't apply to you, that's for needy women!" one of my sisters says. But it does apply to me. I've violated several of *The Rules*:

- Over-sharing too soon

- Being available at the drop of a hat

- Not making him pin down particular days to meet

- Waiting for him to be ready finishing work at whatever time he fancies

- Being available for him at short notice

- Messaging him first

- Answering messages quickly

- Sending him more messages than he sends me

- Sleeping with him before establishing what's what

Oh the list goes on and on….

Meanwhile there are other guys trying to get dates with me and I'm accidentally doing the rules on them. It's not about playing games. It's about creating desire. Creating boundaried expectations. Making sure you have a life that doesn't revolve around what *he* always wants.

Mr Polo had a chance to have something really good with me, but he wasn't paying proper attention. Surely he's had enough bad dates and mismatches to see a perfect match glaring him in the face? I can 'mind wander' into the fantasy world of the perfect life. I often do, but surely I know the difference between real chemistry and creating a fun fantasy? Surely I couldn't have imagined the chemistry between us? How could I have completely misread this? I took the risk, laid it bare, made sure he knew how I felt, and didn't miss the opportunity.

I couldn't have done any more.

In reality, with a clearer head, he's nothing more than a lot of words and charm and sparkling personality. That's a magnetic pull. But he isn't actually brave; not brave enough to close the door. Isn't always being a player and leaving your options open, leaving people dangling, just cowardly and unkind? And a note to self – step away from the overly charming men.

I'm not sure why I still lament him actually? Maybe it was the dream of the organic vegetable patch, of long lazy Sunday afternoons riding, and roaring winter fires.

Maybe it's all just a pretty picture I'm mourning?

30

Mr Vulgar
Elite Singles
Age: 47 or 57
Height: 5'11"

Mr Vulgar looks really nice in his pictures. Relaxed shots of him on a boat with his daughter, a trimmed casual beard, nice shoes. You can even see his face. Smiling. His profile is excellent. At 47 years old he's in corporate business.

He's away the week we message, but he's quick off the mark to book up the following Saturday upon his return. I ask him to meet fairly near me, so I don't have to travel. He readily agrees and says he'll take a hotel in Exeter for the night, as this is miles from home for him. He books a table for dinner, and we decide to meet at his hotel for a drink first. He's been attentive with his messages, but not needy.

"Are you excited?" asks my son's father when I tell him I'm off on another date.

"Good god, darling," I reply, "I've been at this 10 years. Excited? I'm hardly raising a heart beat!"

But what *is* this feeling I do have? Aha, I know! It's reasonably high expectations. I mean, he looks promising.

I take a good amount of time getting ready. I spend so much time in wellington boots it's nice to get dressed for dinner instead. I wear leather skinnies, a thigh-length dress top, low cut (as recommended by Patti

Stranger of *Millionaire Matchmaker*), high-heel strappy gold stilettos (come on, it's Christmas) and a fur jacket.

I've taken time over my hair, which I wear in loose waves. It's simple, but sexy. And I'm feeling good.

I find him in the hotel lobby. He looks like his picture – a good start – but he's in jumper and jeans, and hasn't made an effort at all. It's not that his clothes are bad taste, just that he looks ready for a Sunday afternoon walk.

At the bar he asks what I want to drink.

"Champagne please," I smile.

"Good idea!" he says in his broad Scottish accent. "I've just had my pay review and it went very well."

He orders champagne and starts to talk in a never-ending stream. "I was the only one to go to university in my family. Everyone else is in Scotland. Never left. I saw my daughter yesterday. Took her shopping. That's all teenagers want to do. I've been single a while now. I pay so much to my ex-wife. It took me an hour to get here tonight. Nice hotel. I was in China last week. Here look…"

He shows me a picture of him with his Chinese business colleagues, then dives straight back in.

"Dear lord, she would blow the wax out of your ears!" He gestures towards a large girl in a very short skirt, who looks well on her way to getting drunk. I don't know what that means exactly, but I do know that it's mean. That much I get.

"People having Christmas fun," I respond quickly. I don't want to get into a bitch fest with him, and I'm certainly not willing to play fat shaming.

"I was married for twenty years," he continues. "My wife and I didn't have sex for twelve of those. I mean, it's ridiculous, twelve years! Who wants a sexless marriage? Should have known. She was a Mormon, after all…"

His eyes drop to my chest every other sentence, as if he's hungry. Why did I listen to Patti Stranger. Wearing a low cut top? No no no!

He swallows the last of the champagne while filling me in on some more of his life history.

"I grew up very poor in a mining town. I've done the best out of my siblings. Have done very well in business. I'm in a great place. Oh, by the way, I'm actually 57, not 47. I was getting interest from women my own age, which isn't what I'm looking for. I'm looking for a fun, younger woman to accompany me on holidays. Girlfriend material. I've got money and a good lifestyle."

We walk to the restaurant along cobbled streets. Although generally a fast walker, I struggle in my high heels as he strides on ahead, chattering endlessly. But eventually we reach the restaurant, where he orders more champagne.

Stop it! I think, I love champagne. Champagne is great! But how about a suitable wine with our meal, rather than an expensive way of getting pissed? He then adds on a couple of beers to his order. We share starters and he has steak, me fish. What is it with men and steak?

We talk more about his work successes, where he's lived and travelled and, to be fair, he's interested in my life too. He seems devoted to his teenage daughter, and is generous with food offerings and drink. He's obviously up for a laugh, and really going for the 'life is short, live for now' philosophy. He's fully embracing his newfound freedom post divorce, but is on good terms with his a-sexual ex.

But he's childish. "My ex hasn't ever worked since having our daughter, despite having a Masters. What a waste of an education! Daughter's a teenager now!"

"Really?" I reply. "Did your wife not want to raise the child?"

"Oh yes, but that's all she did."

"So, she did that for her job, right?"

"Och, are you a feminist?"

"Of course! Aren't you?"

He mutters something to try and please me, but clearly has no idea what a feminist even is. Before he digs himself further into a hole, I interrupt him.

"Feminism is the belief in equal opportunities," I tell him. "It doesn't mean that men and women aren't different. Feminism isn't lesbianism either."

"Yes," he says, pretending to know what I'm talking about. "I promote a lot of women at work." He congratulates himself while his eyes dash once more to my chest.

When the bill comes I offer to share it. I don't want him having the privilege. But he refuses, and gets it himself. I thank him for it. We've been merry all night, despite me knowing he's not going to work out. Conversation has been easy. Well, he talked and I listened.

He walks and I hobble the cobbles back to the hotel and, *en route,* he takes the initiative to go in for a kiss. I like a man who isn't afraid to do this. Not in a Donald Trump take-the-initiative kind of way, but a non-faffing kind of way.

The champagne we drank agrees. *What the hell, let's see how this kiss works out.*

Straight away, his beard is the wrong length. It's stubble, not a soft beard, and my face gets scratched up. My eyes actually water.

Then he licks my face rapidly and makes a peculiar gobbling action with his lips, like a fish out of water.

He then stabs his tongue in and out of my mouth, and finally just rests his open mouth on mine. I mirror it to see what happens next. Nothing. Our mouths just sit there, open and void. Then his tongue does a quick stab.

Oh god! Hilarious kisser!

What with the amount of terrible kissers out there, perhaps I should run courses; complete sex courses, to teach these men? I'm pretty sure that the sex would be appalling if his kissing is anything to go by. His a-sexual Mormon wife crosses my mind again.

As we part mouths, his glasses are totally steamed up and we both laugh. We go into the hotel lobby and he makes a line for the bar. I have a fancy lemonade – I'm done on the booze. He goes for two more beers. I keep him company while he drinks it. He then goes in for more kisses.

It's at that point that I tell him I'm off.

"I really want to carry on this night," he says.

"Lovely," I reply, "but I'm gonna go now."

"No," he says. "You don't understand. I really, really want you to stay with me." It seems imperative that I comply with what *he* wants. But it's about midnight now, and I remind myself that what *I* want matters even more.

"I have to go," I repeat.

"Come on," he pleads. "Let's go to my room and have a drink, watch telly and relax."

I shake my head slowly, telling myself I'm not obliged.

The same large girl from earlier in the restaurant walks past us again in the hotel lounge, and he repeats his comment from earlier.

"What does that *mean?*" I say. "That's the second time you've said that about her."

"Oh, it's just lads' talk," he says. "If you had sex with her, you know, those thighs would pop the wax out of your ears."

"Goodness!" I say. "What about your daughter?"

"What?" he says, confused.

"Your daughter?" I continue. "Would wax pop out of her ears too when she has sex with a fat guy?"

"What?" he says.

"I'm off now," I say before he can reply. "Thanks for dinner," I call, gathering speed.

When I get home, I don't bother messaging him – he's probably passed out by now anyway. Which bit of *Lady with bouncy hair, fur coat and fabulous gold shoes* had him thinking it's OK to go all laddish? He's read it all wrong.

The next day he texts. "Did you get home OK? What do you think? Should we go out again? I was thinking a road trip."

"Sadly, I feel we'll be a mismatch," I say. I wait for his reply.

"Yes, I was thinking the same," he lies.

I don't send him any more messages.

And he looked so nice in his photos!

31

Mr Paris

Seeking Arrangements

Age: 55

I'm at the airport. On my way to Paris for dinner with a man I've never met. He booked me the flight and has booked me a hotel with an Eiffel Tower view. We'll meet to see if we get along and, as the website name suggests, potentially make an 'arrangement'.

There's a grey area on *Sugardaddy.com*. A woman can be struggling to pay her bills, yet be treated to expensive dinners that *he* will enjoy. Or maybe she'll receive an expensive gift, or a holiday with him, but be short of cash herself. But *Seeking Arrangements* is more transparent. Everyone seems to lay out what they expect from an arrangement. It could be anything from companionship, to marriage, or anything in between but, as far as I can see, it seems acceptable to talk about money and expectations. Everything is open. Including people's kinks. Well, at least there's no surprises!

Over the last 10 years my income has not gone up, but my outgoings have tripled. It's now pretty much impossible to consider a man who isn't doing well in his career, even if I wanted to. Now there's an element of 'needing someone solvent', though I don't want to be beholden.

On top of that, work in Devon isn't like work in London. I don't pick up the daily rate by photographing an event, or selling one of my knitted jumpers. I do get some work as a supply teacher though, but the pay is low and on zero hours contracts. So I'm picking up work looking after holiday properties as well. All the while applying for (and being turned down for) positions in Plymouth theatre. Is not having enough to live on bringing a new dimension to my dating choices?

Mr Paris contacts me on my second day on *Seeking Arrangements*. "Forget the rest, have me, the best!' Brazen, I think, but it amuses me. How do these men think they'll live up to statements like that?

After a few text messages we agree to have a video chat. He seems a little shy, but nice. His apartment has wooden floors and shelves of cd's in the background.

"Come to meet me in Paris at the weekend," he suddenly suggests. "We'll have such a nice time. I'll take you to a great restaurant."

He feels nice and safe and I'm always up for an adventure. So, there it is… I'm off to Paris for the weekend.

He books me a return ticket and a hotel for one and sends me the details. Everything is correct and courteous. But I don't sleep well on the night of travel and spend hours wondering who it is I'm really going to meet, whether I'll oversleep and miss the plane, or if he'll just turn out to be a twat? Will we get on? He's a French National, born in Tunisia. Now, I lived in Paris for a few years and speak good French. I know Paris well. And I also know the mentality of the North Africans I was acquainted with there.

I already know he won't be the love of my life, put it that way.

He is 50 something. I don't know if he has kids, and I don't think I noted what he does, but what brings him to wanting an 'arrangement', I wonder? And what kind of arrangement does he want? In fact, what kind of arrangement do I even want? I'll have a go at treating this as pleasure with business. I've already ticked the 'high' box on my online profile. Meaning my spending expectations are £6k a month. Plus, I figure, if I'm going to look at the 'arrangement' option, I may as well go in high. I don't know if this will be met at this point and, come to think of it, I don't even know if we'll make an arrangement. We'll simply see if we get on and whether or not we want to see each other again. No further expectations.

I've no idea how these things get worked out, but I guess I'm about to find out.

The only thing I can do to combat my lack of sleep is to drink lots of water. I'm not looking especially fresh or at my best. *If I meet him in the evening I'll have forgiving light on my side and I can dress up*, I think. *I could shimmy into that restaurant and make that fabulous first impression.*

I take one little carry-on suitcase. I like to be able to make easy exits at any point without needing to faff with luggage. I'm wearing a cashmere jumper dress, long boots and a sheepskin coat. Simple, classic, stylish. I tie my hair up for now, so that I can let it down in the evening for a different evening impression.

My gut says that *Mr Paris* hasn't faked his profile information, and I trust strongly in my gut. I've left my youngest son with my friend and given her all the details. I'm only a little nervous but don't feel danger. The paper trail is too long.

When we spot each other at the airport, he confidently comes to me and gives me a warm hug, He carries my bag and we go to his car, one of those big executive BMW's.

Don't fill any awkward silences, tempting as it is, I repeat to myself. *Let him find his strength. Let him be the masculine energy.* I'm on a drive to learn to sit with silence.

His English is really good and we jump between English and French. He says that I must correct his English if he makes a mistake.

"Each time you need to correct me, you have to kiss me," he jokes. It's cute, but doesn't interest me and, when he corrects himself and indicates a kiss, I dismiss him.

"Non, zat's not my 'umour," I say, French style. I'm not playing his kissing game, which he accepts with good grace.

He's in good shape, but has pocked skin from old acne scars. I wonder if he knows just how easy it is to get that lasered, or does he just not care? He's got that generic middle-aged French way: 'Lego hair', light tan leather jacket with poppers and waistband, grey slacks and pointy shoes. My mind immediately gets to work on a makeover.

But the conversation is easy as he drives me to my hotel, and I relax. Ah, Paris!

"I am a very confident man," he tells me, "and very lucky in my life. I'm looking for great conversation and fine dining, I think we are a match."

So far, I'm comfortable. "Do you copy and paste that *You've had the rest now have the best* message to everyone?" I ask. He laughs, suggesting possibly, yes. I don't mind. I like action and can't be bothered with endless messaging back and forth.

We soon arrive at my hotel in central Paris, right by *Rue du Faubourg Saint-Honoré*, Paris's up-market shopping street. The hotel reservation is just for one, and in my name. He takes charge checking me in and we have a little chat in the lobby.

"I want to take a power nap before the evening," he says, "so that I am on form for you. Can I pick you up later?"

"No problem for me," I reply.

"Use the hotel facilities, the spa and so on," he suggests. "I'll come back at 7pm to pick you up for dinner." He subtly puts an envelope on the table. "In case you want to go shopping."

And that's it. Off he goes.

I twiddle with my phone, trying to connect to the hotel Wi-Fi. My room isn't ready yet, so the hotel will keep my case in a locker. I look in his envelope and there's 1,000 euros inside.

Christ, how does this work? Am I meant to sleep with him now? Am I meant to get a dress for the evening? But I already have my evening outfit with me and, besides, that'll do nicely for my imminent MOT back home.

I do however get flashy with tips for the hotel porter.

Is going for a power nap when you have a new guest to entertain an indicator of why men choose to make arrangements with women, instead of having wives, or girlfriends full time? If a man has a wife or a girlfriend, might she have an opinion about being left alone on a city break, while you take an afternoon nap? With an arrangement, can he continue to live exactly how he wants to, without compromise?

I go to get lunch on *Rue de Rivoli*. I wander along by *Les Jardin de Tuileries* until I find a cafe that I like, and order myself some *fois gras* because, in Paris, it doesn't count right? The flirty waiter recommends a glass of sweet wine to go with it, and I remember why I love Paris so much. I people-watch for a good long while thinking, am I actually here?

When I get back to the hotel, I have a nice bath and get ready for dinner. I wear my black skinny leather jeans as pre-planned, but I swap my jumper dress for a bright silk top, a fitted silk smoking jacket and high heels. I wear a chain necklace for a funky edge, and diamond earrings to add a classic touch, but no more jewellery than that. I let my hair down in loose curls for the evening. Classic chic. I don't know where we are going, but this outfit will fit in anywhere.

When he picks me up, he's not especially smart. He *has* changed his clothes, but still with that 'ripe for a makeover' look. We drive through Paris, beautiful at every turn.

In the quiet little restaurant, he's on a first name basis with the staff. "I phoned through earlier to have one of my vintage wines opened," he says. "I keep some here. I like them to pre-open my wine for me, to let it breathe. I also like to let the staff choose what to eat. They always know what will go with the wine and I trust them entirely. Would you to like to join me in the surprise food they will bring, or would you prefer to choose yourself?"

"I trust you know what's best here," I reply. "I'll follow your lead."

The *sommelier* comes to the table with his snazzy wine. They smell it, talk about it, smell it some more and taste it. I taste it too. We smell it and swirl it again.

A long line of mini fish courses arrives, perfectly cooked octopus this, and John Dory that. We drink his vintage wine, which *is* beautiful, as we relax and get to know each other.

I find him very interesting. He's an excellent conversationalist, extremely well travelled, intelligent and there is very little 'small town' Tunisia about him. He's very French. We cover his studies and his business, which is mainly a gambling website. He's also developing some land for building. We cover his atheism and his 'extremely lucky life'.

I also find out that he hasn't had a girlfriend for more than three weeks which, let's face it, isn't a girlfriend at all. "I haven't had a girlfriend because I can't stand their stuff in my bathroom," he says. "It messes up the place. I'm a perfectionist you see. Long term, women just end up annoying me. No really I just like my space."

Well, that's telling it straight! Yet, apart from this, he's non-judgmental in his views – something he learnt on his travels, he says. "When you realise just how much we are made up of the culture from which we come, you understand that there are no judgments to be made on other people."

He tells me about the Russian women he has dated. "Russian women are just the best," he says. "So understanding. They'll do everything in their power to please. They love it."

"Are you sure they love it?" I say, forgetting I'm on a particular kind of date. But his ears prick up.

"I love your age," he says. "You're not worried about challenging me. I like that you have travelled. I love that you won't compromise your opinion to fake it for me. Russian women are great, but they can be empty shells. Maybe we could manage more than three weeks?" he laughs.

I'm interested in just how in-demand more mature women are. Especially if they are in good shape. I think I might have underestimated just how many men are looking for more mature women and didn't expect, at 45 myself now, to still be getting the amount of messages and offers that I am.

This man is growing on me. It's been a while since I've been as engaged in conversation; I'm thoroughly enjoying his bright company.

After dinner, at about 11, the valet brings his car round to the front and we drive around Paris for a bit. We pass his apartment and he points up to a penthouse on a tree-lined road in *Neuilly*.

"My god," I say. "This is the next road along from where I used to live when I worked here in Paris!"

We laugh about it. Then he drives me back to my hotel. Before I get out of the car, we kiss.

But, dear lord… he's a terrible kisser, just terrible. Fumbling, licky kisses. He's doing some weird un-rhythmical thing with his tongue. He doesn't have a clue. I've got a feeling he thinks he's meant to do that. But he's just not letting any of his senses come though. He's thinking, not feeling.

I get into my room, open the balcony doors and look straight onto the Eiffel Tower, lit up in all its glory. Suddenly I'm very lonely. I put the telly on and know exactly why men who travel constantly for work, who sleep and eat in hotels alone, arrange to have company from women whichever way they can. None of these things – beautiful food and wine and beautiful views – are as good if you experience them alone. I almost wish I had a cigarette, sitting here overlooking the twinkly Paris night. If only I still smoked.

In the morning, we've arranged to meet at 10 o'clock, but I wake up at 9.30 and message him to say I'll be ready in an hour. When he's five minutes away, he lets me know, and I go to wait in the lobby. He settles the bill merrily and asks me if I have anything I want to do. I have an exhibition in the *Petit Palais* that I really want to see, and he's happy to take me.

There's a queue to the galley and he drops me off. "Go ahead, I have to park. I'll meet you inside."

Unfortunately, *Mr Paris* doesn't make it back to me before I'm at the front of the queue, so I go in alone. As with the power nap before, if I were his real girlfriend, I'd want a shared experience. A real girlfriend might complain about going alone. But I don't care. I just head in, view the exhibition, and call him when I'm done. He's waiting there in the car.

"Is there anything else you'd like to do before your flight home?" he asks.

"Yes, brunch!" I suggest.

We go to an upmarket *brasserie* and eat crab salad and drink espresso. We chat about business. I tell him about a few ideas that have been swirling around my mind, and I'm reminded that what I've really always wanted is my own business.

He listens intently. "I'm an investor," he says. "I can invest in you if you have a great idea."

Of course, I agree and, for a moment, allow my mind to think of the possibilities. Suddenly it occurs to me, maybe it's an investor I want, not an arrangement!

We finish lunch and he drives me back to the airport, where he asks me what my monthly expenses would be.

Is he planning on making me an offer?

I tell him I'll let him know because, in truth, I don't know. As I get on the plane for home, I realise I loved my little adventure back in Paris, and my break from my Devon wellington boots. And my 1000 euros. I liked them too. I don't know if I'll see *Mr Paris* again, but I do know that I have my MOT covered.

32

Mr Finance

Seeking Arrangements

Age: 36

A nice looking man contacts me on *Seeking Arrangements*. I'm busy looking after holiday properties in Devon while doubling up listening to audio books, and so I get waylaid. I don't respond to him straight away.

The next day there's another message from him.

"Hey hey. I sent a message yesterday. Did you get it? I'm keen to talk to you."

I get back to him. He wants to chat on the phone, which is fine – as we know, messages back and forth forever is not for me.

He calls me. He's 36 and doing very well in his field. "I work 16 hour days and don't have much time for meeting women. I've been divorced three years and haven't been with anyone since." He sounds a little desperate. "I'm craving some contact and affection."

We chat for about 20 minute. *Mr Finance* has an image in his mind, it seems, that he's already decided I'm some kind of goddess, just from my online profile. He's a bit obsessed.

"I could never have a woman like you," he says repeatedly.

"Shall we just meet up and see if we have chemistry?" I say.

"Well, yes. How much would I need to pay you?"

Now, bearing in mind that my profile clearly states I like everything from art to theatre and great food, and that I'm open to finding the love of my life, I don't really think I'm projecting an hourly rate! But I am definitely nosey, and so I suggest we meet up for lunch initially.

"Let's just see how we get on. No money needed for meeting up. If it's near me." I can hear he's uncomfortable. "What is it?" I ask.

"To be honest," he replies, "I haven't been with a woman so long, I… just want to make love with you," he says. "Shall we find a hotel?"

"Well, you may want to jump straight in to bed," I tell him, "but, for me, I need some chemistry. Maybe it's an escort service you're looking for?"

"Yes, yes, I see," he says. "So, after we meet, what would I need to pay?"

He continues with his 'pay for it' routine for a while and, by now, I'm pretty certain we won't be making any kind of arrangement at all! But I'm just such a curious person, and so I carry on.

"Well, £1,000," I throw out there, just for testers. I don't know where that figure came from; it just popped out to see how it feels to throw numbers around.

"What about for just two hours?" he says

"The same," I say. "I'm not an hourly rate kind of girl. And only if we genuinely like each other."

I have no idea what I'm talking about, but I'm getting into a role. Which role, I'm not sure, but I do like a bit of acting.

"I want to send you flowers," he says. "May I?"

"I won't refuse flowers," I reply. But then, to do that I'd have to give him my address. I divert him. Something tells me he could get obsessive.

"I'll be honest," he says. "I know that I want to be with you. I'd like to make love to a woman like you very much. I would like..."

And he's off!

"I would like to kiss you all over, every bit of you, down there, your bottom, I would like to worship you, I'm a very giving man, I like to please a woman, I like to spend hours pleasing a woman, making you come, kissing and licking you all over..."

He carries on like this for a few minutes. I'm not sure if I've suddenly found myself on a free sex line.

"For a woman of your quality," he goes on, "you're very down to earth. Not snotty at all. Most women won't talk for more than two minutes."

I take a deep breath. "So... probably best we meet to see if there's any chemistry." I'm prepared to do it, just for the game.

"Yes," he says. "I suppose I could get a *Travel Lodge*, or something. I live with my parents. £1,000 is quite expensive."

"I'm not interested in cheap men," I say. We've been on the call 15 minutes and I want to wrap it up. "And I am not a *Travel Lodge* kind of woman either," I add. "Why don't you think about if you'd like to meet for lunch? We can see how our chemistry works and go from there?"

"Yes, yes, OK," he says.

"OK, talk later," and, taking charge, I wrap it up.

He goes on to call me every day, as well as sending me messages.

I don't answer any of them, until I've finally had enough.

"I'm not a free sex line," I jot a message to him.

He gives up eventually and I'm glad, but I do rather enjoy trying out this role for size.

The next time I open my *Seeking Arrangements* account a few months later, there he is, popping back up, sending messages to me. I'm glad I can read him. He won't dare actually meet, either for lunch, or a paid *rendezvous*. He's a sad little fantasist who could keep a woman waiting forever.

33

Mr Trophy-Hunter

Elite

Age: 57

Job: Businessman

Mr Trophy-Hunter contacts me on *Elite*, and we strike up a conversation. He sends me a picture of his roaring fire and giant fireplace and I tell him it looks fabulous.

"Looking forward to seeing you here soon," he says. "Should we plan a dinner meeting at Marlows House?"

Is Marlows House his house? He doesn't say and must be assuming that I know.

But I don't want to go to his house straight off like that.

"If that's your house, no, I don't know you yet!" I say.

"I get the feeling my suggestion didn't excite you," he replies. "What do you suggest? I think I'll enjoy your company."

Odd, I think. Why is it always about what *they* will enjoy?

"I suggest you make a proper date, a time and a day. Skipping straight to your house doesn't count."

"I was intending to cook a fabulous meal for you," he says. "My house is a great place to entertain."

I continue to be ruthless with him, no longer caring for this kind of conversation. "That's as well as may be, but you mustn't invite ladies to your house when they haven't met you. It's just not safe, is it!"

He goes on to mention his swimming pool and Jacuzzi and I get bored of him. I don't want to make his choices for him; he needs to choose a date and a venue for *me*! If a man can't even come up with a good meeting place and date and time, then what hope do we have?

This man is trying to sell himself on his money and property alone, which probably means it's all he's got to offer. I let a couple of weeks pass by without any more contact until, one day, I mention him to my married-for-years friend, who promptly goads me in to sending him a message. Cocktails + girlfriend = texting men online.

"How are you?" I message him. "Good day?"

"A beautiful day indeed!" he replies. "Went for a drive in the Porsche to Southampton, with the top down. It was lovely!"

My friend and I fall about laughing. Here we go… couldn't help mentioning the Porsche, could he?

"How about lunch tomorrow? D'you know *Gidleigh Park*? They have an open slot at noon. Menu looks good. What do you say?"

Do I know *Gidleigh Park*? Puh-lease!

But seeing as he has *finally* set a time and place, I agree.

"We'll have time for a glass of champagne on the terrace first," he says.

The next day I'm 10 minutes late. *Gidleigh Park* is a flashy hotel with a Michelin starred restaurant. I have jeans on, a leather jacket and long boots without a high heel. Cool, but daywear. As usual, I'm perfectly happy to be taller than him.

I look around the lounge. There are three men on their own. Not one of them looks up from their phone to catch my eye and, short of going up to each one, I can't tell which one is him. None of them look like the bloody photo on the profile. It's quiet and conservative in the lounge, with silver service waiters everywhere. I feel conspicuous, although the discomfort makes me feel alive. It's very liberating.

I sidle over to the reception and ask for *Mr Trophy-Hunter.* The desk clerk points to him in the lounge. He *is* one of those men who didn't look up from their phone so I couldn't casually catch his eye.

I walk straight up to him and greet him. He's better looking than his photo – slimmer and younger. Late 50s I'm guessing. At first he seems a little uncomfortable and struggles to look me in the eye.

I won't save him. I can, but I won't. I can fill those silences. But I mustn't. I've done way too much of that before. He has to do it for himself.

We order champagne and I wait for him to find his voice. When he does, he talks about himself in his broad Scottish accent. Then he talks some more about himself.

He runs a multi million pound business and made his money buying and selling businesses. Buying them when they've been on their knees, then selling them when they're high again. I love business talk. I love to know how people make their money, how businesses are run, and I just love people's stories.

Finally he asks what I like doing. "What hobbies do you have?" he says as if it's straight out of a *What questions to ask on a date* leaflet. It's a stupid question. Or at least his delivery is. It's not a bloody job interview.

"I like horses," I say, trying to hide my disdain. "I like cross-country and long-distance more than dressage. I like fashion. I made a fashion collection, have my own knitwear label, and had a show once. I'm creative," I go on. "I write and I make films. I model. I've had a photographic exhibition and at the moment, I teach."

Of course this gives him plenty of fodder to converse with me on. He could ask if I actually *have* horses for example. He could ask if I rode as a child. He could ask if I compete. He could expand on fashion, creativity, or teaching.

Does he?

Nope.

Instead, he asks, "Do you ski?"

"No," I say, "but maybe I could."

"Do you sail?" he asks.

"No," I say again, "but maybe I could." I smile and he looks baffled.

"You don't sail and you don't ski! What *do* you do?"

I pause, look at him directly and respond in a clipped, dry tone. "I ride and I'm creative. I just said."

Thankfully, at that moment, the waiter tells us our table is ready and leads us to the dining room, where fussy silver service ensues. The view is splendid out onto the manicured lawns. The sun streams in.

He chooses a truly superb wine, which I appreciate. Great wine and food are winners. But I'd choose good company over both. Hundreds of little taster courses come in a steady stream, each one of them fabulous. He talks about himself. He talks about his divorce – well, his separation.

"My wife and I *were* going to have the best divorce ever, but I don't know what happened," he says. "I went away for a weekend with a woman, with my wife's knowledge – we were separated after all – and she let herself back into the house, took all the business files and vintage wine and actioned lawyers against me!"

There are two reasons why she would do this. Firstly, she knew that he had files he wouldn't let her access. Hiding money or whatever. Or, secondly, she was actually upset about the other woman. I hazard the former.

But he doesn't understand women. And he asks little about me – my children, my work, nothing. I squeeze in how I love knitting.

"I have a Scandinavian hand knit that's years old and very warm," he says.

Fascinating!

But he does manage to ask if I can knit jumpers myself. I start to tell him about my designs and my knitting, but he immediately picks up his phone and I stop, suspended mid-sentence, waiting for him to notice.

Finally he notices, "I have to check the markets," he says. "There are some big changes at the moment."

I link my fingers and stare at him in silence. Eventually he looks up. "Well, I'll leave you to it then while I go to the loo."

Despite his manners, I do enjoy the food, wine and perfect coffee. The lovely setting. And, because my date is oblivious as to how one connects with another person, I don't worry too much about him. I look at him as a specimen to observe.

I think I may be an anthropologist rather than a dater.

When the bill comes, I get a glimpse. Nearly £400. *A la* carte I assume.

He then asks if I'll come to his house for dinner now, "now that we know each other. I'll cook reindeer steak."

I've never had reindeer steak, and I want it. So I agree. I'm not sure that we *do* know each other, though, but a reindeer steak is all it took!

He's clearly unaware that, apart from the food and venue, we haven't had a good date. I don't actually mind. I love all dates, good and bad. I think I just love experiences. He knows nothing about me despite spending perhaps three hours together. Nothing! Why would he want to meet again? Surely it can't just be because I scrub up well? Maybe it was my listening? People do want to be heard after all.

*

A week later, I'm on my way to Marlows House. "I have a guest suite for you," he texts me.

"I may, or may not stay over," I write back.

While I get lost up a lane with no reception, I end up asking a random farmer where Marlows House is.

"Well, my lover," he says – no joke, they really say that down here! – "Go over the ford and turn right. You'll likely get lost though, lover."

As I momentarily wonder if I'm in a dream, or an episode of *Last of the Summer Wine*, my reception kicks in. *Mr Trophy-Hunter* texts to see where I am.

"Lost up a lane, my lover," I reply.

Marlows House has a gate, an intercom and a long drive. As I wind down the driveway, the medieval manor looms into view. Paddocks to either side, and a fountain in front of the house. An array of flashy cars outside. Shamelessly, I pull-up my bashed-up Golf beside them.

"Always late?" *Mr Trophy-Hunter* asks.

"I never give a specific time," I say, briskly. I don't give a fig for what he thinks, which is always rather liberating.

Through the medieval door, with its medieval handle and medieval knocker, we step into a huge, wood-panelled medieval hall, with a sweeping staircase and panelled gallery. Straight out of a movie set. He wasn't joking when he said his place was good for entertaining. It looks like Downton Abbey.

Suddenly *Mr Trophy-Hunter* looks a little more attractive. A regal surge runs through me, and I feel I'm somehow just where I belong...

I can marry him, my kids can have a private education, I can ride horses all day, buy Burberry coats, adopt loads more kids who can build tree houses and I can host the hunt meets at home. I can write books and film scripts with no worry of success, breed horses, have manicures, and eat lunch in Gidleigh Park. Lady of the Manor...

The only problem is *him*. But maybe I can shag the gardener, Lady Chatterley style?

"Can I look round?" I say, practically throwing my coat at him.

"Be my guest," he says.

"Champagne?" I suggest, as my fantasy has me walking around, flute of champers in hand.

In the panelled billiard room just off the main hall, there are some eight taxidermy heads arranged on the walls. Stag heads as usual, yes, but also a huge array of hunting trophies. Beneath each one there's a photo of him and his daughter, proudly holding guns over the dead animal.

"Darling," I say, "You do know we're signing petitions against trophy hunting these days, don't you?"

"Sign away!" he says. "My hunt pays for ten more animals to be entered into the herds. It's conservation."

I let him have it. I don't want to go into some debate about which animal they choose. Today I'm Lady of the god damn Manor!

The kitchen is modern, with hanging pots and a huge Aga. American fridges. Plenty of clear work surfaces. There are jars and jars of homemade fruits and berries. "All from the estate grounds," he says. I suspect it's his ex-wife's doing. From the way he continues with his food prep, though, I can tell he's not well practiced. But I appreciate his effort; the fact that he's really trying. Maybe cooking is a new thing for him? Maybe his ex-wife used to cook? I sit and watch him and I don't offer to help. I don't want him to know I can cook. Yet.

Some while later, the reindeer steak is ready. As is the sauce – a weird mix of many different things. It doesn't work. The combination is all wrong, as is the consistency.

"Fabulous, darling!" I enthuse.

There are new potatoes and asparagus to accompany. We go to the dining room, with its 18-seater table of dark, heavy wood, carved legs, thick cotton napkins in silver rings, and silver cutlery. All laid out and waiting. Heavy carved crystal wine glasses and water tumblers. Silver candelabras. We perch upright at one end. The ancestors stare down from the walls, although I don't think they're *his* ancestors. He's New Money, I think.

It turns out that reindeer steak is really rather good.

34

Mr Trophy-Hunter – Part 2

After dinner, which I complement him on, *Mr Trophy-Hunter* lets me have a guided tour of the house. There are hundreds of rooms, including a temperature controlled wine cellar, to which he has now changed the lock, should his estranged wife happen to resurface. She has apparently moved into the six-bedroom pool-house on the estate, temporarily, while they work out the divorce. We go up the sweeping staircase to the gallery that looks down onto the grand hall. There are many bedrooms, each with a large four-poster bed, the sort you want to dive into, an *en suite* bathroom, and views onto the lawns.

We go back downstairs and take red wine to the fireplace in the grand hall, where two large leather Chesterfields sit waiting for us. The fire is roaring and wood smoke drifts. It's 10 o'clock and I've had too much champagne and wine to leave, so I agree to stay in the guest suite. There's no assumption that I'll stay in his room, and I'm comfortable with that. We sit in the Chesterfields and drink more wine. Him far more than me. He talks about his estranged wife over two more bottles of red. Until 3 a.m.

What would a good counsellor get for a session like that? I think he's got a long way to go before moving on properly from her.

Occasionally he asks me what I like doing, but doesn't log my reply. He then gets enthusiastic and asks where, anywhere in the world, I'd like to go.

"We'll go there," he says. "Anywhere you like! How about snorkelling? Do you sail?" he asks again.

"We've been over this," I reply.

"We could sail in the Bahamas," he continues, not hearing me. "The waters are so clear and it's just the best for sailing. Do you get sea sick?"

"I don't know" I reply. "I don't sail"

"You don't sail?"

He's a bit drunk.

"Anywhere in the world," he says again.

I decide to change my approach. "Oh yes, I want to go to the Bahamas," I say. "I love sailing."

"Me too!" he says.

Finally, I've given him the correct answer. Which must make it time for bed.

"I need to retire to bed now," I tell him. I've had enough of his ex-wife ramblings. He has no idea what went wrong in their marriage. Absolutely none.

"Do you want to sleep in my bed?" he asks enthusiastically.

Bear in mind that we haven't even brushed shoulders yet. I'm pretty sure at this point I don't want to sleep with him, and can't fathom what he thinks he may have offered to have me desire him.

"I don't like to sleep alone," he says.

I stand up and rest my hand on his shoulder, which he grabs, as if thirsty for touch. He squeezes my hand. "No, I say, we're not there yet are we?"

I smile at him, thinking he needs a mercy fuck, but remind myself not to do that out of kindness.

In my bedroom there's a giant bed and a roll top bath with ball-and-claw feet and traditional taps. I don't want to ruin the mini, one-use hand towels placed in a basket next to the sink. I know I'm going to get make up on them. The housekeeper has made a pointy end on the loo roll and I don't want to ruin that either. What's more, that loo's definitely only for a pee.

I close the heavy curtains and dive into bed. It's so high up I practically have to climb in, like the *Princess and the Pea*.

At 9 a.m. the house is quiet. I look out of the window, over the lawns and box hedges and that giant chess set, and wonder if I should hang about, or go.

I go down to the kitchen to get some water. *Mr Trophy-Hunter* is nowhere to be seen. The kitchen is still strewn with last night's mess. The dining room still has our plates. I've helped clean up this kind of aftermath before, but I've noticed it's rarely appreciated. Not by my kids certainly. Nor by any man. If you do it, it becomes expected. So I leave it. I'm currently completely over domesticity anyway. As an older and wiser girlfriend of mine once said, "Never let a man know you know how to cook, clean or iron. Let him hire it instead." And, with that in mind, I touch nothing.

I open that medieval front door, take a good look around the fields and woods, then get in my car and drive away down that long driveway. Somehow I think I might come back again.

A few messages go back and forth over the next month. Then he says that his divorce is nearly done. "We've fast tracked it. I'll be able to start investing again soon."

"What, you couldn't work while the divorce was going through?" I ask.

"No," he replies. "If I invest while I'm still married, my wife will get half of all I make."

That's his business I guess, and I don't question it.

"Anyway, it's all being finalised next week," he says.

I send him a champagne emoji. "Let's celebrate."

Two weeks later, he invites me for dinner at the manor again. I tell him I can do the daytime, as I have child duties.

"What would you like to do?" he asks.

"Eat seafood, drink champagne and get in the Jacuzzi."

The direct route is the best way forward with this man. I'm in the mood for some decadence and I know I'll get it chez *Mr Trophy-Hunter*. I also want to see if he remembers his 'Anywhere in the world' sailing comment.

On the day, I arrive at lunchtime *and* on time, by chance, rather than intention. I decide to loosen things up a bit and give *Mr Trophy-Hunter* a hug when he answers the door. He warmly accepts. I'm introduced to the housekeeper and can see that lunch arrangements are in full flow.

We have starters and nibbles and prawns with chilli dip, followed by fish. He shows me the pheasants hanging in the larder. "We had a shoot here the other day," he says. "An excellent day's shooting!"

I can feel myself slotting straight into my Lady of the Manor role again. I feel so very 'me' here. "Lunch on the terrace, darling!" I say, flouncing around. "Let's get the last of the autumn sun."

Lunch is served on the terrace. Followed by champagne, lying back on sun loungers in the streaming sunshine. It's so relaxed! Conversation is flowing. *Mr Trophy-Hunter* has finally chilled out.

"Do you sail?" he asks.

I raise my eyebrows. How many times!

"Now, we've been here before, haven't we, darling," I say.

"Ah yes, yes. I remember!" and we start to joke. Now he's more relaxed, it all starts to flow more easily. I treat him with more of my own confidence and, interestingly, he responds with more interest himself. Saying exactly what you're thinking, with clarity, no subtlety, relaxes people like him. I wonder if he's somewhere on the spectrum?

By late afternoon there's an autumn nip in the air, though still sunny. "Jacuzzi!" he suddenly announces.

As it happens. I've come prepared. Bikini in the bag.

We take our champagne to the Jacuzzi and he gives me a robe. I put on the bikini that I never got to use in the summer – having gone absolutely nowhere. But I'm fit from all the riding I do, and confident it will look good. Back in the Jacuzzi room, *Mr Trophy-Hunter* has already got in. And, although there are bubbles everywhere, I'm pretty sure he's starkers.

"Oh you came prepared!" he smiles, eyeing my bikini.

"Of course," I say, somehow thinking I'm in an actual movie. "A lady *always* comes prepared." The champagne has made me flamboyant. This is my game, and my house, and my film, and I'm the star of the show.

I climb into the Jacuzzi and we lie opposite each other, legs touching. The champagne bubbles and Jacuzzi bubbles are a heady mix and I take it on myself to lean in.

"Let's see what we've got here," I say.

He obliges and, it turns out, is a good kisser.

I sit back and look at him seductively. This time *he* leans over for another kiss and, as he kisses me, unclips my bikini top.

"Oh yes," he says, licking his lips. He pulls me onto his lap, and we kiss some more. There's something very liberating about not really caring about someone too much. You can be quite free. We play around in the Jacuzzi for a bit and drink some more champagne.

"Come on," he says, "let's go to the bedroom."

We put on our robes and make a cheeky dash for the bedroom, avoiding the housekeeper, all the while giggling like teenagers. We dive straight onto the bed. The room, the giant four-poster bed, the champagne and Jacuzzi… it's all perfect.

That evening we walk around the grounds. He shows me where he plans to grow his vineyard. "I can make about 6,000 bottles of sparkling wine from this field. It won't make that much money. The land hasn't been used for ten years."

"You can do organic then," I say enthusiastically.

"It's well within the criteria, yes," he says, "but I don't believe in it. Science has moved on. There's no need at all for organic now we can cultivate the perfect grape genetically."

"I think you're talking about GM there, not organic," I say.

Lady of the Manor. Vineyard manager. Sparkling wine taster. Organic promoter. British sparkling wine seller extraordinaire... it all flashes through my mind.

Then his ex-wife calls. She's spoken to the lawyers and wants to update him to get some paper work in. If I leave now, he'll wish I was still with him, so I gesture to him that I'm going. I want him to know that I'm now his priority, and he should wrap up his call. He gets off the phone sharpish. But I still go to leave. Leave him wanting more.

I jump into my car. "Bye darling. *A tout a l'heure,*" I say flippantly and drive off.

*

Back at home, I pick up the stupid bills that have flopped through my door. Back down to earth with a bump. What a ridiculous scenario: a couple of bottles of that champagne would cover my bills! I need bloody money more than champagne.

The following day, I'm called by my agency to do a supply job for the day. I earn precisely £55.

Would being Lady of the Manor be so bad? Could I put up with someone who thinks organic is GM? Someone who's somewhere on the spectrum, probably? Could I sacrifice finding true love for security? And not just security, but a life of luxury?

But acting out of amusement for a week or two is not the same as real life. How long could I tolerate him for? Or would I fall in love with him? "Marry for money and the love will come later," my friend once said. Should you marry for happiness, or is marriage all about duty? Could I learn to be happy with this man? I don't know. I haven't decided whether to go back for more, but playing Lady of the Manor was a role I liked playing.

35

Mr Trophy-Hunter – Part 3

New Year's Eve is looming and I haven't arranged anything to do. This isn't unusual for me. I've been known to stay in with a couple of girlfriends, knitting and drinking camomile tea. I'm with an old friend (a previous camomile tea offender also) and her husband. They haven't arranged anything either. "We'll come to you," she says, but my place is so god damn small I can't fit a sofa in it, let alone host a New Year's do. And then, suddenly, *Mr Trophy-Hunter* pops into my mind. He's just sent me some pictures of his Christmas and asked me my plans.

"I know!" I announce to my friends. "I'll invite us all to Marlows House. He loves to entertain at his place, and he's just asked what I'm doing."

"You can't just invite us all!" my friend says.

"Just you watch me," I say. "He can only say no, can't he!" And with that, I shoot him a message.

"How about I come to you for New Year's with my old friends?" And, before I know it, I have a visit arranged for us – New Year's Eve at Marlows House, and an invitation to a shoot he's hosting the next day.

"All sorted!" I laugh to my friends, who shake their heads in amazement. I also pop *Mr Trophy-Hunter* a little add-on. "Oh, I'll have my son with me," I throw into the mix.

"OK!" he replies. "So that's you, me, your couple, your son, my daughter and my housekeeper."

We arrive at the Manor at 5.30 promptly and are greeted by the housekeeper. It's nice to see her. She's jolly and she's taken a shine to me. Then *Mr Trophy-Hunter* comes out. I have my little boy in tow, his long hair bushing out beneath his hat. The housekeeper says "Hi," to him, but *Mr Trophy-Hunter* doesn't seem to notice him at all. I introduce them to each other. My kid is relaxed, but *Mr Trophy-Hunter?* God, he's awkward! He looks at my kid then says, "It's a boy right?" Luckily, my son is not remotely offended.

"Yes, I'm a boy, like you," he laughs.

We troupe inside to the snug with its giant roaring fire, and where *Mr Trophy-Hunter* and his teenage daughter have been playing a game of giant chess. The daughter is as awkward as his father. They quickly round off their game, with the daughter clearly thrashing him.

"It's a draw!" *Mr Trophy-Hunter* announces.

"What?" says the daughter. "But…"

"Same amount of pieces left," says *Mr Trophy-Hunter*. The teenager accepts it with a little scowl. "You can go and do your homework now, or whatever you're doing," he adds.

When the teenager has gone upstairs, *Mr Trophy-Hunter* turns to me. "Shall we wait for your friends, or shall we have a little drink?"

"Let's get a drink," I say, dying to relax.

Luckily, *Mr Trophy-Hunter* does this well: he brings out a bottle of champagne with homemade kir – I bet it was his ex-wife who made it – and nibbles. We settle ourselves by the fire. Yet again I'm right at home.

Half an hour later my friends arrive. We all drink for a bit, and my friend and I team up and chat. My friend's husband entertains *Mr Trophy-Hunter* with talk about cars.

When dinner's announced, we file through to the long dining room table, with its silver candelabras. There are scallops to start and beef for the main. The housekeeper serves some fabulous white wine with the scallops, and a gorgeous red with our main. *Mr Trophy-Hunter's* taste in wine can't be faulted. Truly excellent.

But his daughter doesn't utter a single word during our whole sitting. We – that is, my lot – try to get her involved, but it's clear she's very uncomfortable. She's either very shy or doesn't like her dad. *Mr Trophy-Hunter* talks about his Christmas guests, how it all went and the difficulties of an aging parent. But he doesn't ask any of us where we were for Christmas, or what we did. Neither does he look at me, nor talk to me at all. He doesn't ask my friends where they live or what they do; how many kids they have nor, in fact, anything. Not one thing about them! *Still on the spectrum then*, I suspect.

While dessert is served – a fantastic Black Forest gateau with sweet dessert wine – *Mr Trophy-Hunter* gets on to the subject of diving. Now, I've never dived myself, but my friend has, so he talks to her. About all the places *he* has dived. For an hour!

To me the whole thing is ludicrous, though my friend's husband doesn't seem to care – he just asks for a cheese board and tucks in to that. What on earth am I doing here, in Downton Abbey, with a man who hasn't acknowledged me all evening, who hasn't said a word to my kid, or his kid, and who has talked about himself all night? I may as well not exist.

I can see he's not a bad man, but what he *can* manage – a good dinner, fine wine – is something he's acquired. How to actually communicate with others is another matter entirely. Why did I think I could pretend that I could feel ok here? Why did I think this was a good idea? I thought it would be fun to play Lady of the Manor again. But it's not. It's just lonely. Lonely in a beautiful setting.

By 11.30 I'm suddenly overwhelmed. It has been brewing in me over the dinner, but suddenly I feel the urge to cry. Tough as I am, when that happens to me that's it. I'm a gonner!

I slip away, put my son to bed and head for my four-poster bedroom where I burst into tears. I wash my face, put on my PJs, climb in and weep in the giant bed. I assume no one will notice but, right before midnight, I hear my friend calling for me.

I ignore her, putting a pillow over my head.

Then, suddenly, *Mr Trophy-Hunter* comes into my room, kneels beside the bed and asks me what's wrong.

"You've ignored me all night," I say. "Not a word to me all evening!"

"I didn't know what you'd told your friends about me," he says. "Come down stairs. Please. I'm sorry."

Fuck it, I think. *Better go down.* I'm in shitty, not-to-be-seen PJs, a bad crying face and a weepy mood. But go down I do.

There's my friend waiting at the bottom of the sweeping stairs. I go to the bottom set, sit down, and burst into tears again. And there I am, head in hands, at midnight on New Year's Eve, in shitty PJ's on the staircase of Downton bloody Abbey... crying!

I don't know where *Mr Trophy-Hunter* has disappeared to, but my friend comes and sits with me in her nice New Year's Eve dress and high heels. I start to half laugh through my tears. "I want to be at home," I sob. "Why am I even here with him?"

"You're not here with him. You're here with *us*," my friend says, and that strikes a chord in me. Suddenly I feel much better.

Yes, I'm here with my friends and it's all ok, I think.

Drying my tears, we head into his cinema room off the main hall. Fireworks from around the world are exploding on his screen. We watch for a while, my friend on one side of me and *Mr Trophy-Hunter*, who has re-appeared, on the other. We go through the motions: Auld Lang Syne, hugs and kisses and, at around 1 o'clock everyone drifts off to bed.

I've just fallen asleep when, ping! A text arrives from *Mr Trophy-Hunter*.

"I'm sooo excited to have you next door. Come share my bed, I'd like that."

I remind myself, *no obligations,* and snuggle down into my own bed, switching off my phone and putting in my earplugs. Time for a proper night's sleep.

At 8 in the morning, *Mr Trophy-Hunter* comes to my room, lying down with me and putting his arm around me. "Smell is important," he says, "and you smell good to me."

He however actually smells like fake tan.

"Hmm." I reply and, with my disinterest, he gets up to leave.

"The people will be coming for the shoot at about 10 o'clock," he says.

Oh Christ yes, the shoot, I remember.

Down in the kitchen, the housekeeper is already busy making bacon and sausage baps for breakfast. The dining room is laid out with coffee and juices. We all tuck in. *Mr Trophy-Hunter* doesn't acknowledge me. I honestly think he doesn't know how. At 10, people start arriving. My friend and I mingle a bit as everyone tucks into breakfast. Marlows is feeding the whole shoot party. My son enjoys himself playing the grand piano in the drawing room, playing the tunes he's learning in his school lessons. Then he kicks his shoes off and starts rolling around on the sweeping staircase and I'm not sure if I should let him.

Then it's time for the shoot.

We join the beaters and *Mr Trophy-Hunter* drives the buggy with the guns. We're out from 10.30 until 4, beating bushes and are nicely tired by the end of it all. *Mr Trophy-Hunter* would like nothing more than for his daughter to join him in his sport, but she's nowhere to be seen.

When we get back to the house, the housekeeper has again laid on a table full of canapés and prosecco. Announcements are made on the number of pheasants. The atmosphere's jolly. We spend an hour or two chatting and eating, then ping! My phone again. It's *Mr Trophy-Hunter.*

"Desperately want to have you now," his message reads. "You should stay."

I look around to see where he is, then catch him coming down the staircase. I ping him a message.

"Can't, sorry. Leaving soon." He doesn't reply. Not until I leave.

Ping! *Crying face.*

What the hell? How can someone send messages, but ignore me in person? Does he only feel comfortable through a screen, or is he trying to create some secret mystique? Crying emojis? FFS! Can't he understand that he's got to try and make a proper connection?

Driving away up that long driveway, I know that, just like riding around in Lamborghinis, the novelty of flashy things wears off super fast. What you're left with is just a man. In a better car, or a better house, but ultimately just a man. I had better make sure that that man is the right one; one I can just hang out with when all the flashy things are no longer there.

36

Mr Trophy Hunter – Part 4

I am either:

1. A glutton for punishment,

2. Nosey as hell,

3. Stupid,

or all of the above.

I'm in Geneva, accompanying *Mr Trophy-Hunter* as he hands over 2 million pounds worth of gold to his ex-wife.

Don't ask.

"I have to go to Geneva to hand over gold to my ex-wife, then head to the Alps for 4 or 5 nights. Back to Geneva to pick up some more gold and take it to Germany. Then spend a few days at a spa. Please join me for any, or all, of these things."

Come on now, it's hard to resist a message like that!

"Do it, what the hell!" says my New Year's Eve friend.

Gold what? Gold coins? Gold bloody ingots? I need to know, and start imagining secret vaults, 1960's movies style. How will we hand the gold over? Will we go down into bolted vaults? Where are the buckets of gold kept? When it's handed over, will it be counted out piece-by-piece, or weighed out? I'm simply compelled to know and, before I know it, I shoot him a message back.

"As long as I can sort out childcare, I'm in!" I text, and then message my ex, to see if he can come and be me for two weeks with our son.

Oddly, timing seems to be on my side. Except for having to cancel his old sofa being picked up to be taken to the dump, my son's dad can juggle enough to take over.

"I'm going gold digging," I tell him. Then I ask him to send me a video clip of his hands, to make sure he's not shaking. Meaning that he's currently sober. And not in withdrawal either. I have to have proof. His word doesn't suffice. If he's not sober I can't have him come to take over. Staying sober – his, and our, on-going battle.

Thankfully, his hands aren't shaking.

I promptly spend the next few nights in a state of high anxiety and sleep badly. I'm panicking about spending two weeks with a man who can't read people. I'm anxious about not having an escape should I need to get out. What if he's James Bond-ing it down some black slopes and I'm in baby ski school, fending for myself. I won't even be able to buy coffee and salad – not at ski resort prices.

A couple of friends – blokes – tell me that I'd better air that with him before I go, so as to be clear. Good advice, I decide. So I do. I message him. "I'm really sorry, I just can't afford it."

"The hotels, spas, dinner etc. will all be covered. Whatever could you possibly need?"

I explain that if I need to get home, for example, or need some contingency money, I simply can't cover it on my earnings. "We're not in the same financial bracket," I add. "I don't like asking for money, and it's good to be clear."

He replies promptly. "We're going away together. Nothing extravagant, but perfectly comfortable. I'll cover expenses – travel, hotels, skiing, dinners, spa treatments etc. I'll give you some other money should you need it. If you need to get home, I'll personally get you on a flight. I won't shower you with gifts, or pay for things you buy for yourself. I'm decent and will behave decently. It'll be fun and you won't be disappointed."

Well, can't get clearer than that. Looks like it's sorted, and here's the proof of the pudding. *Mr Trophy-Hunter* needs directness. He's simply incapable of reading a woman's subtle cues and needs everything spelled out.

If he tries it on with me, for example, I'll simply have to say, "I don't, or I do, want to have sex with you *Mr Trophy-Hunter.*" This isn't very romantic, or seductive, and it's definitely a turn off but, if this is going to work at all, I'm going to have to verbalize everything clearly.

I spend the whole week before the trip anxious about any and everything. A couple of friends ask if I'm excited.

"No," I reply. "I simply want to know what he knows about gold. That's all."

"But what about the skiing?" they ask.

"Never had any desire to do it but, while I'm there, I'll bloody well give it a go." It crosses my mind that if I were to break something skiing, I wouldn't be able to work, and then I'd be buggered. It was bad enough when I fell off my horse and nearly sliced my finger off – I had to do the next month's work one-handed. No choice. There's no sick pay for me.

In a moment of forgetting I'm currently poor, I go to *Aveda* and do my hair for the trip, which costs a small fortune compared to the students I normally get to do it. *Mr Trophy-Hunter* messages me constantly about our travels which, in a way, is rather nice. It's nice to know he really wants me there.

My child's father arrives from London to cover the childcare.

"Looking forward to it?" he asks.

"Nope," I say. "I don't know what I was thinking. I think I just impulsively said yes – couldn't resist the story about the gold."

"Perfectly understandable," he replies, amused.

The next morning, *Mr Trophy-Hunter* arrives to pick me up. I'm packed and ready on time, as instructed. There's plenty of room in the boot of his 4x4, for my stuff as well as his, and we set off on the long, long drive to Troyes, in France. It's here we'll stay the night on our way to Geneva.

He chats, relaxed enough, but doesn't seem to want any music on. I'm a sing-along-in-the-car person, and soon learn he's a talk-to-banks-about-gold kind of guy. He makes call after call to financial advisers, banks, vaults, mortgage people, the lot. Big numbers get bandied around. Much as I try – so that I can *Google* what they're talking about later – I can neither remember nor understand what he's talking about. It's simply another language.

After 12 hours, we arrive at our hotel. The hotelier really wants to tell us the history of the building. I actually want to hear about it, but *Mr Trophy-Hunter* doesn't. Instead, we dine quickly and settle down for the evening. *Mr Trophy-Hunter* takes a shower. He strips off starkers and struts around, laying out his vast array of moisturizers and products.

There's just the one bed in the room.

He makes an attempt at getting it on, but I tell him it's the wrong time of the month. He falls asleep, snoring loudly. I can't sleep, even with earplugs. It goes on for hours until he finally stops.

The next day we drive to Geneva. I can feel the tension building as we approach. He's been talking about gold all the way.

"Gold what?" I ask. "Coins? Ingots?"

"Yes," he says. "You must never have all your assets in one place. You have to move it around. Cover all eventualities. If the banks crash, they'll have no qualms about keeping your money. If a government changes, it could be a regime that annuls your property. If you've got your money in shares, the market could crash and you'd lose everything. I had a friend who made £60 million and lost it all in the last crash. Had it all in one place. I learned a lot from that."

This gold in Geneva is all in the bank, however. And he has to split it with his wife. He always refers to his ex-wife as his wife. He hasn't managed to add the 'ex' bit in yet. He seems to be getting really tense about seeing her. We pause outside *Credit Suisse* for a minute while he takes a breath, then go inside. The ex-wife is already waiting, and it appears that she's already pissed off.

She's not very tall, but she's a good-looking woman, well-dressed, casual but expensive – cashmere, Prada flat heels – but she's stern. I can tell already that she doesn't like me.

"Who's this?"

"She's accompanying me," he answers.

"Don't you think you should have come alone?" she snaps.

"We're skiing," he answers blankly.

The bank manager steps in and invites us to the vaults. We're taken in by security men who look like they're practically in riot gear. I say nothing, just watch. One of them punches some numbers into a keypad and the thick doors slide open, just like in the movies. Inside, there are shelves and shelves of gold. Actual ingots. Real coins. They then proceed to count out the gold, and halve it.

After a lot of counting and re-counting the number of coins comes up short, by 50 pieces! I have a strong desire to laugh, but suppress it. The couple start accusing each other of stealing the missing coins.

"It was an estimate," he yells at her.

"You've been in and taken some!" she accuses him.

"I haven't been here for more than a year. We weren't even divorced then. I would have been stealing from myself."

My eyes ping-pong back and forth between them as they hurl accusations at each other.

"That's £60,000 worth of gold coins. Missing!" she says, giving me the ball park of £1,200 per coin.

Would anyone notice, while they're arguing, if I shove a few of those bad boys in my pocket on the way out?

When we come out of the bank, *Mr Trophy-Hunter* is super stressed. He's wired, and in a foul mood. "Does she honestly think I stole my *own* gold?"

The Hilton in Geneva is very… posh. And *Mr trophy-Hunter* is a diamond member. Apparently that means he must have spent at least 60 days a year in Hilton hotels. It gives him some perks. We've been upgraded to a suite, for example. Which means a sitting room, as well as bath and bedrooms. We have dinner in the hotel restaurant. The executive suite is not open; it's being refitted.

"Standards in France are slipping," he hisses. "It gets worse every time." Service is slow. This irritates him further. "See what I mean?" he fumes.

There are starters of self-service canapés, but they look like they might have been sitting there a little while. The smoked salmon is a little dry around the edges, and the crackers are a little soft. *Mr Trophy-Hunter* is, unsurprisingly, unimpressed. Then the mains take a long time to arrive. You could cut the tension with a knife.

Come on food, I think, *don't piss him off even more.*

But when our food does arrive, the sauce is missing from his plate.

We're in for trouble now, I think. And, sure enough, the meal is angrily sent back.

"It's cold now, waiting for the sauce," he snaps.

What is wrong with this man! We made it on time to the gold transaction. We're in a beautiful hotel. We got an upgrade. We're eating decent food, and he's a diamond member! He can drink as much wine as he wants AND he has a smart, attractive woman with him. Jesus! But, oh no! He's just not happy. First World problems, eh?

But then I guess 60k worth of missing gold doesn't help.

The ex-wife is winning alright, I think. He's allowed her to ruin his holiday although, in fact, he seems to be doing a fine job of that on his own.

37

Mr Trophy-Hunter – Part 5

The view across Lake Geneva is not at all bad from our suite. "Such a great view," I say, hopefully. And then, as if I'd told him to get undressed, instead of reminded him how nice this place actually is, off come *Mr Trophy-Hunter's* clothes.

He struts around naked again, with his little willy dangling around his balls, proud as Punch.

He must be pushing 60, I think. Presumably he's either proud of his body, or maybe he thinks this is sexy? He's still refused to tell me his age. Although his hair is quite thick and he has a full head, I can see there's a lot of grey coming through. It seems he's also had a tint a while ago, and now it's fading. He should have done his hair before we left, like me. I look at his face and see that his forehead is a bit more intact than the rest of him. Botox? Botox, fake tan, hair tint – he can try it all he likes, but it won't make up for that bolshy personality that keeps rearing its ugly head.

Drunk on the copious wine at dinner we go to bed and fall asleep. At 6 a.m. I'm woken by a stabbing in my back, but I'm still half asleep and barely *compos mentis*. But as my mind starts to clear, the picture starts to make sense. Hang on a minute, do we have a willy in the back situation here? I thought I might have been dreaming but, no, *Mr Trophy-Hunter* is doing some kind of writhing movement on my back, for real, rubbing his dick up my spine and between my legs. I haven't experienced this since I was a teenager, when no one knew what they were doing, or guys thought they could 'cop a feel', or use a girl's back as a wank platform.

Then, I kid you not... jizz on my knickers.

"You horny old bastard," I shout at him. "Did you just bloody well...?"

But he is merry and blasé and simply skips out of bed to the bathroom, where he has a little wash and gets me a towel.

Honestly, I am lost for words and go for a shower. I can't speak to him, let alone look at the dirty old bastard. The water washes him off me and, as I scrub myself clean, my surprise turns to laughter.

"I'll meet you down there," I hear him say and, satisfied with himself, he leaves me to my shower.

When I get down to breakfast, his laptop is out on the table. He's checking the markets. Not only did he lose £60k in missing gold coins, but it would seem that he also lost £250k on the markets.

I'm not sure why I'm amused, but I am.

"It's very stressful," he tells me.

"Hmm..." I reply in a no-reply kind of way. Try not being able to put petrol in the car to get to work because you haven't got a fiver, I think to myself. That's stressful.

*

We leave the Hilton and head off to Chamonix to ski. One would assume that now the gold has been handed over, we would now be on holiday together and he could relax a bit. But it seems that's not the case.

Mr Trophy-Hunter drinks can after can of *Diet Coke* and *Red Bull*, as well as a stream of double espressos. The hit is just never enough.

En route I learn that he has several theories he would like to share with me. These range from how money works and what shares he invests in, to explaining how he has vaccines for everything in his safe at home.

"When everyone else is dying of a flu epidemic, and the vaccines have all run out, I have enough to survive anything. Antibiotics, flu, you name it, I've got it all in my safe at home. When the markets have crashed and governments failed, and banks have seized everyone's assets, I'll have enough gold stashed away out of the system. I've got enough food to last a year at least."

"Surviving all eventualities then," I say. What is he, a trophy-hunting survivalist?

"Well we must learn from history," he goes on. "We have to prepare."

This survival malarkey is very stressful, whether it's surviving day-to-day like me, or surviving in style like him. Keeping it away from the ex-wife and the government is quite a preoccupation. I contemplate the good life scenario. Surely all we need to be content is a patch big enough to grow a bit of food, some trapping skills and some cool people around us? For all the tight grip he keeps on his gold, *Mr Trophy-Hunter* doesn't seem especially happy.

We arrive at our hotel in Chamonix. It looks like it will have everything we could need, or want. We have a nice suite with a mezzanine bedroom. If there are questions about facilities, *Mr Trophy-*

Hunter will be sure to ask the staff. It's an uncompromising need to let everyone know that he is the customer and he *will* get his money's worth.

We book in to dinner. The menu looks good. The staff are jolly and the hotel buzzing with ski-tired, happy folk.

But *Mr Trophy-Hunter*, like clockwork, isn't happy about dinner.

"I don't know any of these wines," he complains. "Where are the Bordeaux's, the Côte du Rhone's? There's not one wine here I recognise."

He summons the *sommelier* for an in-depth discussion. It turns out that all the wine is local and organic.

"Thrilling," I think. "The world is shifting to organic."

"You can experiment with your organic wines somewhere else," he tells the *sommelier*, totally unabashed, "but I've never tasted a decent organic wine yet, and have no desire to try it out here."

The *sommelier* keeps a neutral, French demeanour. "These are what we have, Sir," he cajoles politely. "I am sure you would enjoy one if you taste it before you buy…?"

We get a nice red.

I'm relieved that it's super tasty.

But apparently it's not good. "Really," *Mr Trophy-Hunter* says, "it's outrageous that after years and years of research we're going backwards. Organic! You know it's full of bugs!" He goes on to tell me about the vineyard he plans to establish on his land, and it certainly won't be organic.

His phone pings, and an email comes in from his ex-wife about the mortgage that he wants to get to buy her out of his property.

"It's good for tax purposes to mortgage the house and pay her off that way," he says. Some kind of financial re-shuffle. But the reply comes back. She doesn't agree the terms. He proceeds to spend the rest of the meal composing emails to her solicitors and mortgage brokers, each of which he reads to me over the dinner table.

I eat my food and watch his courses come and go while his eyes don't leave his phone.

There are people eating all around us, engaged in conversation. But we are *that* couple in the corner. The couple who don't talk. We are the couple you feel sorry for, who sit on their phones instead of enjoying each other's company. *That* couple who miss what's right there in front of them. That's us.

Suddenly I sympathise with Melania Trump, all bouncy hair and nice outfits, silent in the corner, while her rich and powerful husband acts oh-so-important, missing what's right in front of him.

"Would you stop pouting," he suddenly says.

Ah, so he is aware of what's he's doing then!

But I am not a woman to just shut up and can feel the rage brewing inside me. "Did you just tell me to stop pouting?" I glare at him. He's slightly taken aback as I challenge him. "Did I hear that right?"

"It's very important that I send these emails," he says. "There's a lot of money at stake. I have deadlines. I must get it done."

"There's fuck all you can do about deadlines now, darling," I say. "Enough of your ex-wife! Don't talk about her again, please. You have a lovely woman right in front of you. Can you imagine if I sat here emailing and talking constantly about my ex? Rude and inconsiderate. Do you even really want me here?"

He is staring back at me in shock. I lean in towards him across the table and lower my voice.

"And don't be thinking for a second that you can go poking your willy in my back tonight, you disgusting man," and, with that, I defiantly pick up my own phone and start scrolling.

He sits for a few moments in awkward silence.

"You don't want or like sex?" he suddenly offers. I nearly choke on my coffee.

I give it a moment's thought.

"With a self-obsessed, inattentive man who revenge emails his ex-wife, spends all his time on his computer, doesn't notice what's right in front of him, and shows me no interest? No. It's *you* I don't want sex with. You can use your hand and help yourself out."

He looks at me, wounded. "Just a 'No' would have sufficed," he says.

"What! You'd rather not know why?"

"You're a very aggressive woman," he finally says. "Very aggressive indeed. There's no point in talking to someone who likes to attack. And swearing, awful swearing…" he says. "I think we'd better find you that flight home…"

38

Mr Trophy-Hunter – The End

So, *Mr Trophy-Hunter* wants to send me home? Passive-aggressive tantrums. This is pure comedy.

"Sure thing," I tell him. "Book that ticket!"

He starts to look at flights.

"What a shame," he says in a matter of fact manner. "There's one today at 12.30, but we only have 2 hours to get you there. It's too tight. There is one tomorrow though...?"

"Book that one then."

He dithers around. Doesn't seem to be booking it. Is he calling my bluff?

"Well, I've missed my ski time for today," he sighs.

"It's not even lunch time!" I remind him breezily. "Go for a half day."

But he doesn't want to buy a pass for half a day or, maybe, just doesn't feel like it any more.

I get my ski gear and go for my lesson and pray all the time that I won't break anything. When it's over, I put my gear away in the locker and go into the hotel library. I'm happy just watching the world go by, and resist letting *Mr Trophy-Hunter* know I'm back. Until, that is, I get a text message.

"Let me let know when you're back."

I hold off messaging him back a little longer, until he passes by the hotel library and sees me sitting there. "Ah you're here!"

He doesn't ask me how my lesson was, but proceeds to tell me where we'll be having dinner.

"Did you book a flight?" I ask in a blasé way.

"No. We already cut into my ski time and, if I take you tomorrow, that'll be another day wasted. I bought a three day ski pass."

So it seems that I'm staying-on here with him. No choice. I'll have to switch into some kind observant mode and try not to argue with him. He's not really worth arguing with after all. Perhaps I'll make the most of the spa in the mornings, and do some writing in the afternoons. I bought my iPad after all. Then I'll eat decent food in the evening. I'll be civil and polite. Yes, I'll be Melania Trump for a week. I look at him from a distance and even feel a little sorry for him.

That evening, he does make an effort to keep his phone away at dinner. It lies there on the table beside his plate, and he *really, really* wants to check it. I go to the loo a couple of times just to allow him a window to do so. It's like his hand is straining not to touch it. I also want to message a couple of other people. My friend, to tell her about my stories. And someone else – a guy who has messaged me on *Tinder*, and with whom I'm striking up a rapport. I've told him all about my antics in the Alps. It's comical really.

When I return to the table, we're civil with each other. It's all a bit unnatural and weird, but it's interesting. I'm messaging my *Tinder* man, my ex to check-in on my son, and my friend, and he's dying to revenge email his wife. His ex-wife.

"Never mind," my friend messages me. "At least you tried."

"Just because he paid for the trip, doesn't mean he's entitled to sex," texts the *Tinder* man.

"Never mind, darling. Better luck next time," writes my ex.

I take to sleeping on the sofa. Up on the mezzanine. He snores so loud, I can't stand it. Then on, our penultimate night, he says that he's booked the crossing home.

"It's been very disappointing," he says.

"I see these things as a moment in time," I tell him. "An experience. It's all part of life. We always take something away from our experiences, don't you think?"

"Not really," he replies. "I'm running out of time. I don't have time for bad experiences, only good ones."

"Well, you're in control of that I'm afraid," I say.

He doesn't seem the slightest bit impressed. But then I remember how he had previously told me that he'd had a full body scan to detect any diseases. A full DNA test to see about any genetic predispositions. And all those vaccines and antibiotics in his safes. Here's a man who desperately needs to control everything; every experience; every person. His own body.

Well, it's one way to live.

Then, rather oddly, he tells me that all he wanted to do on this trip was to have some fun, some nice company.

"Yes, me too," I say. "I think an ex-wife and your mobile phone might have got in the way though, don't you?"

He seems bemused. "I don't share easily," he says.

"No, no," I say. "You don't talk endlessly about your ex to a new woman. And you don't ignore me in favour of sorting out your dealings with her."

"Is it because I've been sexually inappropriate?" he suddenly asks, out of the blue. I feel truly sorry for him. He doesn't have a clue. "I'd never force myself on someone. I'd only want to have sex with someone who wants to," he adds. "We already had sex, so I didn't see it as a problem."

"Yes. You have indeed been inappropriate, a few times. People have to build a foundation to be intimate. What you did was vile."

"No," he says, "you seem to think there are layers. Stages that need to be passed. Boxes that need to be ticked. There aren't. People are just silly sheep following silly codes."

The poor bastard. He just doesn't get it. I don't think I can be bothered to explain. The guy must be approaching 60. If he hasn't learnt by now...

"I'm glad we had this chat," I say. "I appreciate your effort. I'm sorry you felt you've wasted your time with me. I don't feel it's a waste. It's been interesting, I'd try to look at it like that too, if I were you."

The next morning at breakfast, the laptop is shamelessly out on the breakfast table. He checks his shares and finds that he has lost £1 million since the £4 million investment he made two weeks ago.

"I should have been keeping a better eye on the market this week," he says. "I've never taken my eye off the ball like this. I never put my lap top down for good reason."

So it's my fault his shares are down a million. Some power I must have, eh!

"Never mind," I say breezily. "They'll go up again won't they? That's what shares do right? I'd buy some more now if I were you, while they're low and cheap."

He's not impressed. Doesn't matter. I already know I'm a big disappointment to him. He said so the night before, after all.

I came on this trip to find out about gold and, possibly, make a connection with this man. And to have a bit of fun. I just couldn't resist seeing what happened with the gold. But now I know about the gold, it's a fabulous reminder that no matter how many gold bars a man has, if he can't enjoy what he has, then there's no point in it. He has an ex-wife who hates him. A daughter who doesn't communicate. And so what's all the gold for? It sits in vaults dotted around the world, waiting for a rainy day.

If I were a much better gold digger, I imagine I would have taken over earlier on this trip. Grabbed him and taken him to the bedroom straight away. Changed the whole story of this trip. But I didn't. Instead, here I am, walking through my front door back in Devon. The dog jumps on me and I sit on my armchair in my teeny cottage with its knitted throws and dresser with chipped crockery and I take note: no amount of gold is worth hanging out with men like that. I have no idea how Melania manages it. Either she's dead inside, like her husband, or she has a secret plan. Or she just *can't* leave, for fear of repercussions.

Let's hope it's the 'plan' option.

39

Mr Single-Dad

Tinder

Age: 50

Between all the dates and meetings, there are hundreds of online interactions that never come to anything. Or the little one-off coffee, or lunch dates, that just never go anywhere. The hundreds of *Tinder* matches that sit in your Inbox, without anyone actually sending a message. The *Tinder* matches to whom I send a message, but who don't reply. The *Tinder* matches who chit-chat until you realise you're having an online relationship instead of a real one. You unmatch them. The boring conversations. The *Hi there's!* and *How are you?* messages, so uninspiring you despair and unmatch them without replying. You start out polite but, after hundreds of online chats, realise you've become ruthless. You unmatch with no explanation. Practically mid-chat. Then there are the matches you meet up with and know, straight away, that there's absolutely nothing there. No spark. You know you'll never meet them again.

I leave my memories of the Alps *in* the Alps, and pick up with *Mr Single-Dad*, with whom I'd been conversing while away with *Mr Trophy-Hunter*. *Mr Single-Dad* had been funny in our messages. A festival-going, shaved headed, single dad in a flowery shirt and waistcoat. His son is the same age as my youngest son. He has a nice face and checks out nicely on *Facebook*. We decide to meet up and let our children play. It would be nice to hook up with a single dad with a kid, and his kid seems lovely. I want to persuade myself into it. He seems a nice, normal guy too. Sri Lankan by heritage, and grew up in London.

But as soon as I meet him in his house, where he's invited us for lunch, I know that his nasal North London accent will, sooner or later, drive me potty.

Then there's the biscuit cupboard full of *Lucozade* and junk food that his son raids whenever he wants. My son, not used to free rein on the biscuits, hits that cupboard hard. And then there's the question of the four extra stone he's carrying. Two litre bottles of *Lucozade* perhaps? How would we do long walks or rambling? Could these things be overlooked?

After telling me that he's cleaned the house for a whole day, I wonder what on earth it's normally like? His taste is retro kitsch; I'm more rustic chic. Could I live with that?

He has a nail bar so he gives me a nail consultation as a prelude to doing my manicure and pedicure.

"Ahh," he says, inspecting my hands. "No, no, nooo! You've got to do these nails more often, and what oh what is going on here? You must oil your cuticles in order to keep the nails from breaking!"

Can't he talk about how fabulous he's going to make them, rather than finding everything he thinks has gone wrong with my nails? That's not a consultation; it's a critique. And here's me thinking I've done well on my nails today.

"Ok thanks. I don't really need my pedicure done today too, thanks," I quickly reply, slipping swiftly out of the chair.

A couple of weeks later we met up again, this time at my place.

I decided we should go for a walk in some woods and on to a pub for lunch. My child's father has been for the weekend and hasn't left yet. *Mr Single-Dad* immediately strikes up lad banter with my son's father while ignoring me. He talks incessantly.

"Hang on… she comes to my place and gets a nice home cooked pie, but I come round here and get almond milk in my coffee?" he jokes, North London style.

"Woah… you're a brave man!" my son's father replies. The bantering continues.

All the conversation is directed to my son's father. None to me. I sit making pissed off eyes at my son's dad. Either this guy is nervous, or sexist? Or just a twat? My son's dad looks back at me and withdraws from the chat, experienced enough to know better. But *Mr Single-Dad* continues, oblivious that it's not going down well with me.

My son's dad makes a sharp exit to get back to London, and I drive *Mr Single-Dad* and the kids to the pub on the moor.

"Woah! Ha ha! I don't think you even looked behind there!" he comments on my driving. "Next time, I'm driving." He laughs heartily at himself.

The kids splash in rock pools near the woods. His son seems very cold – he doesn't have the right clothing for the job and he gets upset. "Never mind," he whispers. "We'll go home soon and snuggle up to watch some telly."

Clearly I'm more of a soldier-through-the-moorland-getting-muddy type, and he's more Netflix-and-snacks. But for god's sake, how fussy can I be? I have to give people a chance and live with some differences. Right?

Then the next time we see him – yes, I keep trying! – I choose the beach. I like quiet, secret beaches, usually with a trek to get to them. Beaches that most people can't be bothered to walk to. Before we head down to the sea, I take them to do some crabbing in Dartmouth. I've got some old bait, but my son and I catch no crabs. Our bait's too old. But *Mr Single-Dad* and his son catch loads of crabs. Fresh bait.

"We're winning," he teases. I hadn't wanted it to be a competition anyway.

We get some sandwiches and water, and he gets a giant *Lucozade*. While we're sitting eating, a seagull dive bombs and grabs my sandwich right out of my hand. It flies off leaving me feeling oddly humiliated. Mugged by a fucking bird! My bottle of water promptly falls in to the water beneath where we're sitting. I go to the shop to get myself another sandwich and, when I return, see that he's got some water next to him.

"Is that my water?" I say. "Did you fish it out?"

"Err, yeees. Durrr! It's right there isn't it? What do you think it is?" He laughs like Beavis and Butt Head. On and on. I'm not inclined to answer and, of course, the more I withdraw my attention, the more crass he becomes with insecure put-downs.

After our first meeting he asked me if I liked him. I replied that we would be good as friends. It was an almond milk versus cream in your coffee type thing, I told him.

We will stay *Facebook* friends, but I know, just know, that I can't have a cupboard dedicated to crisps and biscuits. I'd eat them all. And so would my son. I don't want them in the house.

And he said his son has to wear headphones in their tent at festivals, because of his snoring! *And* he's going to stay four stone overweight if he keeps drinking *Lucozade* like water.

I don't want to re-educate him. Or nag him. Forget that!

And also, by the way, almond milk *is* nice!

40

Mr Carpenter

Tinder

Age: 46

There are big difference between dating in London and dating in Devon. But a date is a date is a date. It's good to just get out there and see. You never know when sparks may fly.

I am broadening my horizons yet again and decide that I need to try lots of different types of men. So, when *Mr Carpenter* pops up on *Tinder*, I decide to give him a go, even though he looks every bit 'true Totnes'. Totnes is the magnet town for the alternative lifestyle in Devon, all crystals, salt lamps, African drumming classes, flower remedies and tofu. I noticed a vagina steaming facility recently. Apparently you sit over a steamy pot of water mixed with herbs and the like to… yes, steam your vagina. Really? There's also an alternative supermarket in Totnes, a plastic-free food shop where you bring your own jars to fill, and loads of home-educated children. Hardly anyone wears make-up. Some joker has written 'Twinned with Narnia' on the town road sign. I even did a Trauma Release class, as instigated by a hippie friend who lives in a removal truck that she made into a house. In Trauma Release, you follow a series of exercises and shake your legs, as if in shock, in order to tap into the trauma response that our bodies hold on to from the past. One woman groaned loudly every time she breathed out. It sounded like she was having sex. I don't know about releasing my trauma, more like she was giving me more of my own!

In his photos, *Mr Carpenter* has a nice face, and I'm pretty sure he'll be a nice human being. I know the sort: earthy, and probably mentoring young people. So, I take a punt and swipe right. We match!

I strike up a chat with him and he responds well.

"Do you make homemade wine?" I ask. He feels like a homemade wine kind of guy.

But he doesn't.

"But you do drink, right?" I say.

"I do indeed," he replies.

"Let's drink red wine then," I suggest. He's now supposed to say something like, "Great! How about Friday?"

But he doesn't.

Instead, we become *Facebook* friends which, although it isn't drinking wine together, does provide you with a surprising amount of insight into who a person might be. Though truth be told, I much prefer the approach of the *Seeking Arrangements* or *Sugardaddy* man. They just make a date, and go and get what they want. They're not as cautious, and don't dither about.

When *Mr Carpenter* still doesn't rise to the challenge, I take the initiative.

"Let's meet on Bank Holiday Monday and get a drink?" I suggest, and he agrees.

He then waits for me to tell him where to meet, but on the day of the date calls me up. "I've arrived, but the venue is closed. Bank Holiday! Where shall we meet now?"

Do I have to do everything? Waiting for me, instead of finding somewhere else, he hangs around for me in the street. Oh I do prefer a man who can make a decision!

When I find him, he's actually better looking than his pictures, which are all weird hippie hair and quirky homemade clothes. He's mid-forties and definitely of the alternative ilk and, although this is Devon and I don't dress up much for a date in a Devon pub, I do at least have a shower and make an effort. But *Mr Carpenter* clearly hasn't washed his hair in a while, and hasn't made any effort at all. He smells like earth and coriander.

He hands me a corn on the cob that he's grown in his garden. "A little present for you," he says with a smile.

It only just fits in my bag and sticks out awkwardly. "Goodness, thank you very much."

We go to the only place that's open in my small town. Rustic, but rustic chic. We get a bottle of wine and decide to get some supper too, chit-chatting away. Led by me.

"Have you been a carpenter very long?" I ask him. "What sort of things do you make?"

"Tables and other furniture. Have done for several years," he tells me. He doesn't have kids of his own, but does mentor other kids in his carpentry workshop. My guess was spot on: a worthy, wholemeal, mentoring man.

And he's perfectly nice too.

He grows vegetables in his garden and lives in a hut with wheels next to his vegetable patch. "I grow vegetables that are very connected to the earth and moon's cycles," he says.

Now, I like a bit of organic, and I'm all for free range, but stuffing ground quartz into the horn of a cow and burying it bio-dynamically in order to dig up and use the fabulous compost it's made? I have to draw the line.

People will happily follow their gurus (in this case, Steiner) believing theirs is the only way when, in fact, what people are often following is someone else's mental health issues. Either that, or a ruse. "I'll have to research that before I can comment," I tell him.

Still, *Mr Carpenter* takes my scepticism with a pinch of salt and doesn't raise an eyebrow.

And then it's bill time. I can just tell that he's not the '*get the bill*' sort, and so I suggest splitting it. Spot on again: he doesn't object. I know right there and then that *Mr Carpenter* and I won't become an item, although I wouldn't mind him as an alternative kind of friend from time to time.

So, a week or two later, when he offers a tour of his garden, I take him up on it. But if he likes me in a girlfriend way, I certainly don't pick up on it.

We continue to stay matched on *Tinder* and I send his profile to my friend, to see if she'd like a go. They've now gone on a date, which I arranged, since neither of them would ever have made it happen otherwise. Neither are high energy kind of people.

My friend reports back that there were apparently a lot of silences during their date.

He has since offered my friend a tour of his garden too, and they are going for a walk on Sunday with the dogs.

Welcome to Devon.

41

Mr Architect

Tinder

Age: 44

Tinder seems to have improved in some ways since I last looked at it a couple of years ago. It used to simply be a hook-up app when it first came out, whereas now people are using it as an actual dating app, adding a little write-up about themselves. There's a broad age range and, while the quality of person is hit or miss (*Tinder* is free, after all), it's a usable kind of app. In fact, if people don't write anything, or only add one photo instead of a variety, they're pretty much falling behind their competitors. They don't look serious. Then there's the blank page profile photo, or the photo of a dog. I assume those guys are married, or looking for a quick hook-up. I mean who, we have to ask, would swipe right on a blank page, or want to date a doggie?

But *Tinder* still has its pitfalls.

You'll be scrolling around and suddenly be faced with a dick pic. It's always a hideous shock. And here's the thing. Do men know that we're revolted when we see a dick pic? Do they know that we then take a screen shot and send it to our friends, along with a screen shot of the face belonging to the dick, so our friends can see the offender? Name and shame. I haven't yet met a woman who goes running towards a dick pic in eager anticipation.

And do blokes not know what their pictures or write-ups look like to someone else? Men take obscure selfies, making themselves look weird or, worse, criminal. Or they offer a picture with multiple people in it so you have no idea which one is your potential date. They'll upload a picture of themselves with a pint of beer and a thumbs-up, or a picture with an unappealing background, next to a bin say, or a crooked picture on the wall. A selfie on an unmade bed. Or, especially popular, a topless shot in a bathroom, with products everywhere and soap splashes on the mirror. Maybe, in a way, it's good that they do that? At least you know what you'll be getting and can avoid it.

Guys! Don't take the picture from an unflattering angle. Don't highlight your double chin. Don't put pictures with your kids. Don't write a long list of what you're *not* looking for in a date. Don't point at your own past baggage! And women! What's with the bunny ears and *Snapchat* filters? Pouting after pouting picture! You're in your 40s. No self-respecting guy wants to date a fairy / unicorn / bunny. Grow up!

Swiping through all of this nonsense, I come across *Mr Architect.* He's looking very promising. His first picture is a professional photo, I assume from work, followed by a few others – fun, smiling, good-looking pictures. He has a nice little write up about himself. I swipe right *et voilà!* we match.

As well as being a cutie pie, *Mr Architect* has a good approach. He messages by the end of the day with a nice introduction.

"I've been having a lovely dinner with friends. I just got in, saw we matched and thought I'd message you, sooner rather than later. Whereabouts are you?"

Ending with a question leaves it easy to continue a conversation. We exchange a couple of messages.

"How about a champagne breakfast?" he suggests.

I've never had a breakfast date before, and it seems very appealing. Especially the bubbles. For someone to suggest this kind of date outside of London is impressive. I've certainly been very spoilt up there. Have I got so used to Devon dates now that I can't imagine anyone here having a good idea for a date? Will it always be going Dutch on a coffee in a pub?

"Let me find a venue near you so you don't have to travel," he says, checking that it's ok to come to my town. "Or would you rather go further away from home?"

I'm surprised by this refreshingly thoughtful detail. Is basic courtesy such a rarity that I'm shocked when I see it now?

We arrange to meet the following Sunday morning in my home town. The venue is one that's been newly converted into a great brunch place: wooden benches with rustic, but modern walls. It rivals many a London brunch venue. Proper coffee, almond or oat milk, free range eggs. He reconfirms the evening before, and even confirms when he arrives on the Sunday morning. I arrive shortly after him.

It's 9.30. I wear a black summer dress, knee-length, with a chunky belt, a floaty black cardigan over the top, and some L.K. Bennett espadrilles with straps around my ankles. I've got quite a tan from Devon's summer beaches. My date is instantly recognisable from his pictures. No lies. No pictures ten years out of date.

"You'll recognise me by the rose I'll have clenched in my teeth," he'd messaged me so, on my way, I grab a flower and put it behind my ear. Upon arrival, I take the flower and give it to him.

He laughs and we're off to a good start, immediately chatting.

I rarely sit back and let my date take the lead. Filling silences comes easily to me. Any hesitation and I go right in to the rescue. *Mr Architect* can certainly hold his own, but I still don't let him lead. I watch myself do it, yet can't quite stop myself. Incessant chatter keeps coming out of me.

Blonde, in good shape, educated, charming, easy going and intuitive – this man has it all going on. "You're my first date since my divorce," he says while we wait for our food to arrive.

"I'm on my millionth date!" I laugh, but instantly regret the over share. *Jesus woman!* I tell myself. He doesn't need to know everything right now.

"Ahh," he cringes. "I'm miles behind you then!"

But I still don't shut my mouth. So charming is he that the chit-chat flows and, before I know it, I'm spilling details left, right and centre.

"I've diarized my experiences actually. There've been so many weird and wonderful dates, it all just had to be noted down."

He looks at the menu. "Really! That many dates, hey? Well, you have to kiss a lot of frogs to get a prince," he smiles.

Now that I've hit my 40s, I find that the men I date in their 40s, 50s and even 60s just aren't that sexually attractive anymore. The pool of attractive men has narrowed considerably. I'm sure that it's the same for men. It's not that the signs of age – wrinkles and grey hair – are unattractive *per se*, but being out of shape and overweight *is*. To enter into a relationship with someone unattractive isn't going to be easy. Yes, us middle-aged people are going to have to really pull the personality out of the bag the older we get. The wisdom is going to have to shine on through those wrinkles. Thankfully, *Mr Architect* is not only very easy to talk to, he's insightful and interesting and, what's more, we're not having an attraction problem here, no Siree. He's hot. He's actually, for real, hot.

He does the London thing and picks up the bill.

He's going to meet friends and I'm off to the beach for the afternoon. I want to see him again. I've probably even got a god damn glow on, he's that nice.

The next day I send him a 'thank you for brunch' message and we exchange niceties and updates.

"I've been to a very cool restaurant with friends. You should try it," he says.

I send him a picture of me on my horse.

"How lovely," he replies.

Yes, I could get on board with this guy. We could check out the good restaurants throughout Devon. We could do mini breaks. We could chat in front of fires in the winter and frolic on the Devon beaches in the summer. Maybe our kids could play together on weekends? Maybe I wouldn't have to run back to London for good dates?

I message my friend, rather excited. "My god, there are hot, intelligent *and* lovely men left after all!" I tell her.

The day afterward he sends me a message.

"Hey, I REALLY had such a great time with you on Sunday. We must have chatted for, what, 3 hours? Non-stop. All good too. So, although I don't think we'll date on a romantic level, I'd love, love, love to remain friends. I can't predict what you'll think, but I wanted to be honest."

FFS!! What??

I reply.

"God damn it! I wanted to be saved from a life of boredom, loneliness and tragedy, and it was going to be you to do it. I was going to finish off my memoir with a happy ending... and it was going to be you *Mr Architect*. You!"

He replies. "What a great message, you're a talented writer and very, very funny, xxxxxx"

And there we have it. One date I could actually properly be excited to see again, rather than trying to squeeze a compromise out of. The 'never mind he's 20 years older than me, age is just a number' compromise. The 'never mind he's four stone overweight, I'm sure with my healthy eating plan he'll get in shape' compromise. The 'never mind he's still in love with his ex-wife, I'll move him on' compromise. No. This one was just right. I would have liked to find out a little more for myself at least.

I don't know what it was that meant he didn't want to date me any more. I didn't ask. But I'm pretty sure that revealing I'm writing my dating memoirs on a first date, can't be a great look!

I also had a hole in my top, I now realise, but I don't think that that can have mattered too much on a Sunday morning in Devon, can it?

42

Mr Slave-Man

Seeking Arrangements

Worth: £6million +

Annual income: £140k +

Meeting *Mr Architect* has made me realise something.

I'm looking for a partner. But I'm also a curious and adventurous person. Dating has ended up practically becoming a hobby, I've been at it so long. If I *do* find the love of my life along the way, excellent! But by now, I don't count on it. I still look everywhere. *Tinder, Guardian Soulmates, Elite, Seeking Arrangements*. I use them all, just in case I do bump into the elusive *One*.

Seeking Arrangements is certainly an interesting one. Sifting through and dismissing the married men is a mission of mine. Married men are not for me.

Then you have the confused men. The ones who say they're 'looking for a woman who understands a man's needs'. A woman who 'knows how to please him'. A woman who 'loves to flirt', who 'is sexy' and who is basically up for it whenever he wants. He'll say he wants a 'fun, uncomplicated woman'. The other often-used line that gets me going is 'No drama'. Equally he'll state he's not into paying for a sex exchange, which is fine of course, but a bit off if he's also demanding what he wants for sex.

Cake and eat it comes to mind.

Dismissing these and finding the nice ones, of which there are actually a few, is an effort.

Mr Slave-Man, with no pictures, contacts me. He's in Kensington & Chelsea, my old London borough.

"I live in Kensington," he writes. "I'm single and I'm not looking for sex. But I do want to support a woman. I'm lonely and want someone to live with me, in my house. She'd have her own life and space. I'd like to be a servant to a beautiful woman and support her fully."

What's all this about? I think. I'm curious as usual, about how this would work. You can ask for whatever relationship you want, after all. Has he done this before? Why doesn't he just want a girlfriend? I could do with the financial support, I guess.

I need to understand this more. What exactly does he mean?

"I'd like to serve someone. Support someone," he says.

"Want to serve someone?" I say. "Are you submissive?"

I've heard about this kind of thing, but don't know how it works. I've seen men on *Seeking Arrangements* who specifically request things like this, but I've always dismissed them. I don't really get it and, if it's sexual kinks, I'll leave that to someone else thank you very much.

"Yes," he says. "I'm very submissive. I'm not interested in sex. I'm impotent in fact."

"But I don't get it. You want a woman to serve and financially support, but you don't want a girlfriend?"

"That's right," he says. "I just want to serve and support a beautiful woman. I don't want to socialise with you. You'll be free to do whatever you want. You'll be free to spend my money."

Who on earth is this servant man who wants to surrender his house and money to an unknown woman?

I once had a young guy on *Match.com* message me, to ask if he could come to my house while I held a dinner party with some girlfriends. He wanted to serve us our dinner and drinks in a pinny, and clean the house too. I probed a bit. He wanted to be humiliated, he said. I wished him luck and declined. On reflection, I don't know why I turned him away. I kind of think it might be a good idea now: a free house-clean! Having brought up two boys I'm totally over house cleaning these days.

I'm not into the humiliation thing though. People often fall into the 'serve' or 'be served' category. I'm quite a forthright character myself, so men who need a lead are drawn to me, it seems. But I prefer a strong man, one who can match me. I don't want to dominate or humiliate a man. I tell *Mr Slave-Man* as much.

"I'm a forthright woman," I tell him. "But I'm not a cruel woman. I'm not interested in humiliation. You must understand that?"

He says he doesn't want a domination game. He wants to serve a woman for real. And, yes, he understands.

So, yes! you guessed it… I'm so damn nosey and, already tapping into the role, I suggest we meet.

I can't help wanting to know more. I'm not interested on the 'boyfriend' front. I just want to get into his head and understand how this works.

"You mustn't let me hang out with you like a normal person. I don't deserve it," he says.

"I see. Ok," I agree.

"Will you take me as your servant?" he says.

"Yes. I'm willing to take you on," I tell him. It's all a bit theatrical.

"Do you want a slave?" he asks.

"Not one on a dog lead," I tell him. "Some service wouldn't go amiss though."

"So I can serve you?"

"Yes. I'll come and see you in a couple of days and we can sort out the details."

"You're fast!" he says.

"No point in messing around! Let's just get on with it."

I ask him to book me a train to Paddington

"I can't until we've established something," he says.

"I'm not coming to see you unless you send me the ticket," I say. *He wants a woman to spend his money, but is quibbling over a ticket?*

"No, I can't do it until we're established," he replies and, unsure of how this all works, I don't know if I can agree or not.

"You'll have to wait until next time I'm in London then, you bad servant!" I say.

That's how dominatrix ladies talk isn't it?

43

Mr Slave-Man – Part 2

Mr Slave-Man has sent me a couple of pictures on *WhatsApp* and he does, indeed, look meek. Timid, with a very passive energy. I figure that if he is to be a servant, I'd better make the meeting plans rather than him. I suggest *PJ's* on the Fulham Road, for lunch. Straight away he tells me he doesn't want to have lunch with me, he only wants to serve me.

Hang on, I think, that's not very submissive! Shouldn't he just be saying yes?

"Well, as my servant," I say, "you had jolly well better come and have lunch with me. That's what I want!"

I figure I'm supposed to be calling the shots.

"Ok," he says, "but after this initial meeting it'll be strictly no socialising."

Is that really submissive, I ask myself again?

"Let's just meet and have a chat, and see how we get on," I say. "Discuss the details then."

He agrees.

On the day we're due to meet, I send him a message to tell him I'm nearly in Kensington and to meet me at PJ's in an hour.

"I can't get there in a hour," he replies, even though he only lives a 10 minute walk away. He asks if I can come to Cromwell Road and meet him by the Sainsbury's instead. Apparently he can get there in time.

I don't know why I agree, but I do. I guess I'm just flexible that way. Again, not very obedient for a wannabe servant, I think, and immediately question why I've agreed to do this at all. I'm supposed to call the shots and he's supposed to do as he's told, isn't he?

I message to say I'm at Sainsbury's and he replies that he'll be there in a few minutes. I wait 10 minutes and feel irritated. 10 bloody minutes at Sainsbury's! Then a meek, little man appears, walking towards me. Well dressed in good quality clothes. Nothing flashy. He's about 5'5" in his early 50s. Greying. With olive coloured skin. Neither good looking, nor unattractive. He hardly looks me in the eyes, more sideways.

This'll be an interesting experience, I think. I'm unsure how to play it though. Am I supposed to be bossy straight away? I decide to play it by ear.

"Yes, you look submissive," I say. He looks slightly taken aback.

"Thank you," he answers. "We can go and talk in my house just round the corner."

"OK, but hang on," I say. "Just going to make a call." I call my friend to tell her exactly where I am, and with whom, all within his earshot.

"I'm with a funny little dermatologist in Gloucester Road," I say loudly. "Yes, the one I told you about. Yes, he's a funny little man. Very timid. Just off to interview him. I'll send you a picture."

I turn to *Mr Slave-Man* with my phone camera. "Smile!" I tell him, pointing the camera at him. "Smile more," I instruct. "No, not like that. Better. You don't look any good. Do a better pose than that…"

This is coming easily to me, I think. I send the picture to my friend and then call her back.

"Hi, yes, did you get the picture? No, he's not very photogenic is he? Looks awful!"

Well, he did say he likes humiliation!

We go into his building in virtual silence, past the porter, and into the lift. Up on his floor, we walk along what seems like corridor after corridor. Claustrophobic as hell. I'm not keen on apartment buildings like hotels.

His apartment is split level, with textured wallpaper and minimalist taste in decor. Apart from some slightly gaudy flowerpots with gold rims. The three-piece suite is aubergine, with a matching pouf. He tells me he's Lebanese, and the apartment certainly has a foreign feel to me.

"How long have you been in the UK?" I ask him. He glances down to the floor.

"Since I was 13."

"Hmm. I'll keep your Lebanese accent," I tell him, "but I'll need a refurb in the apartment. Not my taste."

"Yes," he agrees.

"So, you're impotent?" I launch straight in.

"Yes," he replies.

"What, even on your own?" I say.

"Well, yes," he says.

"You've been to the doctor?"

"Yes, it's not physical," he says.

"I heard years ago somewhere that if you put a ring of stamps around the base of it at night, while you sleep, if the ring is broken in the morning, your problem is psychological not physical."

"Yes," he agrees.

"Counsellor then?" I ask.

"I've tried everything," he says. "It doesn't work. I just don't feel worthy. And I've accepted that this is my role. I've made a lot of money, and now I want a woman to spend it, while I take care of the house. Do you think you could treat me like a foreign servant?"

"Christ!" I say. "I can be bossy, but I don't know about *foreign* servant. Jeez, what's the 'foreign' bit got to do with it?"

"Like an African slave," he says. "Or like the Arabs have an Indian servant," he adds.

"I see, let me think," I say, taken aback by the extreme lack of racial awareness. *A foreign slave – my god!*

"I have more responsibility than I can take," he says. "After I retired from being a dermatologist I invested in properties. I now have 14 one-bedroom flats in central London, and I manage them all. I never expected to have so much money coming in each month, It's such a responsibility. I want to be released from it. I'm in the wrong role. I want you to take charge of it all. Can you do that?"

"Have you done this before?" I ask him.

"I've done all the dominatrix things before, yes, but now I want it for real, to actually live like that."

"Look," I say. "I'm not a dominatrix. I'm quite a direct person, and I can get bossy if things aren't done, but there's not going to be any whips, or shit like that."

"That's fine," he says. "A dominatrix is a role play for an hour or two. But I want a real experience. Whatever the woman wants. I just want to serve and be released from all this money and responsibility."

Wants to be released from all the money he has! Is he for real?

"You haven't offered me a drink," I scold him. "Or even offered to take my coat. I'm not sure you're cut out for service. You don't seem to have the basics down."

He gets up to take my coat and I'm still wondering how on earth arrangements like this actually work.

"I'm sorry," he apologises. Please live with me. Treat me like a servant. I'll try and do better."

"I hope so," I tease him.

"Will you have a boyfriend?" he asks. The question seems rather out of the blue.

"Well, yes, probably," I say. "I don't plan on being single all my life!"

"Good," he says. "I want you to have a boyfriend." He gets up to indicate that our chat is coming to an end.

"What would the allowance be?' I ask him. This is *Seeking Arrangements* after all.

"No allowance," he says. "It's whatever you want. You'll spend my money as if it's your money."

"I'll want you to paint my toe nails," I suddenly throw in. "You'll be sat on the floor at my feet." He looks at me. "And you'll call me madam!"

"Yes, whatever you want, madam."

Paint my toe nails, for goodness sake, is that all you've got?

I go to leave, telling him that I'll be in touch. It's bloody tempting… very few strings for the money. And the cleaning. But, equally, I don't believe him. He doesn't feel that submissive and I think, perhaps, that he's playing with me.

A couple of days later I meet up with my older son.

"What d'you know about the submissive man type?" I ask him. "I've got this man who wants to be my servant and be relieved of his wealth. I mean, how would that work?"

"Easy," he answers. "You take his bank cards, take over his accounts, all his passwords etc., take control of his finances and give him a small allowance, just like you would a servant. Maybe no allowance in fact, only food and board."

"Bloody hell,' I say. "You're right, that's exactly how it's done!"

*

Over the next month, back in Devon, messages pop back and forth and, depending on his mood, he's either in slave mode, or in friend mode. When he's in slave mode he starts the conversations with "How are you? Please, take all my money. Own me. Keep me in your basement forever."

And I'll reply, "Stop talking and start doing. Get on a train and meet me, and I'll see what I'll do with you."

And after a couple more messages like that, he'll back out. "No, I don't want this, I can't do it. I'm too vulnerable."

I tell one of my friends about him. "He's lucky it's you he's talking to," she says. "Someone else might go straight in and actually take it all."

A month later, I'm in London and I arrange to meet up with him. We go to a cocktail bar and he's perfectly normal, not being meek or servant like at all. He doesn't look as small now and seems confident and out-going, totally unlike the first day I met him.

"I was only joking about the slave thing," he says.

But I don't believe him.

"Why d'you ask for that then?" I ask.

"Bored," he says smugly. "Got too much time on my hands. My property business is all true though. And I *did* use to visit dominatrix dungeons."

"But what about the slave thing?" I say.

"Just drink your drink," he says, laughing. "Let's go for some Lebanese food."

And I'm confused. Very confused.

And I think that's the point.

44

Mr Slave-Man – Part 3

Little did I know that online dating would lead to the weird world of submissive men and slaves!

If I have any interest in this at all, it's in the psychology of it, rather than any desire for a slave of my own. I simply want to know what it's all about. It's extraordinary how things unfold.

Despite telling me he was joking, when I get back to Devon he's back on the slave thing in his next messages.

"Take everything I have," he says. "I want to be owned. Force me. Take over."

"You'll never be a slave while you have money," I tell him. "It's not possible to truly be a slave when there's a get out clause – money!"

"I can't give it away!" he says' "You must make me do it, so I'll be owned forever and can't back out!"

Slaves are quite demanding it seems. These messages go back and forth for quite some time.

"Then I'd have to kidnap you," I say, thinking this is the only way to actually *make* him.

"What do you mean 'kidnap'?" he says. "How would you do that?"

"Grab you and put you in a lock up, or an abandoned building," I say.

"Yes," he says triumphantly. "Kidnap me. Fantastic!"

Kidnap him! How on earth do you kidnap someone?

My friend and I start to discuss this and, over time, we get more and more elaborately into the details.

I mean, what do you do? Wait outside his house and grab him? What if he struggles? Would he fight back? Run? Would he freeze? Even if he *were* grabbable, what about passers by? What on earth would they think? What would happen then? Would I put him in the car, the boot? Would he be tied up? And where would I take him, even if I did manage to kidnap him? Where would I store him? Hire a lock up? Would I need an accomplice? Or would I do it in his house, maybe keep him prisoner there? What about his cleaner? Would I put a note on the door saying 'No cleaning this week'?

My friend and I spend many an hour laughing about the details of this crazy plan. I *Google* it and, just as my son said, there *are* people who actually live like this.

This is what he's asking me to do. Kidnap him and take over his affairs!

Of course, my mind gets a little carried away with all this. Even if I do manage to kidnap him – maybe I could hire someone for that part – and find a place to keep him, what do I do then? Take his phone? Get him to give me his banking details and transfer his money? How much of it? All of it? How do I transfer his properties over to me? Do I get him to phone the bank and transfer large quantities of money to my account? What about property deeds? I'd need to wait for paper work to be done, surely? What about inheritance tax if he dies within seven years? And what about day-to-day, I mean, would he be tied up? It takes a few months to do the paperwork on buying a property, so will I keep him in a lock up all that time? What if his laptop and phone are thumb ID'd and he's tied up? Am I over thinking things?

The next time I'm in London, I tell him I'm around and we should meet up. We arrange a Monday lunchtime.

He bails on me an hour before meeting. Super annoying!

We arrange the next day for an early supper and I have zip ties in my bag in case the urge to kidnap him becomes apparent, or feasible.

He cancels again, last minute. "Sorry, I'm busy," he says. Can you believe it, the bastard!

I call an old friend for dinner to pick her brains. It just so happens that she used to be pretty involved in the London dominatrix scene for several years.

"How does this stuff work?" I ask her. "See this guy…" I show her a picture of *Mr Slave-Man* on my phone.

My friend flips like a switch on seeing his photo. I've never seen her like it before.

"Pah!" she spits. "Easy, that one! Look at him. You just take him in broad daylight, don't doubt yourself, don't hesitate. In public if necessary. He's 'topping from the bottom'…"

"What's that?" I ask.

"He's said he wants to be relinquished of his power, wants to be the slave, but he's flipped it, and now he's bailing on you. He's not allowed to do that. He's not allowed to do anything you haven't commanded. He's switching roles, making you run after him. It's pretty frowned upon in the Dom/Sub relationship."

"But how do I *make* him turn up then?" I say.

"He's already sussed you out," she says. "He already knows he's on top. Did you tell him you haven't got much money for example?" she asks.

"Well, I may have done, yes…"

"Yeah," she says. "It's a craft, actually, managing this type of man. You may be able to learn it. I'm sure you could in fact, but you may find it more hassle than it's worth. It's a strange thing just how demanding a submissive man can be. They demand that you're more demanding," she laughs. "You'll either have to meet up with him as a normal friend, or lure him into a false sense of security, then get him. Which could be really fun. Or straight-up kidnap him, right off the street. Some men find that extremely exciting. The adrenalin starts pumping and all that."

"Imagine someone calls the police while I'm kidnapping him," I say.

"Who cares? It's unlikely. You can be dying in the street and no one cares in London. And, even if they did, you just say it's a domination game. Do it! It'll be fun. Take his money, if he even has any…"

I've never seen my friend so self-assured!

We decide to text him right then, while I'm taking lessons from her.

"Hey, *Mr Slave-Man.* Come and meet me. I'm near. I'll be outside your place shortly."

"OK, 15 minutes," he replies.

"Yeah, don't be so sure," my friend says and, sure enough, a text pings in from him.

"No, no. I can't do it. I've changed my mind. I don't want to be a slave anymore…"

"You should *so* get him for that," my friend says. "He's really trying to top you. Mine all came to my dungeon and ticked a form for their requirements. I even had security on the door. You can't use a Taser, but you can get some kind of mini electric shocker… they're always fun. Then you do whatever else you fancy."

Christ! I think. *This is quite a thing.*

Then he messages back. "OK. I'll meet you," and, a moment later, "No, I can't." Finally one of the begging messages pings in. "Please, just take me. You have to do it without my permission."

"Yeah," my friend says. "It's kidnap or nothing with him, I'd say."

I send a reply.

"There'll be no kidnapping for you. I'll meet you for a drink at your place tomorrow lunchtime though. Make something nice to eat. I'll bring wine and we'll just have a normal meal."

My friend and I have a plan.

He agrees, but it's perfectly feasible the bugger will bail on me. It wouldn't be the first time.

The next day comes and so far he hasn't backed out. I head to the reception in his building and ask the porter to buzz him. My dominatrix friend is with me. He comes down to the lobby.

"Hi, I've got my friend with me," I say.

"Oh, OK," he says, hesitantly. My friend smiles sweetly.

"Don't worry, I've got wine," I add, showing him the bottle.

We all go up in the lift and he lets us in to his apartment.

"Go ahead," I tell him, "open the wine." He goes into the kitchen and my friend shows me the contents of her large handbag. Inside she's got some kind of electric prodder, some handcuffs and a ball thing for his mouth! I look at her aghast.

She takes the prod and marches without hesitation into the kitchen, poking him in the back with it.

"On you knees," she shouts.

He nearly jumps out of his skin and falls to his knees. I watch, stunned.

She prods him again, and he shrieks. She laughs loudly, looks at me and winks, putting her high heel forward. She stands on his back.

"Hands behind your back," she commands.

He doesn't do it.

She takes her foot off him and prods him again, holding the pulsating prod to him. He shrieks several times.

"I SAID PUT YOUR HANDS BEHIND YOUR BACK!"

He does as he's told.

"I'll give *you* the honour," she says to me, smiling, and nods to her bag. "Handcuffs," she adds.

I get the cuffs out and put them on him.

"And his feet" she says. "With zip ties. We don't want any kicking now, do we?"

She has all sorts in her bag.

"Who's been trying to top your mistress?" she shouts at him.

He doesn't answer. She jabs him with the electric prod.

"I said, who's been trying to be the boss?"

"Me, me!" he answers meekly. "Please, please…" he whines.

"No whining," she says. "This is your punishment. This is what you wanted isn't it? You're making this happen. You'll be punished for messing your woman about."

She looks at me smiling.

"What would you like to do with him?" she asks.

God, I've got to think of something now!

I take the prodder, and she subtly points me to the button. "Don't touch *him* at the same time, or you could get a shock too," she says quietly.

I make a feeble attempt at prodding him, and step back as he squeals from the shock. She grabs it from me and prods him harder.

"You will learn your lesson, you bad, bad slave!" she shouts. "Will you do as you are told?" she demands.

"I will, I will," he answers.

"I can't hear you!" she shouts, shocking him again.

"Yes, yes!" he answers.

"We're going on a journey now," she says, and takes off her coat. Underneath she's pretty much wearing classic dominatrix gear: a rubbery basque, with a corset tie. She already has the heels on. She even gets a little mask from her bag that just covers her eyes.

"Here, one for you too," she says to me.

I find the other one and put it on. A cute little cat mask in black.

"This is for the street," she says. "We're going out. And you, my little slave, you're going to behave yourself, aren't you?" She gives him an impromptu prod.

"Yes," he yells, "yes, yes!"

"You better had," she says, with such authority that I too want to do what she says.

She cuts the zip tie that's restraining his feet.

"Stand up!" she demands.

He does as he's told.

"Where's your ID?" she barks as she gets a chain and collar out of her bag and roughly puts the collar around his neck.

"In my wallet," he says.

"We're going to the bank," she says. "You'll be on the lead! Get your passport, your driving license, a house bill with your address," she says. "Show me where they are."

He goes to his office on the chain lead. All the while I'm watching her – she shows no fear and no hesitation. I totally see why she was so good at this job.

He gets all the bits she asks for.

"What, what are you going to do with me?" he asks.

"Silence!" she shouts.

She gets a long stick out of her bag,

"Apartment keys!" she demands. "Let's go, move it!"

We go down in the lift, past the reception.

"Domination game," she mouths boldly to the porter, who looks completely stunned.

We walk the 10 minute walk to *Barclays* and, yes, indeed, we get *a lot* of stares. And a lot of giggles.

She marches him straight into *Barclays* and up to the counter.

"Get out the money," she says.

"How much?"

"You decide. Just make sure it's an appropriate amount."

He tells the cashier that he wants to withdraw money.

"He loves to hire a dominatrix," my friend tells the cashier, winking. "Don't you?" she says to *Mr Slave-Man*.

"Yes," he replies.

"ID please," the cashier says.

Mr Slave-Man withdraws a sum of money and it all goes surprisingly smoothly. Some people in the bank don't even look at us, and the cashier is amused more than anything. *Mr Slave-Man* isn't even tied, he's just on a lead.

When we have the money, we follow my friend out of the bank and march back towards his apartment.

"Enough, or d'you want him to cook too?" she asks me.

"I could eat," I say.

"Right, let's get him to cook," and we march straight back, brazenly past the porter.

"Serve us wine," my friend demands when we reach his flat. He obliges.

"Take off your clothes and put on that pinny," she continues. He does.

"Cook us lunch."

With each instruction he does exactly as he's told.

"Eh, hem?" she says.

"Yes?" he answers. He looks confused.

"Yes what?" she booms.

"Yes madam," he replies.

"Our glasses need filling. Bad slave!" She gets up from her armchair and prods him with the stick thing. He squeals. "Don't get lazy now!"

"Madam, can I use the bathroom?" he asks.

"No," she says, curtly. "You may not."

When he has prepared the food, he tells us it's ready.

"Give us our plates," she says, and he obliges. "Now get on the floor on your hands and knees. Right there in front of us."

He seems to know where to put himself. She puts her feet on his back, like a footrest, and starts to eat her food.

"He'll do as a table," she says.

I watch her imagination in action. She's incredible! And he's very obliging.

When she's finished eating, she takes her feet off his back and replaces them with her plate. She indicates for me to do the same. She looks at me and raises an eyebrow. "Enough?" it seems to say. I nod. She picks up her bag, checks she has everything and indicates for us to leave. *Mr Slave-Man* is still on all fours with two empty plates on his back as we leave the apartment.

As we go down in the lift, she smiles at me. "And *that's* how it's done!"

We don't have the masks on anymore and she has her coat on over her rubber gear. We stroll out of the building, through the busy reception area, seemingly unnoticed. It's *Mr Slave-Man* who'll have to answer any questions.

"My god," I say, "extreme!"

"I've soooo missed this work," she says. "That'll teach the little fucker a lesson or two, not to mess with you again."

I just stare at her stunned.

"So, did you like it?" she asks. "D'you think you'll take it up?"

"I'll have to sleep on it," I laugh, "though probably not, no."

She laughs. "Let's go for a cocktail and a debrief," she says, pulling out a small wad of his money. "On him."

45

Mr Pheasant-Shooter

Seeking Arrangements

Age: 66

Lifestyle: High [expected £6k per month]

After only one day on *Seeking Arrangements, Mr Pheasant-Shooter* messages me. Three days later, I'm already meeting him for dinner. Speedy date arrangements have always suited me. If I wanted a pen pal I'd... well, go back to the old days.

I'm not actually sure what I'm expecting, or wanting, from *Seeking Arrangements*. Could it be to have clearer details outlined than with *Sugardaddy*.com, or it could be pure nosiness? Am I, in fact, an investigative journalist seeking to plumb the depths of different men's lifestyles? I'm pretty sure having a clear plan is a good idea. Which I don't have. I only agreed to meet him because he got on with it and, at 66, he's no doubt too old for me. But I won't totally rule him out, just in case.

He fixes a time and a venue, since he happens to be in Devon each month for his shooting trips.

When I arrive on the Wednesday evening, I'm underwhelmed with his choice of venue. We meet at a hotel on a roundabout. Did you get that? A hotel on a roundabout, on the outskirts of Exeter!

Seeing me in the bar, he comes over and introduces himself. "So," he says as we sit down and get a drink, "I'll tell you about myself and what I'm looking for…"

Here we go again.

"I've been married for a long time," he says, "and have two grown up children." He's an old Etonian, slightly overweight, with a love of pheasant shooting. He still has most of his hair.

"Don't you think you might have mentioned the married bit?" I say.

"Well, I think it's always best to meet people and then discuss," he replies.

"D'you now," I say, "I think it's probably best to mention it beforehand myself."

And he doesn't look remotely uncomfortable.

We dine together, alongside all those people who dine alone on their middle management business trips. Having been on so many dates, and some quite 'fine dining' ones, I've come to expect a lot more, even on a first meeting. Dating has led me to the very best London restaurants and country hotels, where my dates haven't blinked at spending £400 on lunch. I've got used to that. The food here is fine, but what's the point? What do I want with this guy? Simply to find out what this married life's about? Do I just want to nosey into his life, not into his bed?

I'm assuming *Mr Pheasant-Shooter* isn't prepared to invest in me hugely at this point, despite ticking the 'high earner' box on his profile – that means he's expecting to spend £6k a month on a girlfriend. Now, I've ticked that box because, well, what's to lose, right? But so has he.

Over our meal he wavers between talking too loudly and too quietly. Occasionally he puts his hand to his ear to hear. He has a checked shooting shirt, a tweed tie and a puffer waistcoat. His fingernails are a bit dirty as if he's come straight from the fields.

"Didn't you marry your child's father?" he asks.

"Not in the end."

He shakes his head and tuts. "Why don't you girls get that ring on your finger?" he mutters. "I had a prostate operation not so long ago, so, if you want to swing from chandeliers, that's not me," he adds, bizarrely.

What on earth does he want, this married man?

"I'd like to meet up once or twice a month," he says. "Go to dinner, chat and laugh and spend the night. Affection, yes. And cuddling. But sex is pretty much off the menu."

A relieved look must cross my face.

"Ah, you're pleased about that," he smiles.

"You married men!" I tut, "you really must get hugs from your wives!"

"What?" he asks putting his hand to his ear.

"Oh nothing," I reply.

"Well, let me know what kind of arrangement you'd like," he says.

After dinner, he walks me to the car park and links my arm with his. He asks if we'll see each other again.

"We'll see," I say.

I get in the car and my music pops on. "Ah, you like heavy metal do you?" he says.

Later he messages to check in with me and wish me a good sleep, which I don't have at all. Now, here's the thing. I go to work the next day on my zero hours supply teaching job. I might have a six-week block booking or, like this particular half term, just two days in the whole six weeks. In a very good month I'll earn £800. After bills that leaves very little, and I could end up hitting the food banks. This keeps me awake at night.

Can I get an arrangement where I can cover my expenses, and more? I guess I have to decide how much for a night of company and cuddles? Is this what I'm using *Seeking Arrangements* for? It's a very real thought.

*

Six weeks go by since my meeting with *Mr Pheasant-Shooter*. He's been up and down the country on various shoots. It looks like his accountancy job doesn't take up that much of his time. We do try to meet up once, when he visits nearby, but I had a parents' evening and he wasn't prepared to wait for me. We ended up giving it a miss. He's quite regular with his messages though, so he's not letting me forget him.

He asks a few times what kind of 'arrangement' I'd like, and I never really reply. Mainly because I don't know how much a cuddle costs. What's more, I'm not sure if I really want to cuddle him, whatever the price.

"What would you like?" he messages me once. "£50?"

I message back that we're not on the same page. "I think I'll leave it," I say.

He jumps straight back that he's joking and was expecting me to put another zero on the end.

I don't find that kind of humour funny, so don't reply. Have we all got a figure? Perhaps we have. I'm pretty sure £500 isn't mine.

He *WhatsApp*'s me for a dinner date. He's going to be in the area and has given me a couple of weeks' notice. I'm interested to know what my second opinion of him might be. Is that uncomfortable feeling I've got because he's married? Or is it that he was patronising about *us girls not getting rings on our fingers*? It's been a month and a half now, and I want a re-cap to see what I think of him. Or do I just need some money?

He says to meet at the same place as before. Oh god, the roundabout!

The food is fine, but there's something seedy about it. Maybe there's just something seedy about him? But I agree to meet him and steel myself for the date.

It's early, 6 o'clock, when we sit down to eat. I have to say, I'm really impressed with just how much he's remembered about me – my kids, my work, every little detail. But he seems older than I remember. He still has slightly grubby fingernails, and the same checked shooting shirt, tweed tie and quilted gilet. He jumps up to get drinks before we move into the restaurant to order food.

He tells me about his wife's job. Which actually interests me. She collaborates over horse trial events and property. He seems close to her, and it sounds like they're happy enough. Yet he's a bit shifty about sitting here with me. I just don't get it. Why don't people just have the relationships they want? If they want to be companions, but not have sex anymore, why not just agree to sleep with other people without the guilt? Or don't have sex at all and be fine with it? Why can't people move away from a story they've been sold about how relationships look? So often, after years of marriage, the sex dries up, but couples still want to remain together, financially, with work or family. But they end up feeling guilty because of what society deems 'acceptable'. Guilty for still wanting sex, or guilty for not wanting it. Who even said that people should want to have sex still when they're knackered, or don't fancy their partner anymore, or are just old? People should do what they want. Do people need to open up their ideas of what relationships look like?

If *Mr Pheasant-Shooter* wants to have cuddles, I don't know why he doesn't just ask his wife. And, if she doesn't want to cuddle him, fine! He should be able to say, 'If it's ok with you Darling, I think I'll go and get me some cuddles somewhere.' But he doesn't do that. He deceives her. Those societal norms get him sneaking around behind her back, which is plain silly, because, from what he tells me, they seem pretty happy together otherwise.

He asks me if I know *Gidleigh* Park. "Yes, I've often been there for lunch," I tell him. "How do you know it?"

"Family celebration," he says. "If you're a good girl and very nice to me, I may take you there."

I should probably say, *Fuck right off you patronising old twat,* which is what pops into my mind. But I don't. "Is that what you want, a good little girl?" I say. *Oh yes Daddy! I'll be a good little girl if we can go to Gidleigh fucking Park. Fuck off!* He has this spectacular knack of being patronising and belittling. Entitled. But we both know that it's me holding the cards. He needs someone to cuddle, and dine with him. He has to make the arrangement, although I would never belittle him just because he wants some attention.

After dinner he walks me to my car. "This is the second time we've met up," he says. "Is dinner sufficient, or did you want something?"

"I wouldn't say no," I say.

He pulls out a roll of cash and peels off a number of 20's, slowly, one by one, until he reaches £100. "There," he says "£100." He reaches over and slips it down my top. So, what the hell am I now, a fucking lap dancer!

I whip it off him and put it in my pocket, before he can get it into my bra.

"How about we spend the night next time?" he says. "I'll get a *Travel Lodge*. How much would you want for that? £400?"

I curl my lip, unimpressed.

"More?" he says. "£500 then?"

Interesting conversation, I think.

"We'll only be sleeping," he adds.

"Are you punting for a straight up hooker?" I say. "I wonder what your wife would think?"

He looks bemused.

"I'm really not a *Travel Lodge* kind of lady," I say, "nor am I a £400 a night girl. So, thanks, but no thanks." And with that I slip into my car and leave him there, cuddle-less and a hundred pound lighter, on the tarmac of a roundabout hotel car park.

46

Mr Great-Grandpa

Tinder

Age: 61

Here, in beautiful Devon, us women have a narrow pool of options on the men front. And with 10 years of dating experience under my belt, I know that being open-minded and broadening my search criteria is a necessity.

"For god's sake mum, don't be so picky," says my older son. He's 26 now, and nicely ensconced in a five year relationship himself. "Everyone has faults you know."

I screen shoot a dick pic I received yesterday, along with the message "Babe, you're gorgeous, I'd love to hook up with you. What underwear d'you like wearing?" and send it to my son.

"You're right, I shouldn't be so picky," I say. "How about him? He seems nice…?"

I spend very little time on *Tinder*. At a guess, 10 swipes or so every three days. I spend slightly more time on it when I'm in London – the choice is so much broader there and, anyway, I date more when I'm in London. For two reasons. Firstly, the venues. And, secondly, the standard of man is just so much better. Simple as that. And my youngest child hangs out with his dad, so I have childcare covered. In Devon, my *Tinder* radius settings of 30 miles includes Plymouth. Plymouth has a lot of sailors and a lot of high viz vests. Lots of full-body tattoos, and men who look like they may possibly have a crack problem. In Devon we also have, farmers, hippies, surfers and alternative people. And *Mr Great-Grandpa*.

On a casual *Tinder* gander one day, *Mr Great-Grandpa* pops up in my scroll. In my mid 40s myself, a 61 year-old date is really pushing my search criteria out, but with my son's words ringing in my ears, I decide to swipe right. There's also the fact that *Mr Great-Grandpa* is sitting on a horse in his picture.

Lo and behold, it's a match!

Admittedly, nine out of ten 'swipe right's' that I make, are matches, so it doesn't really get me excited.

He's written in his profile that he has two horses, a cat and a dog and is looking for someone to enjoy the countryside with. And fancy restaurants. He's done a good write-up on himself, certainly compared to the usual low efforts *Tinder* offers. But is this the choice now? A 61 year-old? Are there *no* other men in Devon?

He's only a few miles away. Fantastic for falling madly in love while not having to change my child's school. For moving my horses onto his farm. All balanced with potentially 'shitting on one's doorstep'.

A message pops up.

"Hello, it seems we have a lot in common! Let's chat."

He gives me his phone number, but I don't call. I've gone off phone calls. Instead, I send him a message and include my number.

He calls me a couple of times, both of which I miss. I'm so used to messaging these days, I can't remember how to talk on the phone. He has given me a landline number, but I literally do not know my own. I'm not even sure that phone's plugged in anymore. He messages again. We're misfiring here. Him on a landline and me on *WhatsApp*. Apparently he doesn't have *WhatsApp*.

Finally, I concede I'm going to have to call him. On a landline!

Straight away I can tell that he's rural Devon, born and bred.

Don't be so fussy! rings in my ears.

We have a slow Devon chat then agree a time for dinner. "Shall we try the *Dartbridge Inn*, that's a nice place?" he suggests. Nearby for both of us.

"OK then," I agree. *Dartbridge Inn* is part of a chain. Didn't he say 'fancy dining' on his profile?

Friday evening comes, and I don't dress up too much, just jeans and boots. I'm relaxed – this is hardly my first date, after all!

Thankfully, he seems relaxed too and there's no issue recognising each other. The approach is easy and so is the chat. We get a drink and take it to the table.

6'2" with a sizable belly and a deeply-lined face, he's charming nevertheless. He wears a navy double-breasted jacket with gold buttons. Thin, receding hair, and gums that have seen a dentist for implants.

I look at him across the table. *So, is this what 61 looks like then? Can I date 61?*

And then he starts talking. And doesn't stop. "I've been in Devon all my life," he says. "My daughter's just come to live with me. My son lives with me too. I had a lovely housekeeper once. She cooked the best food, every single day. I was once swindled out of half a million pounds by my PA. I'd love to go on a cruise. I asked my friend to come with me, but he couldn't get the time off work. Crazy really! I was offering to pay for it! Let's have starters. I think I'll have the lasagne for my main. Shall we have another drink? Where was I? Oh yes, I'd love to go on a cruise. I've been to a lot of places. My granddaughter is very lazy…spends all her time on the phone. No get up and go. D'you have horses then…?"

I spot the gap and try and get a few words in edgeways. "Yes. I've got one horse, and my son has a pony… I…"

"Ahh that's good," he says quickly. "It's good to have something in common. Can you cook? I love a woman who can cook. Not saying a woman *should* cook, but I do like a woman who can. I did love the food that that old housekeeper made! Wonderful meals, every day. I'm taking this Chinese medicine. It tastes really disgusting. I'm a property developer. Been developing all my life. There's nothing I don't know about finding a good property deal…"

Our deep-fried seafood sharing platter arrives.

"You can have the mushrooms," he says. "I don't like them there mushrooms."

I dip the mushrooms into the garlic mayo and accept the offer of another wine.

I have fish cakes for my main – also deep-fried – and sit listening to *Mr Great-Grandpa* while I pick at them.

"You see, it's good that you look like your picture. A lot of people don't, do they? No point in that now, is there? You'll only be disappointed when you meet them and how's that going to help anyone, that's what I say?"

He tucks into his microwaved frozen lasagne. "Not bad at all this food," he says. "One thing I do like is good food. Very important."

At 9.30 I'm pretty exhausted with all the listening. "I'm going to have to go soon," I tell him. "My son's at that in-between age – doesn't need a baby sitter, but I do need to make sure he gets in to bed."

"Ah yes," he says, pulling out his phone. "See these pictures, they're of the last building I did up. Oh, and that's the last holiday I went on. I have a boat. I went out with some friends. What a good time we had! Oh, and that's my last house. I sold it. Couldn't refuse the offer. I'll do the same again with the house I'm in now. I do them up, and sell them. Ah, that's me with my dog. He died last year, sadly..."

"Ahh, that's sad," I say, "but I really do have to go now." It's 10 o'clock.

"Oh, and this is my son. He lives in a property I have on site."

I get up from the table. "Lovely to meet you! Thanks for dinner. Let's take the horses out one day."

I think he's still talking as I wander out to my car.

*

A week later, I get a call from a landline number. "Hello there, I was wondering if you'd like to go to lunch. Do you know the *Cott Inn?*"

"I do indeed, and yes please," I say. The *Cott* is certainly worth a visit. He picks me up *en route* and we head for the thatched, gastro pub he's chosen, for a spot of lunch.

We sit by the blazing fire and, just like last time, *Mr Great-Grandpa* talks. As we wait for our food, someone I know bounces over to say Hi, having spotted me. It occurs to me he may wonder what my relationship is to *Mr Great-Grandpa*… a date? A relation? My Father!

Who cares. I banish the thought from my mind and eat the chef's *poulet au cidre*.

"It may not be popular with most," I confess to *Mr Great-Grandpa* as we chat over lunch, "but I have a penchant for taxidermy. I love a stag's head in a hunting lodge. I really want one."

"Ah," he says. "I have a couple of them in my house. Come and take a look."

"I'll take you up on that! I'm passing your way tomorrow. I'll pop by for a cuppa."

Then I get a call from my son's school. I need to come in. "Your son has had a fight. He's bumped his head. Can you come in early to get him?"

"Seems my son has had a fisty-cuffs with another boy at school and banged his head," I tell my date. "They've asked me to come and collect him. Sorry, going to have to go."

"Let's look at the dessert menu," he says. "Won't be too long."

"No, I've been asked to come in now actually. Sorry about dessert."

He orders dessert.

I arrive at school at the normal pick up time.

*

Several weeks later, I get a call from a landline number. "Hello, it's *Mr Great-Grandpa*. I have to go into Exeter to do some Christmas shopping. Would you like to join me? We could have lunch after shopping."

I need to go into Exeter myself for a few Christmas bits, so I agree.

He picks me up and chatters all the way there. We browse the Christmas market, I pick up the few bits that I need and, as we head to a café for lunch, we pass the *Anne Summers* store.

"I love an *Anne Summers* I do!" he says. "Love to see the things they have in the back. Very funny."

I ignore him.

We pass one of many homeless people around Exeter's Cathedral Green. "These guys," he comments. "I love the way they leave all the coppers in the cup and take out all the silver, making us think that's all they've got."

I ignore him.

He links my arm conspiratorially. "These guys, honestly! You'd think they'd want to work instead of this. I've always worked." He shakes his head disapprovingly.

"Well, *Mr Great-Grandpa*," I respond, holding on to a very contained explosion. "There are many reasons a person ends up homeless. PTSD. Addiction. Domestic abuse. Mental health issues. All sorts. Not everyone is as lucky as you."

"Thing is," he says, knowingly, "I worked from the age of 15, all hours. Always have, always will. No need to rely on anyone else."

"Then you've been a very lucky man," I say. "We should never ever judge someone else's story." I'm just shy of one of my very explosive rants but, luckily for him, the restaurant is upon us. Over lunch, I'm able to compartmentalise his views and enjoy some prosecco and Christmas lunch atmosphere. We talk about the country pursuits that we both enjoy then he drops me back home.

He pops a Christmas card for me through my letterbox later that week, but I don't see him at the Boxing Day drag hunt that my son and I ride on. Not even at the meet. Odd, considering he said he'd be there.

*

I have been invited for tea. I drive up to *Mr Great-Grandpa's* house – electric gates, a little drive way, a couple of stables – and pop in for that cup of tea and stag head viewing. I have my kid with me.

His house is decked with mahogany furniture and thick-pile, light peach carpets throughout. Plenty of pictures in free-standing frames on side tables. Relatives. And two, navy blue reclining armchairs, complete with matching footstools. Matching sofa. Grandpa furniture. He offers me a cup of tea and proceeds to show me every room in his house, like an estate agent and prospective buyer. There on the stairwell are the stag heads.

"I had loads more of these in my old house," he says. "They're in storage."

We go back to the kitchen. "Do you want a piece of cake?" he asks my son.

"Ah," I butt in, "It's a bit close to supper time! Very kind though."

My son scowls at me.

"Sorry, it's what your mum says," he apologises to my son, and turns to his sideboard, picking up a bottle. "See this here," he says in his slow Devon drawl. He hands me the bottle, unscrewed. "This is that Chinese medicine I told you about. Tastes horrible. Smell that!"

I oblige. "It's not *that* bad is it?" I say. "What's in it?" I search the label for the ingredients. Mainly Echinacea and a few other herbs.

And then, in prescription print, his name. And date of birth.

10th of March, 1943.

Making him 75 years old.

The average age of death for a man in the UK is 79, I looked that up. And lying about your age by 15 years or so can actually be considered deception.

I looked that up too.

47

Mr Establishment

Seeking Arrangements

Age: 54

   &

Mr Arrangement

Seeking Arrangements

Age: 44

A little splattering of messages hits my inbox as I have a quick flutter on *Seeking Arrangements* again. *Mr Establishment* and *Mr Arrangement* are amongst the flurry of men to get in touch.

Mr Establishment is very efficient. Two messages on the dating site, then on to *WhatsApp,* and promptly on to a thoroughly efficient call. I'm immediately put into sceptical mode – after complimenting him on his wild and funky red glasses he replies 'Oh that was a one off' and proudly labels himself as *very* 'establishment'. I've just finished reading Owen Jones' book, *The Establishment,* for goodness sake!

Still, mustn't judge right?

I agree to a date because, by this point, that's just what I do…

Simultaneously *Mr Arrangement* gets in touch. A divorced businessman living in Essex. He's got a smiley face, a bald head, and a toned torso. I know this because he – I assume proudly – sends me a whole bunch of topless beach shots on *WhatsApp*.

I don't reciprocate.

Then *Facebook's* creepy algorithm shows me his profile and suggests him as a friend. The algorithm clearly knows that we are connected on *WhatsApp*, so I promptly entertain a spot of *Facebook* stalking, followed by a friend request in order to see his full profile.

He accepts the friend request and messages me.

"How's my lady then?" he says.

"Fine," I reply. But 'my lady'…WTF?!

"You're flippin' gorgeous," he says. "When are you coming to London?"

"Soon, maybe," I say.

Meanwhile, I see that he's often on *Facebook,* and start to build a picture of him. Firstly, he has a man friend whom he tags in almost every post, and who tags him equally in equal measures. They have a constant flow of man banter and in-jokes. I also note his preferred reading. He regularly shares articles on things like immigration, from *The Sun*. He shares meme's with captions like 'This is what real men look like (Showing a picture of a soldier carrying a wounded man) Not a man in a skirt'.

He often mentions 'The British People' and what they 'want'. I see he is rather keen on Donald Trump and says 'Make Nigel Farage Prime Minister'. He posts quizzes on 'How good are you in bed?' He posts articles on the legal aid that immigrants can get. He captions the Katie Hopkins video that he shares 'damn right Katie!' and he mentions how 'easily offended' everyone is these days. 'Snowflakes, the lot of them'. Yet, in contrast, he seems offended by the transgender community. When he travelled to Amsterdam, it wasn't only his best mate that joked with him that he was going there for the red light area.

Yes, it's amazing what you can get from an active social media profile. I've got him down good and proper.

He also has a habit of sending me messages with maps of how many miles he has run that morning. When I ask him why he's spamming me with it, he says he thought I'd be interested.

I try to stop myself, but I can't help commenting on one of his posts. He counters with a message. "Apart from my sexist jokes, are you still up for a date?"

"I can't say that sexism, trans comments, the red light district comments, the serial dater comments, the snowflake and 'remoaner' talk is really my thing," I reply.

"Oh come on! I'm not a bad person. You might enjoy yourself."

"Well, we don't share the same values," I say, "but maybe I'll get a coffee with you, just to see in person."

"Great!" he says "It'll be interesting to see just how morally degenerate you think I am. I'm hardly Charles Manson."

Odd choice of comparison, I think.

*

A month or so after my phone conversation with *Mr Establishment,* there's not much contact arising, as is often the way, but he suddenly calls me.

"I normally have a video conversation with someone before meeting them," he says, but why don't you pop on a train and come for lunch this Thursday? I've been a while out of my last relationship and I'm quite convinced you'll be delightful. I'll book *The Ivy*, Kings Road and we can see how we go?"

As we know, an affirmative approach goes a long way with me and, along with being on the spot when he asks, I agree. But there is the little issue of a train ticket. A day return is around £100, and I still haven't yet got my head around how this 'arrangement' thing works. Do I ask him to get the ticket for me? Should he offer? Should I get it? As usual I'm an unclear and very bad sugar babe. I ponder for a day, then bite the bullet and send a message – a screen shot of the train ticket. "Hi there, here's the ticket and my bank details. Looking forward to seeing you on Thursday.'

This is *Seeking Arrangements* after all.

He replies. "Great, see you Thursday." It looks like that's that sorted then.

He keeps on confirming throughout the week and I keep reassuring him that I'm coming. Just one thing though, he hasn't yet sent me my fare, so I prompt him.

"Yes, I'll reimburse you when I see you," he says.

I scrutinise the pictures on his profile and think he may be a little fuddy-duddy for me, in his pressed shirts and cream trousers. He seems much older, in ways than years and, I assume, has always been like that, even when young.

He messages me on the Thursday morning, to check I'm still coming, and I reassure him that I am. At 10 o'clock, he asks if I'm at the station yet, and I assure him I am. At 10.15, he messages me to check that the train is on time and I assure him it is. At 10.25, he checks that I'm on the train and, of course, I tell him that I am, indeed, on the train.

"Send me a selfie of you on the train," he requests.

I snap a picture, making sure that the train seat is clearly visible.

"Fabulous, see you at *The Ivy* soon!" he messages. I bed in to my seat and get some reading.

At 11.30 he sends another message. "Better turn around at the next stop. Sorry. Work emergency has come up. I have to go to Brussels!"

What! Is he serious? Surely this is a joke?

"Are you serious, or is that a joke?" I message him.

"Oh yes, indeed, no joke, sorry." But it doesn't feel like he's sorry at all.

Well for goodness sake, I think, *do I turn round and waste my day, or take a day in London anyway?*

One of my best qualities is adaptability, and it takes me all of two minutes to create a new plan. What can I do at short notice now I'm nearly in London? I'm damned if I'm going to simply turn round and go home again. So, who haven't I met yet?

I send *Mr Arrangement* a message,

"I'm unexpectedly free for lunch," I say. "Are you by any chance around at 1 o'clock?"

"Hello, babe, nice surprise," he replies. "I can get available for you, gorgeous, if you know what I mean." And then there's a wink emoji.

I'm immediately reminded of his character, just in case I'd forgotten.

"Meet me in *The Ivy*, Kings Road," I say.

It occurs to me that, if *Mr Establishment* is fucking with me and hasn't actually been called away on business but is, in fact, indulging in a quick change of date, then it's not impossible that he might well be sitting in

The Ivy too! Something about this delights me. It could be amusing to watch that unfold.

I arrive at *The Ivy* a little while before *Mr Arrangement* and, after my impromptu morning, I'm in an especially feisty mood. If this is what arrangement dating looks like, I may have to flip this nonsense round. *Mr Arrangement* arrives, tall, toned, bald, in his 40s, with his shirt a button or two too many undone. His jacket is slung over his shoulder. His flounce as he walks towards me, having spotted me waving at him, is bigger even than my best flounce.

"Alright babe?" he says.

I stand up to greet him. "Do sit down," I say, smiling. I beckon the waiter over. "Two prosecco's and some water, please."

"I don't normally drink at lunchtime," he says.

"You don't normally see me at lunchtime," I smile.

I tell him that I had a meeting that ended early and now I'm free. *Well, it's not untrue, is it!*

"What would you like to eat? Anything you like," I say. I take the initiative and call the waiter again. "Another drink?" I ask him. "I'll take another prosecco," I tell the waiter, "and for the gentleman?" I look at *Mr Arrangement* who takes another drink. "So, tell me everything," I say. "How long have you been divorced?"

We chat easily over lunch.

"I love women, I do," he says. "And respect 'em."

"Ah, very nice," I reply. "So, *The Sun,* hey? Your favourite paper?"

"Great sports section," he quips.

"Ahh, speedy get out!" I reply. *Well done.* We sip our drinks. "Now then," I say, putting my glass down. "What kind of arrangement are you looking for?" My two proseccos have made me bold. *Enough of this skirting around the edges.* "Let's talk numbers."

For the first time, he looks a little uncomfortable.

"Now, now!" I say. "Don't be shy! What sort of number are you thinking and I'll see what I can do…"

"Well, I've got around the £1,000 a month mark in mind, I guess," he says.

"Hmm, £1,000 a month? I see. Well. I'm a very busy woman, so probably only have time to see you two or three times a month. Will you be available when I'm free?"

"Well, within reason," he says.

"Well, you see, I do need someone to be free when I am," I say. "I have a child and a busy schedule. I may be able to go a little higher than £1,000 if that helps…."

He looks confused.

"And I'll cover your expenses," I go on. "You just keep going to that gym and running. Keep in good shape. I could get you a little extra for shopping too, if you'd like that. Would you like that?" I say. "I'm going to Malta on holiday, maybe you could come?"

He looks utterly stunned.

"But... what...?" he splutters.

"Shopping," I say. "You look like a guy who likes shopping. You do like shopping don't you?"

"Well, I do but... but..."

"What's the matter, sweetie," I say. "I don't know if I want to stretch to more, since I'll only be seeing you two or three times a month."

"You want to give *me* a monthly allowance?" he chokes.

"Well of course!" I say. "What did you think we were doing here?"

And before he can reply, I get up and go to the bathroom. "Back in a minute," I say, leaving the table.

I head past reception, order coffee and pay the bill before it can come to the table. So, *this* is what it feels like to be them! It's an extraordinarily presumptive position and, when it's turned on its head, it highlights just how extreme gender roles still are.

Every one of those things I said to him have all been said to me, on more than one occasion. When an arrangement is reversed to have the man at the woman's beck and call, it just highlights all the absurd assumptions that these men are making.

When I return, the coffee is on the table. I drink it quickly then stand up. "So, have a little think. I'm seeing a couple of other boys too, so let's just see shall we? Train to catch… bye!"

"Er, we need to get the bill…" he falters.

"All done, sweetie," I say, and give him a wink. "Here…" I pop a twenty on the table. "Get yourself a little drink if you like." And, with that, I leave.

I can't afford this lunch, but I leave with a better understanding of the roles we're all playing. They go so unnoticed! And for that insight, it's worth it. Oddly, I feel a bit bad for him. I hadn't planned to go this route. It just popped out of me. I'm not sure he enjoyed it but, hey! he got a free lunch and, I assume, he'll just go back to Katie Hopkins anyway.

Back in Devon that evening, I send *Mr Establishment* a message.

"Hope your trip is going well. Here are my bank details for the ticket".

"Will see to it later," he replies.

He doesn't see to it later.

Two days later I send him another message. "Doesn't seem to have come through?"

"Odd," he says and sends me a screen shot of his attempted transaction. It has everything but the 'make payment' step.

"Yeah, you have to press 'Send' to make the payment…"

I follow this with another message.

"Never mind, you don't have to make the payment for the day you cancelled. My mistake. Enjoy the rest of your trip and take care."

He replies. "Paid."

I check my account and he has finally refunded the ticket. And it's now that I get to see his full name. I have a quick *Google* stalk. A well-known investment banker turned financial advisor. He is indeed *very* 'establishment', with some political wrangling in his past too, as well as some pretty poor reviews from disgruntled ex-employees.

It was an expensive, if interesting day. I had better not name him, but I'm pretty sure I should have billed him for lunch with *Mr Arrangement* too. One man paying for lunch with another. That's the ticket!

48

Mr Campervan

Tinder

Age: 48

I'm broadening my horizons, casting my net far and wide. Rich men, poor men… maybe not beggar men or thieves… but, young men, old men, 'normal' men too. Down-to-earth, 9 to 5 types. No Lamborghini's or manor houses. I'm in Devon after all.

Swiping around on *Tinder*, I match with *Mr Campervan*, a man wearing nice hats, with a very nice face and a tidy beard. I can just tell he'll be nice, kind and wholesome. He has pictures of himself on beaches in linen shirts, with a dog. Normal clothes. Smiling pictures. We may or may not be a great match, but we will not have a horrible time. Of this much I'm convinced.

We exchange some messages and I find that he does a lot of singing. In a folk band, and in a couple of choirs. He's a Russian language translator. And he chats really well. Just one problem. Every message he sends, he ends with *Take care,* or *Hope you find what you're looking for,* or *Have a good day*. Conversation closers. All you can say is 'Thanks'.

I ignore his closing sentences assuming he's just being polite and we become *Facebook* friends. Viewing his page, I see that it's perfectly normal and healthy. We chit-chat for probably around two months before we meet.

One day, when my son is camping overnight with his dad who is down from London for the weekend, I message *Mr Campervan* to ask him what he's up to. I'm pretty sure I'm going to have to instigate a meeting, otherwise we'd just float around chatting online forever. "What are you up to right now?" I ask. "My boy is with his dad and I'm free."

He agrees to meet. *Et voila*, we have a date.

He moseys down my way and lets me know when he arrives. It's nice not to have to travel when I meet someone in my town but, also, it means it's up to me to choose the venue. I prefer the man to do this. I'm perfectly able to choose a venue, but it's nice to know a man can take care of things. Can make a decision. Is able to handle situations. Choosing a meeting place, and picking up a bill shows character straight away.

"Meet me by the ice cream shop," I say when he messages me to say he's arrived. "We'll get an ice cream and go from there."

An easy, casual, friendly meeting.

I instantly recognise him. He's exactly as his picture, but he's really short. I'm tall anyway, but he's shorter than me by a good hand or two. Not dismissing men on height, I'm undeterred. That lovely smiley face he wears in all his pictures is right there.

We get an ice cream and go to sit on the village green by the stream. We chat easily for about an hour before he suddenly makes a suggestion.

"Look," he says, "I've got my camper van here. It's stuffed with food. I'm on my way to Cornwall for the weekend, maybe even a few days, I'll see how I go, but why don't you grab a jumper and come up onto Dartmoor. We could camp overnight. I've got wine, a BBQ, everything…"

The weather is amazing, I'm an adventurous lass and I don't have a childcare issue. So, yes! I agree.

We whip past my house, I grab some jeans and a jumper, a toothbrush, the dog, and off we go.

I know the perfect spot on the moor for wild camping and we plant ourselves there. First things first, we crack open some wine. Neither of us are uncomfortable, but wine gets the conversation flowing and some life stories. Relationship history. Family stories. Even some sad ones.

Mr Campervan gets the BBQ going. "I'm pleasantly surprised you didn't blink an eyelid at my very un-posh camper van," he says.

"I do like the flashy things in life," I say, "but I'm no princess. I'll pee in a bush, or wash in a stream if I have to. And I'll clamber through mud. I'm a country girl at heart. An un-posh camper van is no problem!"

He starts to cook up dinner and we drink some more wine. He even gets out his guitar and strums a few tunes. I watch as he cooks. He's standing with one knee bent, relaxed. And when he chats to me, he waves his hand around in the most camp fashion imaginable.

The night sky is totally clear and absolutely packed with bright stars. At just about midnight, hundreds – literally hundreds! – of shooting stars start falling all over the place, the likes of which I've never seen before. It's extraordinary. But, when the bushes rustle, *Mr Campervan* squeals and jumps up waving his hands around.

"Oh my goodness!" he shrieks. "Oh gosh! What's that in the bushes?"

Am I going to have to protect him from whatever scary things lurk in the dark!

The noises settle down, as does he, and we stay watching the stars with a fire and blanket until 2 a.m. A rare, clear, night sky. He gives me the van to sleep in while he takes a pop up tent outside.

In the morning, I wander across the moor to find somewhere to pee and pick up a phone signal. I'm currently on a 'don't be glued to the phone drive', especially when I'm with someone, so I wasn't concerned about phone reception all evening – we don't need to be glued to our phones constantly, right?

As soon as I open my phone, it starts popping with messages. One from the camp leader where my son is camping with his dad. *Could you pick your son up?* it reads from the night before. I then see there are a couple of missed calls from him too.

Immediately, I call him back.

"There was a bit of trouble between your son and his dad last night," he tells me.

I ask to speak to my son who is cagey. "Well, Daddy was a bit drunk last night," he tells me awkwardly. "He was mean to me. He's ok now though, and we're playing football in a field."

My heart sinks. I know exactly what that means. The ongoing trouble we have with my son's father's drinking is ever present. Even during the very short-lived, fortnightly sober patches. We live in the prison of knowing that any day will be the day it all starts again. As is repeatedly the case. But never has he ever turned on his own son. On me, yes. On my older son, yes. Random people in the street, friends… we've all had the drunken, aggressive rambling of a true alcoholic, but it has never, until now, been projected onto our little boy.

The father/son camping night had been instigated by me. I'd wanted my little boy's dad to be *that Dad*. The outdoor, bonding-with-your-son Dad. The cook-sausages-on-the-campfire Dad. The whittle-bows-and-arrows-together Dad. It was all my idea. None of it was his. He's a London guy through and through. Should I have known better than to expect him to stay sober for one night?

"I'll come and get you now," I tell my son.

"No, no," he says," we're playing football. I'll be fine till later."

He will be ok for the daytime and, as it was a one-night camp only, they'll be returning later. So I go back to our base where *Mr Campervan* is cooking up breakfast. Coffee, juice, *rosti* even!

I briefly tell him what happened, but don't want to go into it much, though it's playing on my mind. *Can't I leave my child with his dad, even for one night now?*

The sun is already very hot, so we get a blanket out and lie by the stream with some cows and Dartmoor ponies wandering by. Our dogs wander around together enjoying themselves.

As I lie sunbathing, I wonder how on earth I can even go on dates if I have to always worry about childcare. I'm in Devon, my son's father is in London and, although he's willing, I have to constantly monitor what phase of drinking he's in. And because he lies, I don't always know until we meet up and I see for myself what state he's currently in. I can pop out for short dates locally – my son is old enough for that – but, overnight, I have to rely on friends, or his father. How, exactly, are mothers without childcare meant to strike up a new relationship?

I've done angry to the maximum, but this time I just feel resigned, or is it despair? I'm not sure which. I do know, though, that without going out and meeting people, I'm not going to find *Mr Right* sitting at home.

As we lie in the warm sun, *Mr Campervan* asks, "Should we have a hug?"

Does he mean 'snog' when he says 'hug'?

I'm really not sure, but shrug and say "Nah, thanks."

He's like an old friend. I just don't feel that kind of attraction. He's just a bit too camp for me. Then again, I hardly ever fancy my dates any more. Should I just override that? Would a physical attraction come in time? Should I kiss him and find out? He's a really nice bet after all.

We carry on chatting and relaxing in the sun then head back. I want to be back when my son gets home.

"I'll show you some of the great beaches I've found this summer," I tell him on our way home. "I've discovered some great ones."

He enthusiastically agrees and sets off on his own for his campsite down in Cornwall.

*

When they arrive home, my son's father busies himself unloading the car and putting things away, avoiding eye contact with me, or saying anything. When he finally sits down, I ask him if he's going to tell me what happened. He bursts into tears and says he can't remember too much.

It turns out he ended up sleeping in the car, as persuaded by the camp organizers, because my son didn't want to sleep in the tent with a 'ranting, mean daddy.'

He mainly denies everything he does, but I prefer tears. It's better than denial. More real. Still, I know we've been here before. The *I'll go to AA*. The *this is the last time*. We've heard it all before.

On the Monday, my son goes to school and I haven't been booked in to any supply work, so I message *Mr Campervan* to say that I can show him a nice beach. He trundles back from Cornwall in the van and we drive to one of my newly found beach delights, hanging out there for the day, relaxing, doing nothing.

"I'm not a big risk taker," he says.

"Me neither," I agree.

"Isn't spending the night on the moor with a random stranger taking a risk?" he asks.

"Nah," I say. "There's such a long paper trail to where we were. People knew. Anyway," I add, "I consider myself more of an adventurer. It's things like drugs I'm not risky with. I don't even like hanging out with people who take drugs. Gives me the creeps. I can't read those people. Ever considered it was *you* taking the risk going onto the moor with *me*?" I laugh.

"Good point!" he says as we both laugh.

As we drive back he muses over where we would go in his campervan if we got together. "You, me and your son could all go wild camping tomorrow evening," he says.

It's not an unappealing idea, but I somehow think we won't become an item. Should I just try anyway? He's a good man. He cooks *rosti* for goodness sake. But I decline. You know, the camp man thing.

When he drops me home, my son comes to take a look at his van parked up outside my cottage. He's suitably impressed by all the nooks and crannies. We say goodbye and, back inside, my son asks, "Do you like this one mummy?"

"Well, he's very nice," I say, "But I think he's going to be more of a friend."

Later that evening, to make sure *Mr Campervan* doesn't let his mind run away with itself, I send him a message:

Hey, I really had such a great time with you on Sunday. I was just this minute telling my friend that, and saying we chatted non-stop and all about good stuff too. So, although I don't think we'll date on a romantic level I'd love to remain friends. I can't predict what you'll think, but I wanted to be honest.

Sound familiar?

Yes, *Mr Architect's* message to me was such a good one way back when, I sent it to *Mr Campervan*.

Because, well, it's true. And, maybe in time, we could have had something more. But I see on *Facebook* that he soon becomes happily ensconced in a new relationship and is looking very happy.

And that in turn makes me happy too.

49

Epilogue

Dating the over 40s, especially if you're a woman in your 40s, often means you'll be dating men in their 50s, even in their 60s, and this can be a whole new ball game, unless you're doing the hot cougar thing. And here's the harsh reality: many men do not care how *old* a woman is. They care how *hot* she is. If a woman is 60 and hot, a man will likely be interested. A woman's worth in our society is based on her sexual allure. Do men approve of her? Do men want her? Does she have any value for men? And for men, unless they are equally hot, their exchange will likely be based on status, success, and money. Which can be just as damaging for them too.

My friend — a man — said to me only this week that he changed his age from 58 on *Tinder* to 52. When I questioned his reasoning, he answered "I don't want a woman my own age. I want a woman your age. I don't find women my own age attractive." I wondered what he was going to do after a few years when she got older? Trade her in? I also pointed out to him that he himself is not very hot, and a bit overweight.

"Are you really entitled to a hot, younger woman?" I asked.

"It's just what I want," he answered with a shrug. And he thought no more about it.

And it's true. He wants what he wants.

In fact, I find his response quite refreshingly simple. It makes life simple for him I guess, whereas I try to persuade myself into being attracted to men's personality, because, let's face it, hardly any of them are attractive over 40, and even less after 50.

"Do you fancy me?" I've been asked by men who are 50 and four stone overweight.

No, no, I don't fancy you! Maybe, just maybe if we hang out a bit, I'll grow to see other things in you, I tell myself. It all hangs in balance with the hot young guys I've dated here who start to look rather less attractive once you get to spend time with them.

Maybe I just don't want a man? Maybe it's a good career I really want? After all, each time I've met one of these *Sugardaddy* types, I always end up talking business, far more interested in their careers than I am in *them* as a date. One of these guys I met – a Ray Winston sound alike – I actually sent a business proposal to. He could have been a very good match for one of my business ideas. I proposed a business partnership. But I had to nag him to read it, just like he had nagged me for a follow-up date. After finally reading my proposal, he replied, *Well, you have been busy haven't you? I'm very impressed with what you've come up with. Very interested to talk to you more about it. It's refreshing to see a beautiful girl with a brain. Aren't you a clever girl!'*

Would he have said something similar to a man who showed him a business proposal?

And what about the sugar daddies? I've been a very bad sugar babe. They're so often good at business, but rather crass at dating. To my mind anyway. How simple it could be, fluffing around being pretty. Why can't I just shut the fuck up and just be pretty?

In these ten years of dating, I've actually only been properly taken with two of my dates. *Mr Polo* and *Mr Architect* and they were pretty much the only ones not interested in me. How is that even possible? I even thought for a moment that I had unwittingly fallen upon the only man in Devon with a Ferrari, when I went out a few times with this cutie in his 40's whom I met on *Tinder.* I sent him an appallingly rude message telling him to 'Get on with it' in arranging a date. Of course he hadn't been at it as long as me so, probably, had more patience for online ramblings, or hadn't yet learnt that there's no point in online chat when the likelihood is you'll be ghosted anyway. But my rudeness didn't put him off. On the contrary, he apologised and made a date.

I saw him several times.

On one meeting he rocked up in his Ferrari. We met up several times and I really did try to like him. He was cute, had a cool beard, and was a good kisser. But as I got to know him and his constant critiquing – *dairy intolerance? that's not even a thing!* and *I think the sexism war has been won don't you?!* – I found myself shutting down with nothing to say. We didn't share *any* common ground, except that we both have children. I was willing to overlook the fact that he holds his knife like a pen, but as he argued the toss over everything, I just couldn't be bothered and let it fizzle out.

Then there was the nice-looking, posh, 50-something widower who liked horses. After two dates he sent me holiday pictures and clumsy messages. "Are you a good kisser?" I assume he was looking for some sexting. I replied with the number of a sex chat line telling him he should try that instead.

There was even the guy who asked me for boob pictures for money. I said OK, found some boobs online and sent them to him, for which I was remunerated with £50 in my bank account!

And there was the guy who wanted to go to *Harrods* to take me shopping on his hands and knees while being led in a dog collar in full view of everyone, burning a hole in his credit card. If he hadn't backed out, I dare say I might have considered trying it, to see what happened. But the dominatrix thing isn't really my bag. *Mr Slave-Man* showed me that.

Maybe investigative journalism is, in fact, my calling?

Am I terribly bothered by my single status? I would like to go to events with someone. I would like to have a partnership with someone. I would like to have security and contentment with someone. And I would like to have a deep connection with someone too. It would be nice not to be looking all the time. Nice to be ensconced happily with someone. So, yes, I'm still looking.

Terribly bothered? Probably not.

I remember, in the early days, I assumed that meeting a lot of different dates would be a simple numbers game and I would almost certainly meet at the very least one very good match. I therefore invested more time in these early dates. I now notice that I hardly get excited at all by the prospect of a date. It's almost become a habit instead of an actual quest.

Does that mean I'm jaded? That I've lost hope?

I think not. More like 'take it as it comes'. No need for expectations. What will be will be. If he turns up, he turns up.

Do I regret any of my choices? Nope. I simply enjoy my experiences for what they are. Except *Mr Architect* – surely it wasn't a good idea to reveal on date number one that I had ended up making a book out of my dating experiences? I regret that.

It should be no surprise at this stage in my dating life that I have some dating tips. I've tried to keep them few, and simple. Here they are. For the men first:

1) Be clean. Make an effort. Shave if you don't sport a beard. Trim it, if you do. Smell nice and clean. Wear clean clothes. Obvious? Yeah, you'd think so, right?

2) Pay for the date. You're not buying your date. You're not dominating your date. And you're not buying sex. And don't worry, you're not

paying forever. You are taking part in a dating/mating ritual. Did you get that? You're letting a woman know you've got this, you're capable, you can take care of things. Genders are equal, but we are not the same. Women put effort and money into their outfits, their hair and make up, their nails and, sometimes, a babysitter. Which probably costs more than this drink or meal. It's rather like a Sunday lunch being prepared, or Christmas dinner – the woman cooks it all for hours, and the man carves the joint and gets all the praise. The time, effort and money that a woman puts into a date means the man gets to pay the bill and hit the glory button. Go ahead men, take the glory.

3) Be on time. Don't leave women waiting around in bars or restaurants.

4) Listen to her. Ask her questions and try not to talk non-stop about yourself. It's not a job interview, or a counselling session.

5) Talk well of your ex. Slagging off the mother of your children is a *very* bad look.

And for all you women:
1) Make an effort. Everyone likes to feel like they're worth the effort.

2) Fashionably late is one thing, but more than half an hour late is a No No. It's rude and presumptuous.

3) Try not to sound bitter (even if you are). Your new date is not your counsellor any more than you are his.

4) Your children may be the main thing in *your* life but, at this point, your new date wants to know about *you* first. Have other interests to talk about.

And for both men and women: don't build up an expectation or fantasy in your mind about your new date before you have even met. You are very likely to be disappointed. You may have a preconceived idea, but s/he is just a person. Give each other a break and go with the flow. Accept that s/he may not be a match, and that's OK.

And what have *I* learned in all this time?

Be softer.   Be tougher.

Be more girly.

Let the man take the lead.   Take more of a lead.

Initiate.   Don't initiate.

Wear less make up.   Wear more make up.

Be less opinionated. Yes, definitely that one!

Or how about *just be you*? There really is someone for everyone.

Maybe I'm too fussy? But then again, looking back at all of my dates, would you have settled for one of them? Should I carry on looking? I have several conversations on the go, and some dates lined up in both Devon and London so, yes, I dare say I will carry on. I bumped into a friend at a party the other day. She told me that she hadn't met her partner of 15 years until she was 49. Before that, although she had had children, she hadn't had long or functioning relationships until this one. Her little story inspires. So do I expect to meet a good match at some point? Despite my track record, interestingly, yes I do. There are good quality dude's getting divorced all the time, so the selection is opening up again. Let's see what the next 10 years may bring.

And Just Before We Go...

I wrote a Moon Letter. I am in the hippie bit of Devon after all.

A Moon Letter is a letter of intention and desire. You write it in very specific detail, on the New Moon with its powerful manifesting energy. You put it away until the next Full Moon, re-read it, and then burn it to allow the full moon energy to bring all your intentions to fruition. "Om..."

Despite not being a fully paid up member of Hippiedom, but with nothing at all to lose, I follow these specific Moon Letter instructions and detail all my man desires. I write for example, that I want a clever, honest, kind, grown up man, emotionally intelligent and together. A man who grows vegetables. I write that I want to let go of my continued pull back to London and settle myself properly in Devon.

I occasionally swipe around on *Tinder* and, one week after writing my Moon Letter – and within precisely one week of finishing this book! – I match with a man with a very nice write up and photos. He promptly messages me and wastes no time at all in making a date. As we know by now, getting on with it is an absolute winning approach for me.

We meet the next day for coffee in my hometown. He lives fairly close by. Tick. He has grown up children, so knows what it's about. Tick. And, guess what? He's all the things I included in my Moon Letter. He even has a house in France. *And* he grows vegetables, to boot!

We meet the next day too, for dinner. Then, at the end of the week, we meet again for a third time for a picnic on the moor. He brings pink prosecco and a spread of lovely nibbles from the deli. We go for a walk. Sit on the rocks and look over the landscape. We link arms. And we kiss.

Then, six weeks later, we decide we will marry. And my friends are totally on board.

"Fantastic! Well, by now you should know, after all!' is the general consensus.

There's the odd sceptic. "But why do you need to actually *marry*?" has been said. More than once.

And I reply, "Oh, you know, because of love. You know, that *love thing*? Plus he grows vegetables."

"I can't believe you're going to marry before me!" says my oldest son.

Was it the Moon Letter? Was it finishing this book? Was it simply a numbers game? Who knows. But we do know that we have to be out there, in it, to find it.

And the particulars of this special *Mr*, and the details of our dates?

Well, that's all for another story… I said in an earlier episode of this memoir that I was going to finish it off with a happy ending, so here it is. After all this time, the pressing question of do I still think I'll find *Mr Right* has been very nicely answered. Very nicely answered indeed.